Best wishes

J.C.Lee

SEVEN CURSES © 2024 J C Lee

Published by Graveside Press
graveside-press.com

All rights reserved.

This novel is entirely a work of fiction. The names, characters, businesses, places, events and incidents portrayed in it are the work of the author's imagination or are used fictitiously. Any resemblance to actual persons, living or dead, events or localities is entirely coincidental. No part of this book may be reproduced or transmitted in any form or by any means, electronic or mechanical, except for the purpose of review and/or reference, without explicit permission in writing from the publishers.

Editing: K. York
Cover Design: Sleepy Fox Studio – sleepyfoxstudio.net
Interior Formatting: Sleepy Fox Studio – sleepyfoxstudio.net

eBook 978-1-964952-21-5
Print (KDP paperback) 978-1-964952-17-8
Print (Paperback) 978-1-964952-13-0
Print (Hardcover) 978-1-964952-20-8

No part of this book has been created using Generative AI.

GRAVESIDE PRESS

SEVEN CURSES

J C LEE

CONTENT WARNING

For a list of potential trigger warnings, please turn to page 300
or visit our website:
graveside-press.com/cw/seven-curses

PROLOGUE

One upon a time...

Once upon a time...

THERE WAS, IN a far-off eastern land, a young orphan girl who was brought up by her grandmother. She was a difficult and naughty child, so much so that her grandmother often chided her that she must have been swapped in the cradle for a fox fairy.

The orphan girl never believed this but liked the idea nonetheless, for she spent much of her childhood lost in storybooks, many of which featured fairies, demons, and magic spirits of all kinds. These, she felt, were her only true friends, and she loved them.

When her grandmother died, the orphan girl—now a young woman—found herself alone, so she set out to explore the world. First, she travelled to a nearby country, the land of the shaking earth. And while there, the earth and seas did indeed grow fierce, killing many thousands as they shook with anger. But she had by then met a beautiful young man whose foxy eyes knew where and how to lead her to safety.

Once the land was calm again and the sea had withdrawn to its bed, and as they looked and saw the destruction around them, the young couple made a vow. Together, they would seek a language to calm the earth; he through music, she through poetry.

With this as their newly shared purpose, they travelled many miles westward, first to a city of poetry and light, where they studied and

SEVEN CURSES

worked and played. It was a happy time, but still they did not find what they were seeking so they travelled further west still, to a country of rain and mists where, she told him, there dwelt a master wordsmith who taught in the centre of that land and from whom she hoped to learn much. He, her beautiful friend, followed her to study under a master musician in a city close by, close enough for him to visit her often…

CONFIDENTIAL NOTES FOR THE ATTENTION OF THE SENIOR REGISTRAR ON THE DISAPPEARANCE OF DOCTORAL STUDENT XIE FEI (AKA ROSE) FROM WEST MIDLANDS UNIVERSITY ON OCTOBER 15TH.

Ms. Xie arrived at the start of the last academic year to study with Professor Dominic James. Following his sudden departure to take up a chair at Cambridge, she was allocated associate professors, Charles Towne (Cultural Studies) and Catrina Whitehead (Sociology), as replacement supervisors. During the course of the year,

Ms. Xie made official complaints about both. She also brought forth charges of sexual assault against Mr. Scott Lyle, a security guard, and of gross carelessness leading to food poisoning against her then resident tutor, Dr. Terence Usgood. Details of the charges and the action taken by the university in response to each case can be found in the appropriate files, copies of which accompany these notes.

Her disappearance occurred immediately after the sudden death of a male friend in the university's guest accommodation. Her then flatmate, Mrs. Serena Lai, reports that Ms. Xie suffered a nervous breakdown so violent that Mrs. Lai felt she had to leave the apartment in fear for her own safety. Security personnel arrived within fifteen minutes, by which time Ms. Xie had disappeared. The extent of the wreckage can be viewed in the accompanying photographs. None at the scene could understand how one young woman had wrought such destruction on her own.

There have been no sightings of Ms. Xie in the fortnight since her disappearance. She has only distant family members in China still living. They have been informed, and her passport has been flagged by the immigration authorities and border control. Fortunately, the story has not been picked up by Chinese media and ran for only two days in a minor capacity in local and national press (articles attached).

The university has discouraged the flurry of conspiracy theories currently on social media. Most have, however, cast Ms. Xie rather than the university in a poor light, as she was not a popular student. Some of the stories circulating on Chinese social media (principally on Weibo) are more sympathetic to her and less helpful to the university's image. Some suggest the pressure of work caused her to lose her mind, others that she may have been kidnapped and even murdered. More outlandishly, a number have focused on sightings of a white fox in the vicinity on the night of the fifteenth they are identifying as a fox fairy. The fox fairy is a semi-immortal, shape-shifting female spirit, common in Chinese folklore and ghost stories—beautiful, seductive, and sometimes vengeful. This is evidently a somewhat tasteless joke and is, at least, one theory we can readily ignore.

We are fortunate that none of this appears to have damaged our reputation either at home or in China, where recruitment is still on course to meet targets for the next academic year, and where our new motto *Educating minds, transforming lives* is, our Shanghai office informs us, being met with approval.

Those staff and peers who had an association with Ms. Xie are being asked to remain vigilant and to inform Senate House should she make contact of any kind.

Dated: October 29th

SEVEN CURSES

Song of the Weeping Fox

See the sun rise over eastern hills,
As western plains grow dark.
Hear whirlwinds blow like thunderous drums
As Fox runs through the clouds.
Then painted flutes and zithers sound
A softer, subtler tune.
To the rustle of embroidered silks,
She treads now through the autumn gloom.

Countless flowers stripped by the wind
Their petals, drifting, fall.
And Fox now weeping tears of blood
Is shivering, close to death.
But tales are told on ancient scrolls
Where demon fairies wake and rise,
And cowering scholars, powerless, learn
That emerald fire, laughing wildly,
Leaps from Fox's eyes.

Song of the Fairy's Curse

The Fairy pours libations,
Viscous, pale, and blue.
Smoke rises from jade braziers
And sparks crackle like drums,
Releasing perfumes, pungent, sweet;
The mirror clouds with lies, deceit.

As sunset colours western skies,
As ghosts rise up and demons stir,
She knits her brows and plucks the lute,
A different note for each word sung.
The Fairy's anger, rage and spite
Show on her face, sound in her voice,
And echo through the emerald hills;
The scent of bat flowers fills the night.

J C LEE

"Through air and liquid, touch and taste,
Through fragrance foul or fair,
Oh curse, infect my enemies,
Pursue them everywhere.

Infect their pride, their arrogance,
Their curiosity;
Punish their damned delusions
And their foolish vanity;
Be cruel, relentless, merciless,
Deal just revenge for me.

I'll oversee their destiny;
My presence they will never see;
My vengeance will forever be,
In curses seven, my legacy."

Children's Rhyme

Fox Fairy,
Scarred and scary,
Nothing worse
Than her curse.
When you listen
To her story,
Heed her words
And fear her fury.

From *Final Poems* by Dominic James

CURSE ONE
OIL

One is for she who silenced me;

May silence be her destiny…

Hong Kong, November 25th

Edited extract from interview between Associate Professor Catrina Whitehead (CATE) and Cong Yang (Lucy) Leung (LUCY), young Cantonese actress.

Location: Hong Kong University, Room 404

Interpreter: Assistant Professor Ka Yee (Carly) Shu (CARLY), research partner in Hong Kong

NOTE: The Cantonese is not included in this extract but can be found on the original recording

-

CATE: Mr. Golden Turtle? You're kidding me!

CARLY: No. You haven't heard that expression before? I can explain. [turns and speaks briefly in Cantonese to LUCY, then back to CATE] It dates back to the Tang dynasty, I think. He represents wealth and a long life. You marry someone like that, you gain all the advantages of social privilege.

CATE: So, it's about getting a rich husband.

CARLY: Not just that. She says the wizard can help you be successful in your career, too. She is telling us about a famous Taiwanese dancer who went to visit him in Thailand. She went on to have a brilliant career for the next three years.

CATE: Only three years…

CARLY: Yes. She died of a heart attack because she didn't listen to the dashi[1], the wizard. She carried on buying shoes.

CATE: Buying shoes?

CARLY: She was a shopaholic. For shoes. Everyone knows this now, but not then. But the wizard knew. He knew her weakness. He always knows your weakness. He told her she must stop buying so many shoes, but she didn't. And she died. You see, you must not ignore his advice. [pause] She wants to know if you heard about Amelia Choi. She is an actress at the centre of a sex scandal a few years ago.

CATE: Remind me, Carly. Of the details.

CARLY: Well, she and her boyfriend liked to make videos of themselves, you know, having sex. But then they got a problem with their computer. A virus. They deleted the videos and sent it to be repaired, but the technician found them on the hard drive and put them out on social media. It ruined her career.

CATE: Yes, yes. I think I remember reading about it. In The Guardian. But what's that got to do with this [pause] this wizard?

CARLY: She says that people say she owed her famous career to the same dashi. He lives in Thailand. "He is the best, the king of wizards," she says. He collects the bodies of dead babies…

CARLY: What?!

---

1 **dashi:** A Buddhist monk or priest.

CARLY: You adopt the ghost of one, a little ghost, to do your dirty business for you.

CATE: [indistinct muttering] So, what went wrong? This time, what did she do wrong?

CARLY: She says, "That is a mystery."

CATE: Well, it's a mystery to me that anyone be… [sighs] These are just urban myths… Wha-what is she telling us now?

CARLY: About Arabella Chung.

CATE: I've not heard of her.

CARLY: Very famous in Hong Kong. She had a romance with the son of one of the wealthiest men here. He gave her lots of money. I know of this, but Lucy says it is because she visited the dashi, and he smeared oil over her lips and tongue. This means she will get what she desires through either talk or sex.

[pause]

CATE: Hmm. Through talk and sex, perhaps. What happened to her? Did she marry this guy?

CARLY: No. She had his baby, but he left her. Not the right social class, you see.

CATE: Another one that didn't work, then. … [pause] Lucy is shaking her head. Why?

CARLY: She says, "It did work until the father found a rival wizard to break the spell."

CATE: [laughs] I'm sorry. Tell her, tell her I do appreciate her stories, really. Tell her it is very helpful for our research. She isn't smiling, though.

CARLY: No. And she says she is very lucky. You have to wait a very long time to get an appointment to see this dashi, and he has refused to see even some very famous people. But she is going to see a wizard who has trained under him next week.

CATE: She's still staring at me. What is she saying?

[pause]

CARLY: She says, "You are very beautiful and very clever." But she can tell you are not… What is the English word? Fulfilled. Yes, not fulfilled. [pause] She says you should go see the wizard. He will help you get what you desire.

"Oh, I have all the lovers I want, believe me!"

"I *can* believe it," said Carly.

They had returned to Catrina's hotel room to discuss the afternoon's interview. It was a very pleasant room. Expensive, too. Catrina had insisted on the Renaissance Harbour View for her week's stay, saying she would find the extra funding needed herself if necessary.

"The view—I've heard it is rather like New York," she had said.

Carly had been to New York and had seen the Manhattan skyline but preferred the view on display through these plate-glass windows over the narrow waters that separated Wanchai from Kowloon. It was a sight she particularly appreciated at night when she took the ferry home to her apartment.

She'd first met Catrina one year before, sitting next to her by chance for the opening keynote speech at a conference in Singapore. "Call me Cate, please!" she'd said, introducing herself with a broad smile so charming Carly could not help but feel flattered by this invitation to a first stage of intimacy. With her slim figure, wavy blond hair, puckish nose, broad mouth, full sensuous lips and, above all, her piercing blue eyes, Catrina struck her as a fine image of Western female beauty.

But it was her evident intelligence and supreme self-confidence that had most captivated Carly in the ensuing days as the pair regularly sought each other's company. Over lunches and beers in the evening, they had shared opinions and criticisms of the various speakers and research papers, discussing their own ideas and theories as well as the numerous frustrations of being a female academic, agreeing that their respective faculties were dominated by men.

"They're either patronising or predatory, or more likely both!" commented Catrina, and Carly laughed.

In fact, she laughed a lot, despite herself, at Catrina's wicked sense of humour. She had a lot of fun with some of the names of the conference attendees in particular.

"Did you go and hear that Professor Dymm? I did, and I must say he is aptly named. And what about that local guy, Dr. Wei Hung? Is that a misprint? I'd love to introduce his paper. 'Here is the man we have all been waiting to see—Dr. Wel Hung!'"

Carly had laughed politely but hadn't really appreciated that last joke. She did, however, enjoy the many personal stories Catrina regaled her with, her favourite being when a waiter in a New York restaurant had mistaken her for Cate Blanchett and brought out the entire kitchen staff to ask for her autograph.

"That's when I decided that people from now on could call me Cate," she concluded.

Carly's topics of conversation were a lot more serious. She'd just been awarded quite a generous level of funding for a new research project that would, she explained, focus on the careers of young Cantonese actresses from unprivileged backgrounds and the social factors that they felt impeded their ambitions. Catrina had listened with interest, lauding the pragmatic aims of the project—to seek out and propose practical solutions to counter these factors—but had strongly argued that it needed a more robust theoretical framework.

"After all, we are sociologists, not social workers," she'd commented. Then, suddenly excited, her eyes had lit up. "Say, why don't you invite me to join you in this, to add an international dimension to the project? And to work specifically on the theoretical implications of what you uncover?"

Her enthusiasm had been as infectious as her self-confidence had been overwhelming. Over the next few months, Carly's research had evolved into a joint project. Now Catrina was here with her for a week of joint field work.

This focus on rumours and mythmaking had emerged as an unexpected area of interest in response to early interviews Carly conducted with several female actors. For her part, she saw such stories, generated by local superstitions, as a communal coping mechanism, offering salutary fables for these young women to explain the success of the few by offering the compensation of schadenfreude to the many. On the other hand, Catrina was more interested in positioning them, as she put it, within "globalised theories of gender oppression."

Carly was not entirely happy with this.

"God, the drinks in this place are so expensive," Catrina said, looking at the mini bar price list. "Fortunately, I bought some beers earlier at the 7/11. Here, have one."

Carly accepted the can of Tsingtao, putting it aside while she took a sip from her bottle of water. Catrina was pouring her own beer into a glass when her mobile phone began to ring urgently. She picked it up, saw who was calling, and pursing her lips, rejected the call.

"She'll have to stop calling me so often," she muttered before turning back to Carly. "You know, when you come over to the UK, you can stay in my apartment. I hope you realise what a privilege that is," she added, taking a long drink of her beer as Carly gave her an embarrassed smile. "It's only a few girlfriends and my cleaner who normally get through the door. Oh, and sometimes my cleaner's daughter. God! Children are definitely not allowed inside! She's the exception. Besides," another long drink, "she's quiet. She doesn't disturb me."

Catrina put her glass down on the table and sighed.

"So, what do we make of the lovely Lucy? I thought it was an interesting tactic of hers, to turn the focus away from herself on to me. She could no doubt sense my… Well, to call it scepticism would be an understatement."

"I think we shouldn't judge her too quickly as a person less educated and therefore more superstitious, more gullible, than educated women such as ourselves."

Catrina looked doubtful, so Carly continued.

"Take my university. You know that building on the hill you called a labyrinth, where you got totally lost the other day?"

"Oh God, do you have to remind me? Let's see… The entrance I took brings you in on the fifth floor. To get out on to the main campus you take a lift down to the second floor—it doesn't go any lower—then the long escalator that goes all the way down to the cellar, then you walk back up to the ground floor and find the exit behind the staircase on your left, right?"

Carly smiled. She did enjoy telling this tale to visitors. "It's so weird, yes. The rumour in the university is that the designer was told to build it like that. It's not just because we are situated on the side of a mountain. You remember that story Lucy told about the father who found a rival dashi? Well, he paid for its construction as a gift to the university just after his wife died. What a big-hearted, generous man, you may think. But everyone knew that he and his wife did not get on at all. The rumour is he had her ashes buried secretly in one of the walls and the building is designed so her ghost cannot escape to haunt him." Catrina was looking at her with an incredulous expression. "You see, she was confined to a wheelchair when she died."

Catrina laughed heartily.

"My point is," concluded Carly, "Whatever you think of the story, it circulates in a very prestigious university. Anyone can be susceptible to…"

She was interrupted by the sound of a mobile phone ringing. This time, it was her own.

"Hello? Oh, hello!" To Catrina: "It's Lucy." Her smile changed to a look of concern. She listened for a while and then spoke in Cantonese while Catrina sat waiting impassively, although Carly sensed some tension in her look. Eventually, she turned away from her phone.

"Lucy's lost her passport. It was in her bag. When she left us, she went straight to the Thai embassy to sort out a visa and then found out it was missing. I told her she didn't need a visa to travel to Thailand from Hong Kong. This only made her more upset. She is in tears and asking if either of us has found it."

Catrina shook her head and mirrored Carly's look of concern. After a few more exchanges on the phone, Carly said, "She's crying. She waited months for this appointment, and now she'll have to cancel it."

"No, no, tell her not to do that so hastily," Catrina said quickly. "Look, tell her we'll go back to the university ourselves right now and have a good look for it. Say that we'll report it as missing to the departmental office and ask if anyone has handed it in. Tell her not to lose hope. It's bound to show up."

Carly turned back to her phone and relayed this plan to Lucy, who, though still in tears, seemed to calm down a little and thanked them both.

"I'm surprised," Carly said as they both picked up their bags and got ready to leave. "From your response this morning, I didn't think you'd have been so concerned. But I do appreciate it, and so does Lucy."

"Well, whatever I think, it means a lot to her. Besides," Catrina continued with a smile as she closed the door, "think of the story she can tell us when she gets back. There's nothing like a firsthand account in our type of work."

Bangkok, December 2nd

Catrina sipped at her coffee and looked at her watch. She still had thirty minutes before her appointment. Looking out from the corner where she had ensconced herself, she smiled sardonically. The bar was open to the street from where a mixture of pungent smells drifted in to mingle with the acrid smoke of cheap cigarettes.

My god, the company I keep!

An assortment of tattooed Western males were scattered around her, some on their own, some chatting loudly in groups, all leering openly at the bar girls and ladyboys[2] who were serving or flirting or just playing pool at the other end of the bar. She knew she was far more attractive than any of them but had long ago learned how to keep men at bay as well as how to attract their attention. Besides, she could tell these men were here to prey on flesh younger than her own, and it was too early for any of them to be drunk. Although barely comfortable, she didn't feel at all threatened.

Bangkok was much as she had imagined it. Just as busy as Hong Kong but crazier—more and varied crowds in the airport, a more chaotic road system once you got into the city, more traffic jams, more air pollution, more blatant sex work. She'd been surprised to discover that the so-called "temple" where this particular wizard practised was actually on a floor above a massage parlour in one of Bangkok's notorious sex districts. The information she had found on Wikipedia had suggested that these wizards, or lersi[3] as they were called in Thai, were to be found living as hermits in forests.

---

    2   **ladyboy**: A trans woman or transfeminine person in or from Asia. The use of *ladyboy* to refer to trans women is common and accepted in Southeast Asia (primarily Thailand) but considered offensive outside of it.

    3   **lersi**: A Thai word used to describe a spiritual person with mind powers, commonly depicted as hermits.

SEVEN CURSES

It hadn't been hard for her to find him. Lucy had already shared the address confidentially with Carly, and Catrina had known how to ask for it without showing too much interest, and so avoid any suspicion over the unexplained disappearance of the passport.

She hadn't planned to steal it. She'd simply acted on sudden impulse to the presented opportunity when Carly had accompanied Lucy to the restroom at the end of the interview. They'd both left their bags behind, and Catrina couldn't resist having a look inside Lucy's while she had the chance. *Ethnography trumps ethics every time,* she'd thought with a wry smile. On finding Lucy's passport tucked into a side pocket, she'd instinctively taken it and slipped it into her own bag, a plan quickly forming in her mind.

In spite of herself, Catrina had been impressed by Lucy's insight, for she didn't, in fact, feel fulfilled. It was nothing to do with her sex life—what she had later said to Carly was true—and she certainly didn't secretly hanker after marriage and motherhood. Christ! Certainly not motherhood.

But as far as her career was concerned, she was frustrated by her lack of fame, power and influence, both in her workplace and beyond. The senior positions in UWM were held almost exclusively by men. At first, she'd thought she could use her beauty and charm to aid her advancement, but this had proven not to be the case. The cultural trope that beautiful blonde equals bimbo ran deep, she discovered, even in what claimed to be one of England's leading universities. Her publications were always well received, but her reputation, good as it was, was limited to a narrow academic field. This had been frustrating her for some time and was what had immediately attracted her to Carly's project—that, and her need to respond to a complaint that awful Chinese student had officially made against her insinuating, among other things, that she'd shown contempt in class for her culture.

Anyway, she was sure she could make something sexy out of this project, even if Carly wasn't exactly on board with the idea. And how sexy would it be to write from her own firsthand experience about a visit to a mysterious Asian magician, who apparently could make one's dark desires come true? Surely, she could get media attention from this. Let her rival academics rail all they might against exoticism; she would make the exotic work in her favour.

Poor Lucy. Catrina had persuaded her not to cancel her appointment until the last minute. Meanwhile, she'd emailed the wizard herself, claiming to be Lucy, explaining that her email account had been hacked, so she was using a friend's. She confirmed her appointment and asked that any emails from Lucy's own address be subsequently ignored. Now here she was, and it was time to set off and get there punctually.

Switching to Google maps on her phone, she stepped from the shade of the bar into the street outside. It was like stepping into a steam oven, and soon she could feel the discomfort of damp perspiration in the roots of her hair and across her back. She twisted her shoulders awkwardly as she walked, trying to release her dress from its sweaty hold on her skin. At least she didn't have too far to go, and the relatively early hour meant the more sordid and rowdy aspects of the street had yet to make an appearance. Some girls seated outside the massage parlours were already plying their trade. "Massage?" they would call out to her and to any other passers-by, sometimes with an inviting smile. The sheer ugliness of most of them repulsed Catrina, and she wondered how any man, no matter how drunk or desperate, could be tempted to take up their offers.

She finally found the address hidden down a narrow passageway between a greasy-looking restaurant and another massage parlour, where the girls gave her only a cursory glance as she turned into the alley, removing her sunglasses to see better in the deep shade. Covering her nose to protect it from the stink of sewage rising from the drains and rancid cooking oil from the restaurant, she made her way along the passage, gradually leaving the sounds of the street behind her. At the far end, she climbed up a metal staircase to a door, tarnished and weathered but solid.

SEVEN CURSES

She pressed a buzzer on the wall beside it and waited, marvelling at the sudden quiet, a quiet that was eventually broken by the sound of footsteps approaching along what must have been a bare, echoing corridor. They stopped at the other side of the door. Bolts were drawn and hinges creaked as it was pulled half open. A small young woman with a shaven head gave her a sceptical, albeit a rather knowing, look.

Catrina put on her most confident smile.

"Hi. I'm clearly not Miss Leung. Unfortunately, she couldn't make it. But I'm a friend of hers and I see no reason why her appointment should be wasted. I've travelled here from Hong Kong especially to see the lersi. Look, I have the payment right here."

She opened her purse and drew out a thin wad of thousand baht[4] notes, which she had converted from dollars at the airport. Lucy had been quite open about how much the session was going to cost her and how long it had taken her to save the money for the trip.

The woman paused for a few seconds, all the while staring at Catrina with a curious look. Then "Wait here," she said and closed the door.

As the minutes drew by, Catrina wondered for the first time if she had made an error of judgement. She'd known it was a gamble, of course, but she figured there was less chance of the wizard refusing to see her if she showed up in person than if she had requested an appointment earlier via email. She was growing increasingly anxious when, finally, she heard the same footsteps approaching again and the door was opened.

To her immense relief, the young woman signalled for her to step inside. Ahead of her stretched a dingy, windowless corridor lit only by a single light bulb that hung shadeless from the ceiling. Catrina noted with distaste the faded cream coloured paint on the walls and the scratches on the floor tiles but appreciated the cooler temperature, nonetheless. The door behind her closed, and she turned to look at the woman.

She was quite young, dressed in white robes like those of a Buddhist

---

4   **baht:** The basic monetary unit of Thailand.

nun. Her face looked vaguely familiar, more Chinese than Thai, Catrina thought, but given the shaven head, she couldn't place the resemblance. The woman led Catrina along the corridor to a bare wooden staircase, which stopped abruptly outside a single white door that looked clean and new compared to its surroundings. Climbing the stairs, Catrina felt a mixture of excitement and apprehension. Once they had reached the door, the nun—for this she surely was—turned and looked at her dispassionately.

"Please remove your shoes now."

Catrina did so. The woman spoke English well but with a strong Chinese accent.

"Once inside the temple, remain silent until you are spoken to and answer any questions truthfully. The lersi knows who you are, Professor."

If this was supposed to impress her, it didn't. He'd evidently got her name from the address of the emails she'd sent while claiming to be Lucy.

"He will decide whether to help you or not after you have talked a little. And one word of advice," she added. "Don't mention or show your money until he has made his decision. It will only insult him."

Bangkok airport, December 3rd just after midnight

SITTING UPRIGHT IN her seat, waiting for the plane to take off, Catrina covered her ears with a set of headphones purely to signal to the spotty young man seated next to her she was in no mood to engage in conversation with him. She had her notebook on her lap and had intended to jot down the details of her extraordinary day as an aide-mémoire[5] for the account she would write up later in her research journal. But she couldn't concentrate. Two bizarre incidents had

---

5   **aide-mémoire:** A French loanword; something, usually written, that helps you to remember something.

occurred since she had left the temple, and they still had her shaken.

Thinking the experience might provide her account with some useful local colour, she'd journeyed back to the airport via the sky train and metro. The sky train had been extremely crowded with passengers crushed together along the central aisle, but Catrina had found a vacant seat and pushed her way into it next to a young mother who had a child, a little girl seated on her lap clutching a doll in her hands. The girl had stared at Catrina, her eyes moving from somewhere near her stomach, then up to her face and back. Suddenly she'd begun to cry, struggling away from her, burying her face in her mother's shoulder and hiding her doll from sight. She pointed to Catrina, sobbing the same phrase over and over again. Her mother's attempts to calm her proved to be futile. Other passengers were by then staring with some interest, and the whole scene was becoming embarrassing. Catrina looked inquisitively at the mother, who shook her head in puzzlement.

"She saying, 'He want my doll! He want my doll!'" and, vacating the seat, the woman squeezed her way down the carriage, the child still visibly fearful, snivelling and staring over her mother's shoulder at Catrina until the crowd had hidden her from view.

The second incident happened at the airport when she tried to scan her boarding card at the gate and pass through into security. No matter which gate she tried, it would open but close again as soon as she began to walk through it. Nor was the assistant able to help her, her own card proving equally erratic.

"I don't understand that at all," the assistant had told her as she had manually let her through the staff gate at the side. "It's like something's deliberately playing with it."

Catrina could shrug off the wild imaginings of a frightened child and incomprehensible glitches in technology, but what unnerved her was the way in which these events chimed with words the wizard had spoken to her earlier. Closing her eyes, she put her notebook aside and lay back in her seat in a vain attempt to sleep.

Cate Whitehead: Extract from research journal, written December 4th, describing events of December 2nd

What struck me most as I first entered the temple was the contrast it offered to everything in its immediate surroundings. The light was subtle, unlike the glaring sunlight of the busy street, the grimy shadows of the alleyway, and the dingy light of the corridor outside. Here there was neither the noise of traffic nor the echoing emptiness of the entrance hall, just the gentle sound of religious chanting and the soft, rhythmic pulse of gamelan music coming through a hidden speaker. The soothing perfume of incense emanated from a corner of the room. And it was cool, comfortably cool with no evidence, visual or aural, of air conditioning. So far, so stereotypical, I thought. Everything was deliberately concocted to offer an illusion of spiritual refuge to the tortured soul, a sense of serenity, a feeling that here was a place where you could unburden your troubles and find some peace. In preparation for what? I wondered.

The light, as I mentioned, was subtle. Lamps with coloured bulbs gave off different shades of green, perhaps to suggest the more rural setting in which a dashi or lersi would traditionally have practised. Above each of the lamps—four in all—was a different framed print of what looked like battle scenes from ancient Eastern mythology. These were grey in colour. Everything else was white—the walls, the floor tiles, the curtains, the drapes that hung over a door that led into an adjacent chamber. White, too, were the robes of the nun, who now sat on a stool in a corner behind me, and the more ornate wooden chair that faced me on the opposite wall, alongside which was a small table upon which I could see a porcelain jug and two glasses.

In the chair sat a man of over fifty years of age, lean and fit-looking, clothed in white robes like those of the nun. He had short, cropped hair and a neatly trimmed goatee and dark, piercing eyes that were studying me closely. Once again, I was surprised; he was not what I had expected. Pictures of the dashi I had seen on the internet were of thin old men with long white hair and beards.

SEVEN CURSES

The nun had told me, in no uncertain terms, that I had to wait until I was spoken to. I obeyed, returning the stare of the dashi, refusing to be cowered. After a notable silence he eventually spoke but in Thai, to the nun, who got up from her stool and walked over to the table, picked up the jug and poured out a colourless liquid into one of the glasses and handed it to me. She then fetched her stool, placing it behind me, and gestured for me to sit down. I did so and tasted the drink. Its flavour was unusual, sweet, not unpleasant. I drank some more and waited.

NOTE: The following conversation is as true to the original as I can recall. In order not to appear condescending to my interlocutors, I have corrected the frequent grammatical errors of their English.

"Epic scenes from the Ramayana." The dashi indicated to the prints as he spoke. "Taken from the magnificently sculpted tableaux in Angkor Wat, in Cambodia. I saw your gaze was inquisitive. Did you know it is the largest religious building in the world?"

I looked at him and said nothing. He held my gaze.

"So Ms. Leung could not keep her appointment."

"No. Unfortunately not."

"And you decided to come in her place."

"She offered no objection."

"But it is not her who will make the decision."

I began to reach for my purse but remembered what the nun had told me. Instead, I sat still and gave him a warm smile.

"Tell me," he said, "are you a spiritual person?"

"I'm a sociologist," I replied. "A professor. It's curiosity that brings me here."

Then I told him of the stories I had heard from Lucy, and he nodded, saying nothing to confirm or deny them. Finally, I told him I wanted to physically experience firsthand what these young women had, so I could…

"So you can write about it," he interrupted. "Yes, yes, I know what you people do."

I assured him of my academic integrity.

"Everything will be accurate and anonymous. I promise you that."

He waved a hand dismissively.

"And how many people read these journals you publish in, Professor? No!"

I held my tongue. Now was not the time to challenge him.

"What you do or do not write does not bother me. No," he repeated. "I am not concerned for myself." He paused. "My concern is for you."

I gave a short laugh, which he ignored. Instead, he stood from his chair and approached me. Taking my face in his hands, he stared into my eyes. His hands were soft and cold and felt strangely soothing. I did not feel as though his touch was a violation, more like a medical examination.

"When it comes to ritual practices such as mine, curiosity without belief is dangerous," he said. "There is oil, as you have heard. Ritual oil. And curiosity without belief can lead to unforeseen outcomes. If you do not respect the ritual," he paused, "then the ghost of the dead person who has supplied the oil may pursue you rather than protect you."

I tried not to react to these words.

"But there is something you want from this oil," he continued. "I can see it in your eyes. Desire more than belief, yes. But desire often feeds belief. I often wonder where one ends and the other begins."

I flinched as he suddenly let go of my face. He returned to his chair and sat down.

"You are an ambitious woman. I see that clearly. As with all ambitious women, the oil can indeed help you. It is true what you have heard. Like the master who taught me, I only use oil extracted from a young child or a baby, whose spirit is more likely to attach itself to you as it would in life to its mother."

He leaned forward towards me.

"But you must be very, very careful how you treat such a ghost if it is to bring you joy and not ruin your life. I will give you advice but, once you leave, it will be your responsibility. Now you must decide if you want to go ahead with the ritual or not."

Writing down the last few sentences brought back the sense of eerie discomfort Catrina had felt at the time. Later, she would embellish her reaction with more descriptive prose, but right now, she needed a break. Overall, she was being as truthful as she could be, she felt. Maybe too truthful. She might edit out the wizard's words about ambition and desire and find another angle there.

She had decided to use the term "dashi." This was the Chinese term Lucy had used. It sounded more authentic than 'wizard,' with its *Lord of the Rings* connotations. And lersi didn't feel like the right word, either.

The dashi had realised her subterfuge almost immediately but had not admonished her, and most of the rest of what she had written was as accurate as she could recall. She also consoled herself with the fact that, in essence, what she had written about Lucy was misleading without being false: it *was* unfortunate for her that she couldn't come, and she had *not* raised any objection to Catrina taking her appointment. How could she? She knew nothing about it.

Catrina looked at her watch. After 2:00 a.m. Her mind was fuzzy. Jet lag, of course. She poured herself a glass of wine and turned back to the journal.

The next section was going to be trickier. When she had asked, the dashi had refused to say how he gained access to these dead children, but he told her he only used certain parts of their corpses to make the oil—principally the lips and tongues but, on occasion, the male foreskin. Perhaps with this latter detail, he had been playing a deliberately ghoulish joke on this faithless Western woman. She'd remained impassive, not wanting to risk this appointment being brought to a premature end through any inappropriate reaction. But how to write such details down without them sounding like something from a cheap horror film? How to make it believable? She decided to leave this section for now and move on to her anointment with the oil.

The nun led me through the door into the adjacent chamber. This was smaller, with what looked like a massage couch in its centre and a chair to the side. Next to the chair was a small cupboard. The same subtle lighting as the neighbouring room, though somewhat dimmer, the same music, the same wafts of perfume in the sleepy air.

The dashi spoke from the doorway. "Now I will leave you. My assistant will help you prepare for the ritual."

The nun joined her hands and, in the Thai manner, gave him a slight curtsy as he left.

The preparation was simple enough. I was asked to remove my clothes and put on a thin white robe made of silk. I luxuriated in its touch. It felt light and smooth as it caressed my skin, and a drowsy pleasure began to flow through me.

"What was in that drink you gave me?" I asked the nun.

She didn't answer but indicated for me to sit in the chair. She drew out a cushion from the cupboard, which she placed at one end of the couch. She then took a brush from a pocket in her robe and ran it through my hair quite expertly with soft, regular, sensual strokes. When she finally stopped, I sighed, feeling pampered and extremely relaxed. She replaced the brush in her pocket and asked me to lie down on the couch and wait for the dashi.

He was alone when he re-entered the chamber. I had expected some ritual chanting, the uttering of archaic phrases, and had visualised the oil in a chalice of some kind, carried in on a silver platter. None of this proved to be the case. Instead, he drew a small, thin, tubular bottle out of his pocket, very ordinary, with a screw top, which he removed carefully.

"What happens now?" I asked.

"It is very simple. I will ask you a series of questions that you must agree to if the ritual is to go ahead. The ritual itself is very short and straightforward and will be over in seconds. Are you ready?"

There I was, naked under silk, lying on a bed, my hair loose, alone in a room with a man who claimed to have great powers. No one knew I was there. No one even knew what country I was in. I should have felt profoundly vulnerable, but I didn't. There was nothing sexual in this man's attention. I can only compare my situation to that of being in the presence of a trusted doctor. Strange as it might sound, I felt completely safe and nodded my agreement.

"Then, as long as you answer 'I do' to the following questions, I will proceed."

Very solemnly he held the bottle over me and asked me first if I believed in the oil. Of course I did; I was looking straight at it. He then asked if I believed in the spirit of this oil. Again, I answered "I do." In any case, I believed I knew what the spirit of this oil was meant to represent—success, sexual and professional success, and I certainly believed in that. His third and final question was more baffling: did I accept responsibility for the spirit of this oil? I hesitated, unsure what this meant, but only for a few moments. "I do!" I answered, whereupon he emptied a few colourless and viscous drops onto his forefinger and smeared it gently around my lips, uttering words in Thai that I could not understand. He then asked me to show the tip of my tongue and dropped the oil directly on to it, again speaking softly in Thai. Then he stood back.

"Now, lick your lips and roll your tongue round your mouth and we shall see if the ritual has been successful."

How best to describe the sensation that followed?

It was like that of a first kiss. The oil felt alive, sensuous and organic, as though it were exploring my lips like a new lover, licking and sucking at my tongue as if it were the object of someone else's pleasure. More than pleasure, *hunger*. It could so easily have felt like a violation, but instead it was like feeling wanted and desired for the first time.

The sensation began to diminish, and I didn't want it to. I wanted more. Opening my eyes, I could see the dashi looking at me rather than at the bottle that was still open in his hand and which he was handing to the nun. As she took it, I snatched it from her and shook much of its contents over my lips and onto my tongue before either could wrench the bottle away from me. The dashi cried out and struggled with me, but I was only aware of this somewhere at the edge of my consciousness. Instead, I revelled in the immensity of the pleasure, as though there was nothing in this world other than my lips, my tongue, and the sensuous power of the oil.

Catrina took another break from her writing. It was well after 3:00 a.m. now. She read through what she had just written, satisfied she had captured the essence of the experience. Closing her eyes, she recalled the moments when she'd fully regained her senses, exhilarated, still with a feeling of thrilled exhaustion. The dashi and the nun stood over her with very different expressions in their eyes, the one full of worried concern, the other with a look that had puzzled her at the time and still puzzled her now. It almost looked *triumphant*. They left her to get dressed, and she had done so slowly, gradually regaining her strength and simultaneously losing her sense of exhilaration. Instead, she had begun to feel embarrassed at the thought of the spectacle she must have made of herself, losing all rational control in that way. Already the sensation of the oil was becoming only a memory, one that generated a sense of loss, of emptiness and regret.

She had paid the money, and the dashi had taken it dispassionately, not bothering to count it. He wasn't angry, she could tell, but a deep frown furrowed his brow. Before she left, he had asked her in a voice full of urgency to listen carefully to his advice.

"You have taken far more oil than anyone I have ever known before. There are likely to be unforeseeable consequences for this. It may mean that your own power increases substantially. I rather hope this will be the case, for your own sake. But it could equally mean that the ghost who will now travel with you will be very needy, very demanding. I advise you to honour and care for its childish spirit by keeping a candle lit at all times and surrounding it with toys and playthings. Read to it before bedtime, as you would to a child. And above all, feed it, feed it well. Otherwise, it will likely feed on you."

She said nothing, just bade them both a polite goodbye. But his words had left her feeling cold towards him. How patronising. He seemed to be forgetting she wasn't one of his gullible young actresses. How ridiculous of him to think that she, a reputable academic, would take such advice seriously or heed such a warning.

But then she remembered the incident on the sky train and at the airport. Although she had experienced nothing similar since, recalling them, a chill slithered down the length of her spine. She shivered, then yawned and decided now she might actually be able to sleep. As she undressed, however, she still couldn't shake that uneasy feeling. Maybe tomorrow she would buy a candle after all, she thought sleepily as she lay her head on her pillow. It might work on her subconscious, calm her fears…

Then she lurched awake, her eyes popping open. Wait! What was she thinking? Was she losing her senses? She needed to own this thing. If writing about it wasn't enough, if she had to play with this whole superstitious nonsense, then she would do so on terms that would amuse her, that might work to her advantage. She puckered her lips and rolled her tongue around them. Who could she trap with this enhanced sexual magnetism of hers? Who might she lure under the mistletoe at the departmental Christmas party?

Smiling as she thought of a number of possible victims, she finally fell asleep.

December 6th

THE TWO MEN sat in a corner of an empty bar near a Christmas tree, the same one that was retrieved, polished, and erected in the same place with the same decorations every year. Teaching had finished for the term; the undergraduate students had all left the previous weekend, so there was peace on the campus—if not on earth—for the next four weeks at least.

It was early evening, around 5:30 p.m. The two men, senior academics in the faculty, were friends as well as close colleagues and had started to drink early in preparation for the annual Christmas social later that evening. Neither was particularly looking forward to it. The elder of the two was in his fifties, tall, bald, with a small, tidy beard. As head of faculty, he wore his authority as impeccably as his suit and carried it as comfortably as his smart leather briefcase. It was common knowledge that a number of female graduate students found him very sexy; such is the allure of power. He had no choice but to attend this event and had been bemoaning the fact to his colleague—a younger man who spoke jovially but deferentially to his friend, never forgetting that he was also his boss.

"Well, I suppose it is the one day of the year when we can all get drunk together and let our hair down—no offence, H."

"H" stood for "Head." H was used to this term of address. All members of staff called him "H." Even his wife did now and again.

H accepted his companion's comment as the joke it was but didn't smile. The pair had previously been discussing the vexed question of next term's staff development interviews—who was likely to apply for promotion and which candidates they thought should be supported.

"What about our lovely Cate?" The younger man had a mischievous twinkle in his eye as he spoke.

"Well, it's no secret that *you've* always fancied her," H replied. "She's too mouthy for my taste. Besides, she leans the other way."

"Oh, I'm sure she'll lean whichever way suits her career best."

They smiled conspiratorially. The two enjoyed this private, transgressive banter, though they were far too careful to engage in it when in company.

"Seriously," the younger man continued, "didn't she make a good case in the last round?"

H leant back in his seat. "Not bad, but it did fall short. Her publication profile is good, certainly, but evidence of impact is slim. And she was told she needed to develop her international reputation. Which, in fairness, she has started to do with this recent Hong Kong collaboration. She might have to wait another year or two, though, before we can support her case."

His colleague looked about him. Two members of the secretarial staff had just entered the bar, but they could tell the pair were in conference and knew enough to keep their distance. He lowered his voice, regardless.

"And her student satisfaction score must have been hit by that problem with the Chinese girl, the one she was jointly supervising."

H shrugged. "That Chinese girl seems to have had a problem with everyone, and not just with teaching staff. She also complained formally about one of the security staff and even one of her housemates."

"Yes, so I've heard. Were the complaints all as petty as the one Cate faced?"

H shook his head. He looked edgy, like a man who needed a cigarette. "Well, Xie Fei didn't see it as petty. She said Cate refused to give her a tutorial until she had attended a course of seminars she was giving to a group of undergraduates. This she found insulting enough, but then Cate apparently continually mispronounced her name in the seminar group. Xie is the family name, pronounced *Shui*. When she pointed this out to Cate in class—and told her she was pronouncing it wrongly—Cate didn't take kindly to being publicly corrected like that."

"Well, why not call her by her English name? What was it again?"

"Rose."

There was a pause, and they both shook their heads in silently shared amusement before taking a drink.

"Anyway," continued H, "Cate apparently saw this as a further insult. So, she began ignoring the girl in class, never inviting her to contribute to discussions. If ever she did speak up, Cate would deliberately mispronounce her name as some kind of joke. 'Oh, *She* has spoken!' and once she silenced her with 'Oh, *She* has spoken enough!' Apparently, this amused many of the home students, especially the boys, so Xie said she felt shamed into remaining silent."

The younger man laughed. "Sorry. Cate evidently never went through cultural sensitivity training."

H raised his eyes to the ceiling. "Keep your voice down. Someone might hear you, design the course, and make us all attend it." He laughed sardonically. "How to be culturally compassionate as well as critically clever." He practically emptied his beer glass. "Anyway," he continued, "one of the male students saw this as a licence to be offensive and began to refer to Xie Fei as 'Shitface' in her hearing."

The younger man raised an eyebrow. "Well, that's going a bit far…"

"Cate said she never knew about this, but Xie Fei blamed her for setting the precedent."

"Hmm. Well, *She* left, didn't she?"

"Left us and the country. Just disappeared one morning after wrecking her flat and causing hundreds of pounds worth of damage. The university was very anxious to keep a lid on the whole affair."

"Cate must have been relieved about that."

"Cate's popular. None of the home students will say a word against her." He frowned. "But I did have to give her a pretty stiff dressing down."

"Lucky you!" The younger man gave a lewd laugh and took a drink from his pint. Then, looking towards the door, "Uh-oh, talk of the devil—or rather, the she-devil…"

H followed his colleague's gaze and saw Catrina at the entrance of the bar. She looked good, which was no surprise.

More surprising was the fact that she was walking towards him, a brazen look in her eye, an alluring smile on her lips, and a large sprig of mistletoe in her hand.

December 20th

H MADE HIMSELF comfortable on the settee and cast his eyes about the apartment. It was sizable, tastefully furnished, and very tidy. He had expected no less. He took a sip from his scotch and waited for Cate to finish readying herself. She was in her bedroom—a fortress he had yet to penetrate, but he knew it was only a question of time.

He still couldn't credit it. If you had told him two weeks ago where and with whom he would be spending the Friday before Christmas, he wouldn't have believed you. If you had mentioned that he would be passing most of his days in a state of delirious desire and ardent anticipation like a besotted teenager, he would have laughed in your face. Any suggestion that his obsession with a woman would make him reckless to the point of risking his marriage he would have dismissed out of hand. He would have told you that you didn't know what you were talking about and certainly didn't know *him*.

Yet just one kiss had changed all of that.

He sang to himself about being kissed like never before and wanting to be kissed like that forever more. How ridiculous that such a banal lyric from an old pop song should define his feelings so well. But it was true. It was her kiss, more than anything else, that he longed for, that he could not get enough of. She had so far resisted all other advances, coldly and persistently. Even her kisses could hardly be described as passionate. But it didn't seem to matter. Each kiss that he snatched from her, however brief, served only to bewitch him all the more.

He looked at his watch. The play didn't start for another hour. Plenty of time. But he could do with another drink to calm himself. After all, this was his first proper "date with Cate" (the phrase both amused and excited him). Before tonight, he'd had to limit himself to forays into her office and brief kisses in the corridor when no one was about. This was the first time she'd agreed to go out publicly with him. The first time he'd been allowed into her private space. He lured her with tickets for *The Taming of the Shrew*. "*God, that dreadful, sexist play!*" had been her first predictable response. But then she'd become intrigued when he told her that the male parts were being played by women and the women's parts by men. Not at all H's cup of tea, but he didn't care. He doubted whether he would be able to concentrate on it, anyway.

He got up and found the whisky bottle perched invitingly on a desk over by the window next to a laptop and a sheaf of printed papers. He picked up the bottle and looked at the label. Glen Moray, no wonder he was enjoying it. Then he picked up the papers. As he had thought, it was a draft for an article, one she was probably working on now. Maybe he could help her. And maybe… He looked towards the bedroom and smiled. Sitting down at the desk, H poured himself a generous measure and began to read. After two pages, he threw it down. This wasn't Cate, evidently. It was very poor, undergraduate level. Limited language, incoherent referencing, poor focus, no theory. Probably one she had been asked to review.

He looked at his watch again. Cate was taking an inordinately long time. "Cate?" he called out. No response. Earlier, he told himself he wouldn't rush her, would try his best to act cool in her presence. "Cate?" he called out again, this time approaching the bedroom. Still no answer. He knocked and gently turned the handle.

She was sitting at her dresser, staring blankly at her reflection in the mirror. She'd changed into a tight-fitting red dress and her body looked stunning, but her face looked as drawn and tired as it had done when she'd answered the door to him earlier. Her makeup remained untouched in front of her, and he wondered what she had been doing for the past twenty minutes.

"Cate?" This time his voice was inquisitive, concerned. "What's up? We really need to go soon."

"What?" She turned and looked at him, as though surprised. He noticed the bags under her eyes and the wrinkles around them. This did nothing to diminish his desire for her.

"Did you hear it?" she asked, looking around the room.

"Hear what?"

"The baby crying. He sounds hungry."

"What baby? Does your neighbour have a baby? How annoying! No wonder you look so tired." He forced a laugh. *'God, she looks spooked,'* he thought.

Suddenly, her eyes cleared, as if she were snapping out of a trance. She looked at him, seeming to notice his presence for the first time.

"H? Oh yes, the play. The bloody play."

He sat on the edge of the bed, near enough to take her hand. She didn't resist, and it thrilled him.

"You look dreadfully tired. Are you not sleeping?"

"Yes, yes, I am—too much. I wake up exhausted every morning. Unable to think clearly. Sometimes it takes a while for me to work out where I am. And… And… I'm forgetting things."

"You need to rest."

She sighed. "But I *can't*. I have that article to finish. The deadline is next week."

He asked her which journal it was for, and she told him. He nodded. "You've published there before, haven't you?"

"Yes, yes. But I'm struggling with it. It's been on my desk untouched for two days."

H couldn't hide his astonishment.

"That one? Surely not!"

She looked at him accusingly, almost in tears.

"You looked at it?"

"I… I…just glanced at it."

"And…?"

He paused.

"It's not to your usual standard, I must say."

The tears began to flow.

"Look, look, don't worry. I know the editor of that journal quite well. I'll contact him. I'll explain that you've been under the weather. I'll ask if you can have a few more weeks. I'm sure he will agree. And…" another pause, longer this time, "why don't I have a look at it for you? I'll revise what you have written, make it acceptable. You need to forget about things for a while. Just take a rest. Trust me."

The tears didn't stop, but she didn't disagree.

Excited by her newfound helplessness, by her sudden dependence on him, H couldn't hold back any longer. He leant forward and kissed her. The feel of those lips, the touch of that tongue. *Ecstasy*. He drew her into his arms.

"Let me take care of you. And let's forget about the bloody play."

He picked her up and lay her on the bed, and he felt the thrill of arousal as she offered him no resistance.

Email from Carly Shu, December 23rd

Catrina, I haven't heard from you since your return to the UK, and you haven't responded to my previous two emails. I won't repeat myself, but I am now more angry than disappointed. It was cowardly to leave Lucy's passport in the office anonymously like that. Cowardly and unfeeling. You haven't tried to deny that it was you. This lack of response only serves to confirm my sad suspicions.

Lucy has lost a lot of money. The dashi won't confirm or deny whether you took her appointment or not, but we know you must have. I cannot work with someone so unethical. I will take steps to terminate our partnership. Should you publish about your experience, I will expose what you did.

I liked you. Your cleverness, your sense of humour. You were full of life, and I was a victim of your charm. You have taught me a painful lesson.

Carly

December 28th

It was the same every morning. Cate would wake up exhausted after a night so vividly awful that the experience was less like sleep and rather like living in some hellish alternative reality. And every morning, she would struggle but fail to recall her dreams.

This morning, however, the phone rang and awoke her near the end of the nightmare. When she had put it down again, she found she could remember everything clearly.

It always began in a private, air-conditioned room in Bangkok. She was lying with her eyes closed, comfortably naked on a couch, being massaged by a beautiful young woman who was smiling at her. Catrina was smiling too, enjoying the strong touch of the fingers as they worked over her scalp and forehead.

Her pleasure would then be broken by the cry of a baby. The massage would stop, and she would open her eyes to see that the masseuse had transformed shockingly into a bearded, white-haired old man. His smile was sinister, and he held a bottle she recognised in his hands whose contents he began to pour onto her lips. As she opened her mouth to tell him to stop, the oil would flood down into her throat. Choking on the warm, viscous fluid, she would turn her head aside as the oil continued to pour on to her exposed cheek. It was then that she would see the baby for the first time, and she knew he was slightly bigger and stronger than on the previous night, a baby boy with Asian features, crawling across the floor towards her.

That was the point when she always woke up, drenched in sweat, gasping for breath. Too exhausted to get out of bed, she would try to stay awake at all costs by thinking of something stimulating or puzzling she'd recently read. But this was bound to fail. Terrified of what might come next, she would feel her mind slowly and inevitably drifting back to sleep.

Only it never felt like sleep. Each night, unable to move, she was aware of lying on a bed—her own bed this time—blanketed in darkness, breathing heavily, waiting. She would hear it before she felt it, an invisible presence crawling up her body. She would thrash her head from side to side, but it always managed to find her face, covering her mouth so she couldn't scream, leaving her barely able to breathe, weighing her head down deeper into the pillow.

Then she would feel what she could only describe as a snake-like gust of air writhing its way over her tongue, into her throat, through her facial tissue into her skull, and up into her brain, where she could feel it sucking and biting and flicking its tongue, feeding voraciously, emptying her mind as it did so. How long this would go on for, she had no idea, but it always felt like an eternity.

It had been H on the phone—again. He wanted to see her soon after the New Year, when he could safely escape the torture of his family Christmas, as he put it. She sat still and thought for a minute. No matter how curt she was, how difficult, how unresponsive to his advances, it seemed to make no difference to his desire for her—or rather, his need for the physical contact of his lips pressing against hers, his tongue entwining itself around her own. She had willed this upon herself, not believing it would work, of course.

And it *hadn't* worked as it was supposed to. Instead of using H to gain influence and power, she would be fortunate if he managed to help her keep her job. How much longer would she have to put up with him? Three years, was it? Is that what Lucy had said? Could she bear it?

She was suddenly aware she was having a rare moment of clarity and recalled the advice of the dashi. She went into the bathroom and gazed into the mirror, shocked to see how thin and drawn she looked. What had she been eating? How had she spent Christmas Day? She was appalled to realise she had no idea. A wave of tearful regret passed through her as she thought about how her ex-lovers would shun her if they saw her like this. But there was no time for self-pity. She had to act while she could think straight.

At her laptop, she typed a few words into the search engine and after several minutes, she'd learned enough. Without caring about her appearance, she threw on a thick coat and warm scarf, pulled on a pair of winter boots, grabbed her bag, and hurried out of the apartment, slamming the door forcefully and locking it behind her.

Seven Curses

January 6th

THE FIRST THING that struck Mrs. Gee when she stepped into the apartment was the smell. Incense, like in a church, but with something pungent and unpleasant to it. Looking about her, she shook her head. She had always considered Dr. Whitehead's apartment one of her easier jobs, done in ninety minutes, but this mess would take her all morning. If things continued like this, she would have to ask for a lot more money.

Mandy was already searching in her bag for toys as her mother placed it on the floor and took out a prettily decorated, child-sized mask she had found online, cheap now that the pandemic was over.

"Here, let me put this on you," she said, drawing her daughter towards her. Mandy put up no resistance; for a three-year-old, she was very well-behaved, and Mrs. Gee was forever grateful for that. Taking out a box of building bricks, the little girl skipped to the settee and sat on the floor while her mother adjusted her own mask, then put on a pair of thin gloves and took a bottle of disinfectant spray out of the bag.

She had noticed the change in Dr. Whitehead before Christmas, soon after her return from Asia. She must have picked up something nasty over there; she looked so pale and thin. Brought some horrible virus back from Hong Kong. Well, that was part of China, wasn't it, and that was where Covid had started. She couldn't understand why anyone would want to go there. She imagined it as a dirty, overcrowded, disease-ridden place. If she hadn't been in such need of the money, she would have handed in her notice immediately to avoid contamination. Instead, she would take precautions, do the job, and leave as quickly as she could. And, as for her next visit, double her fee.

But the smell! What was it exactly? Mandy had emptied the bricks onto the floor and was carefully trying to build a tower with them as Mrs. Gee followed her nose through an open door into the bedroom.

In the middle of a low table, new to the room, stood a tall, coloured wax candle with a yellow flame flickering from its wick. Gathered around it were a bowl of cooked rice, a dish of segmented oranges and chopped banana, and a plate of cooked meat—chicken and pork, she thought. The fruit had liquified, and the meat was discoloured. Perched in the centre of the rice, an incense stick burned gently, sending tiny swirls of smoke into the air. The food had evidently been there for some days, and the smell was overpowering. A bottle of red liquid had been positioned in the middle of the food. It was most likely a fizzy fruit drink with a straw poking from it but, from the doorway, it looked more like blood.

On the floor, in front of the table, were some toys—some stickle bricks, a couple of colourful plastic cars, a Barbie doll, and what looked like a white furry fox perched on top of a small pile of picture books.

Catrina sat on the edge of the bed, wearing only a dressing gown and looking much worse than the last time Mrs. Gee had seen her. The bedsheets were a grubby mess, and Dr. Whitehead stared at her as though she barely recognised her. Mrs. Gee was so shocked that she could hardly speak. When she did, her voice shook.

"Dr. Whitehead! What is this?" She pointed to the table. "What is happening?"

Catrina followed the direction of her finger and spoke listlessly.

"He likes dolls. I know he likes dolls. But I bought him some boys' toys, just in case."

"Who…who likes dolls?"

"Max. Max does." She coughed. "I call him Max. A good name for a boy, don't you think? Hmm?"

Mrs. Gee glanced about her. Had someone left a baby in this woman's charge? She was in no state to look after a child; she couldn't even look after herself.

"But, Dr. Whitehead, where is he? Where is…Max? And…and who does he belong to?"

"Oh, I suppose… I suppose he belongs to me."

"Really, Dr. Whitehead. You need to see a doctor. Urgently."

Catrina shook her head.

"Oh no, no, I don't need a doctor. I've seen a wizard."

Backing towards the door, a concerned look on her face, Mrs. Gee was beginning to think that this Asian virus, whatever it was, must attack the brain. No amount of money was worth this.

"The food," she said, "it's putrid. No one can eat that. Certainly not a baby."

"No," came the answer. "I don't think he likes it. But he's supposed to. And the wizard told me to feed him." She gave Mrs. Gee a vacant stare and started to tap the side of her head with one finger. "But...*this* is what he likes. My brain. He likes to feed on my brain."

At that moment, there came a crash from the living room, followed by a little girl's cries. Mrs. Gee rushed into the room. Mandy was sitting there, sobbing loudly, her building bricks scattered across the floor.

"He knocked them down!" she screamed. "He knocked them all down!"

Mrs. Gee picked up Mandy to comfort her and cast a fearful look towards the bedroom. Catrina stood in the doorway, leaning against the architrave. Her voice was sleepy.

"Max doesn't like other children, I'm afraid."

January 9th

H hadn't been able to see Cate when he planned to. Flu. An evil dose of it had hit him soon after he'd called her before the new year. He'd only recovered just in time for yesterday's faculty leaders' away day, which had been predictably dreary and pointless, and today's pre-term departmental meeting, which he had to chair, of course. The two or three times he tried to call Cate since his recovery, she hadn't answered her phone.

He only got wind of how bad things were through the gossip swirling around the room before the meeting. Different groups had gathered in different parts of the room, but they all seemed to be focused on the one topic: Cate. Cate was ill; she had picked up a horrible virus in Asia; Cate had lost her good looks, had become a dowdy spinster overnight; Cate was consumed with regret, indulging in fantasies of motherhood; Cate had joined a bizarre religious cult that followed the teachings of some mysterious Asian wizard; Cate had gone crazy, had lost her mind. Each group was discussing some of these things, maybe all of these things.

Before opening the meeting, H had managed to trace the source of these rumours to a Mrs. Gee, a cleaner who was employed by a few members of the teaching staff and was a friend of one of the secretaries. He calmed the room by assuring everyone he would make it a priority to investigate and report back to them before the end of the week. He praised them for their humane concern.

He ended the meeting early and drove over to Cate's apartment, where it took a few minutes for her to answer the door. She looked as bad as he had anticipated. He embraced her, nonetheless, but recoiled at the strong odour of stale sweat and bad breath. He asked her, gently, what on earth was wrong but received no verbal response, so he led her to an armchair, sat her down, went into the bathroom and began to run a bath.

He then went into her bedroom. The candle had burnt down and hadn't been relit. There was no sign of the food Mrs. Gee had spoken of; evidently, she'd thrown it away. Some toys and a couple of dolls were on the floor still, and H tripped over a pile of children's books as he moved to the other side of the bed to straighten the sheets, which were relatively clean. Mercifully, Mrs. Gee had completed her tasks before rushing out to tell all and sundry her story. No doubt greatly embellishing the details. He went into the kitchen and looked inside the bin; there were one or two cans and an empty milk carton in it, nothing else. All the time he spoke loudly to Cate about how concerned everyone was for her health, how they all wished her a speedy recovery, how they all missed her lively sense of humour. She still wasn't answering him, so he went into the living room to check on her. A single tear had welled in her eye and was trickling down her cheek.

After he bathed and dried her, he found a clean dressing gown and helped her into it, then helped her clean her teeth, talking to her, gently chiding her, like he used to with his daughter when she was a little girl. He then led her back into the bedroom and sat her carefully on the newly made bed, where he had plumped up some pillows to make her comfortable. Sitting on the edge of the bed, facing her, he placed a hand gently on her cheek.

"You mustn't worry," he said, softly. "I'll get a nurse to come in every day to look after you until you're feeling better. I'll get her to clean you and feed you properly and take you for walks. Food and exercise will soon get you your figure back. She'll put your makeup on for you and dress you in nice clothes. And every evening I'll come and take care of you."

He bent forward, slid his hand down from her cheek and on to her breast, pressed his erection into her thigh and kissed her long and hard.

Cate offered no resistance. She was barely aware of his presence and only occasionally had his words made sense to her. Her eyes were open, however, and she was peering over his shoulder into the corner of the bedroom, where the toys lay scattered across the floor and where she could see the shadow of a child materialise before her eyes, cuddling up next to the furry white fox she couldn't recall buying and that seemed to be staring at her. The little boy clenched and unclenched his tiny fists and blinked his tiny eyes, a look of fury on his little face. And she could hear him burbling, rhythmically, the same phrases over and over again.

Whether it was Thai or baby talk or some demonic tongue, as she listened, the words began to make sense to her, tapping their rhythm into what remained of her mind:

"You belong to me, just me! Me alone and no one else!"

CURSE TWO
SOUL

May number two, who dared touch me,

Be untouched for eternity…

January 17th, evening

"So, this is me grabbing her tit and giving it a good grope."

The bar was open at two sides and the three men were gathered in an airy corner of it, laughing loudly as they crouched together, staring avidly at an iPhone.

"And this is me tonguing her other tit."

The laughter grew more raucous and startled a young Russian couple who were walking past the bar just a few yards away.

"They look nice and firm, Scott!" The man who spoke was very fat and looked over fifty years old. He had an untidy, grey beard and thick glasses.

"Nipples hard as rock, if you ask me." The third man was unhealthily thin with greasy, grey hair. He must have been over sixty, with a wrinkled face that had never been handsome. "Hard as your prick, I bet."

As his two companions laughed uproariously at their own jokes, Scott closed his phone and took a large swig of beer. He made no comment, just smirked to himself. Eventually, the fat one spoke again.

"I'll be surprised if security didn't throw you out of the temple, though. I mean, these sculptures are hundreds of years old and supposed to be sacred, aren't they? Heavenly dancers, so I've heard."

Scott wiped his mouth with the back of his hand. "Fuck 'em! Security, my arse." He took another swig from his bottle and belched loudly. "Bunch of wimps. They wouldn't last two minutes on the job back home."

The bar was filling up nicely, mainly with old ex-pats like his two companions. Scott felt younger, fitter, better looking than all of them.

"But I thought you were working at a university now. Surely that's easy stuff."

Scott guffawed.

"Don't you bloody believe it. A few drinks, and they're like fucking animals, some of them." He drank deeply and waved over to the bar, holding up his empty bottle, before turning back to his companions. "Eighteen years old and they can't hold their beer." He shook his head contemptuously. "They're not men."

His companions started talking about molly-coddled youth who didn't know they were born, wasting their time learning useless rubbish when they ought to be out earning a living. Scott said nothing, but he caught the eye of a young waitress and pointed again to his empty bottle.

"Still, what about the girls then, Scott?" The leer on the wrinkly face made it even uglier. "All that posh totty? I bet some of them are gagging for it." He leant over the table, smirking lecherously. "Got any juicy tales for us?"

Scott's face stiffened. The old man couldn't see his eyes behind the shades he always wore, but he sensed the anger in them and drew back apprehensively. He was relieved to see the face finally soften a little.

"Ah fuck off, will you? This is the totty I like!"

At this, Scott grabbed hold of the girl who had just placed his beer on the table and slipped his hand under her skimpy top, pulling her towards him. She let out a scream of surprise, to the men's evident delight. "Hey, hey," she called out, pouting and sulking as she struggled to release herself from his grip. His other hand was by now firmly squeezing one of her buttocks. "You wanna party, you buy me drink, okay?" she said loudly and called out something in Thai to two girls loitering at the bar, who came quickly over to the table. They were older, skinnier, flat-chested and far less attractive than her. She let Scott pull her on to his knee but didn't smile. "You buy us all drinks, okay kha[6]?"

Scott looked at the two men.

"Are we gonna party, guys? You gonna buy these two lovely girls a drink or not?"

There were only two girls in this bar that Scott was remotely interested in. This was one of them, and she told him her name was Ory. The other was over at the counter, fussing around some young guy who was grossly overweight and had been mauling her since he came in. She seemed happy enough until he had sent her off, scowling, to the restaurant next door to buy him a meal of pad Thai noodles and a large plate of chips. He was now ignoring her and concentrating on his food. Ory told him the girl's name was Yahi.

"You do have some daft sounding names!" he laughed.

They danced together on the small makeshift dance floor set between the tables. Ory evidently enjoyed dancing and soon asked him to buy her another drink. Scott didn't mind because the music was good, and he knew he'd be shagging her later. The bar was called *Blues Bar*, but what music it played was Soul, classic Soul—Ray Charles, Otis Redding, Isaac Hayes. "Your taste is distinctly retro!" called out the bearded fat man from the table, where the two girls who'd joined them were chatting together in Thai over their drinks. All four were smoking.

"Mug's game," muttered Scott, at which point Otis Redding singing "I Can't Turn You Loose" came blasting through the speakers. He grabbed Ory and twirled her around, at which she let out a scream that Scott interpreted as one of pleasure.

"You sexy bitch, kha!" he called out to her over the music, mimicking her Thai accent.

"What you say? I not hear!"

---

6   Kha: In Thai, the words "kha" (female) and "khrap" (male) make the sentence more polite. On their own, they can indicate agreement.

"Never mind." He pulled her body to his, making sure that she could feel his six-pack pressing hard against her breasts. "Let's go party."

The condo he was renting for the month was only a ten-minute walk away, situated on the thirteenth floor of a tall apartment block with a balcony, a sea view, and the use of a gym and a pool where he liked to work out in the afternoon. This was only his second week in Pattaya. He'd already slept with two bar girls, but Ory was the first he had really fancied.

A cool, refreshing breeze blew up the street from the beach when they left the bar. As they rounded the corner from the main strip on to the much darker and quieter soi[7] that led to his apartment block, a young Asian woman emerged suddenly from the shadows holding two bunches of flowers in her hands.

"Sawadee Kha!" she called out as she approached them. Strange—she didn't look or sound Thai to Scott.

"Flowers for your lady!" she said in English, holding out a bunch of orchids. "Just one hundred baht."

He was about to ignore her and walk on when she held out a second, very different bunch. He stopped to study it. Three flowers: black, or maybe purple, with petals that formed the shape of a bat, and each with a circle of long, white stamens cascading from the central pistils.

"I give you these for free if you buy orchids for your lady."

Ory began to speak harshly to her in Thai, but the flower seller ignored her completely. Instead, she held the black flowers closer to Scott's face. The scent was powerful, some would say unpleasant, but he found it strangely appealing. Speaking in a soft voice as if she didn't want Ory to hear, she said, "These we call bat flowers. They will help you harness the power of your anger and overcome your fears. A strong man like you will be even stronger. Here, take them."

She was staring intensely at him. Her face was striking, good-looking,

---

7   In Thailand, a side street branching off a major street.

one he vaguely recognised but couldn't place. She certainly wasn't the usual flower seller he had seen here once or twice before, and these two bunches appeared to be all she had for sale. On an impulse, he took the bat flowers from her hand and held out a hundred baht note. She shook her head. "The lady doesn't want the orchids. But you can keep these. As a gift."

He turned to Ory to find her staring at him with a look somewhere between concern and anger. When he looked back along the street, the flower lady had already disappeared into the shadows.

January 18th, morning

It took Scott a minute or two to find his bearings when he woke up. His head was woozy, which was strange, as he had drunk little the night before. Ory wasn't to be seen, but that didn't worry him. He'd got what he wanted from her last night and felt too exhausted to be in the mood for another round. The sex hadn't been great, he could remember that much, so it couldn't be the cause of his tiredness. He had a vague feeling that he'd gone out afterwards but dismissed this as ridiculous.

With a loud groan, he pulled himself out of bed and walked naked into the next room. It was a small apartment with just the one bedroom, bathroom, and living area. Ory was dressed and sitting on the balcony, a glass of fruit juice poured from the carton in his fridge on the table beside her. The balcony doors were fully open, letting in a pleasantly fresh morning breeze. She didn't lift her head from her phone when he stood a few feet behind her to gaze for a minute at the sunlit sea, where a few passenger boats were speeding quietly along the coastline. The view lifted his spirits, as it did every morning.

"Good morning to you, too!" he said. Getting no response, he shook his head and went back into the bedroom to slip on his sunglasses and a pair of shorts before returning to join her on the balcony. He tried to kiss her neck as he sat down, but she shrugged him off. He helped himself to her fruit juice instead.

"You slept well then," he said

"You come quick, then sleep. So, I sleep too."

She hadn't raised her eyes from her phone yet. He felt the urge to shake her or give her a slap but resisted it. After all, she was young and pretty and he might want to see her again.

Finally, she looked up at him. "But you wake me up later. You shake door very loud. You still sleep but you shake door with this hand." She mimed the action, vigorously shaking her right hand. "And you hold the horrible flowers with this hand."

Scott frowned as he stared at her. Her words had conjured up images that were now surfacing from his subconscious.

"There was a dancer," he muttered. "I was trying to join the dancer."

"What you say?"

"The doors were made of glass. The woman was dancing on the other side of them. I wanted to dance with her." He looked at Ory, snapping out of his reverie. "It was a dream. I was having a very strange dream."

Stranger still was the fact that, as far as he knew, he had never been prone to sleepwalking. With a sudden movement, he turned his head to scan the room behind him. "You said I was holding those flowers. So where are they?"

Ory leant across to pick up and drink what remained of her fruit juice.

"They outside your door. I not sit with them. They smell very, very bad. Devil flowers, they bring very, very bad luck."

He got up, walked across the room and opened the door to the apartment. They were there on the floor outside, in the makeshift vase he had placed them in the previous evening. He picked them up. Their fragrance was no longer as pungent but was still powerful. He looked at the petals, at their angular blackness, at the dark heart of each flower and found them rather beautiful. He brought them back into the room and put them in the centre of the table, at which point Ory stood up from her chair.

"I go now," she said. "You give me money."

Scott smiled grimly. His wallet and valuables were locked safely in a drawer, so he knew she couldn't have helped herself to any of his cash. Truth be told, he was never sure if this, the moment when he paid the girl, was a sign of power or weakness. Still, he didn't want to be thought of as just another cheap Charlie, too stingy to pay his way.

As he retrieved his wallet from the bedroom, he called out to her, asking where she would go now, what with it being so early in the day. He had checked his watch, and it was still only 8:00 a.m. She replied she would walk up the hill to the temple of the Buddha to pray "for luck."

He laughed. He had seen bar girls and ladyboys do the same, offering brief prayers before the tiny shrines that dotted the streets. The thought of a hooker visiting a church before her shift back home seemed grossly incongruous to him. But as he handed a couple of notes over to Ory, he suddenly didn't want to be left alone. He would join her for a vigorous uphill walk in the fresh air. She didn't look so happy at this suggestion until he offered to buy her breakfast afterwards at one of the expensive cliff top bars that overlooked the sea.

"Okay, kha," she said, her face still expressionless. "You get dressed now?"

THE WALK UP the hill took only twenty minutes, but it was steep enough to get the heart pumping. Ory kept pace with him, and Scott felt more alive. They passed several meek-looking dogs on their way, strays evidently, but seemingly well fed. When he asked, Ory told him that local people would feed them to be granted luck by the Buddha.

Luck again.

They seemed to be obsessed by it. Lucky for the dogs anyway, he thought. Or not. He swung his leg in the direction of one of them, ignoring Ory's protests and laughing as it skulked away with its tail between its legs.

The temple, it turned out, was situated in the middle of a park, which Scott hadn't even realised was there, hidden as it was from the road. He nodded his approval at the early morning runners. "I'll be joining you as from tomorrow!" he called out to a fit-looking Thai woman as she ran past him.

Further up a steep incline, they came across four or five coaches, disgorging groups of tourists who flocked to the steps of the temple.

"Christ, they're keen!" he muttered. "At this hour?"

They walked past the shops that were selling various religious artefacts and he waited as Ory hired a shawl for fifteen baht to cover her naked shoulders, giving an exasperated sigh as she called him over to pay for it.

They had to negotiate their way past various parties being photographed at the foot of the steps leading up to the temple. Once climbing them, Scott was impressed, despite himself, by the ornate bannisters on either side that took the form of two long, many-headed snake-like creatures with scales of red and gold. Most impressive of all was the sight at the summit—an enormous golden statue of the Buddha, seated and smiling enigmatically, displaying a serenity Scott found annoying.

"Life isn't like that," he muttered to himself as he left Ory praying in front of it and quickly toured the rest of the temple. It was open to the air, but the smell from the incense sticks was strong and he enjoyed breathing it in. He shook his head disdainfully at the various donation boxes but appreciated being surrounded by the bright colours in the warm morning sunlight, the golden statues, the red roof tiles, the white marble balustrades, from where you could view the whole of Pattaya. It was all clean, neat, and well-maintained, and he liked that.

Ory appeared to be praying in front of another statue when he finished his tour, and he was irritated to see her drop a few coins in the donation box.

"That's my bloody money you're wasting," he said. "Come on, let's get going." He walked past her, and she descended the steps behind him. At the bottom, he paused to look along a path to his left that skirted the summit of the hill just below the temple. It appeared to be completely deserted of people, though there were small buildings with glass frontages and terracotta tiled roofs dotted along its length.

"What are those?" he asked.

"Families visit their dead. Their spirits live there. Nothing for you." Ory seemed anxious to leave now. Perhaps she was hungry. But something stirred in Scott's subconscious again.

"Let's walk around. I'm curious," he said, setting off.

After a few paces, he noticed Ory hadn't moved and was staring after him.

"Not take long!" he called to her in his mock Thai accent. "Then we go breakfast in nice bar! Okay, kha?"

With some reluctance, she began to follow him.

He stopped in front of the first of the mausoleums. It was about three- or four-square metres in size, he speculated, with what looked like a small altar inside, on which he could see an unlit candle and three statuettes of the Buddha. There were framed photos on the walls, all perfectly visible through the glass frontage, which consisted of two large sliding doors. He tried to open them but, unsurprisingly, they were locked. Ory hung back, a scowl on her face.

"You don't understand," he said to her. "I've never been here before, but these are just like the doors in my dream."

"But show respect!" she snapped. "This not your family."

They walked on, and he stopped briefly to peer inside the next mausoleum, similar to but cleaner than the previous one. A vase of flowers on a table in front of a framed portrait made him frown as another image from his dream stirred vaguely in his brain. Others they passed had open frontages and looked abandoned apart from the many dolls and statuettes crowded along their length, where people had also placed small offerings of food and drink.

"Food for the dead?" he inquired. "Their spirits still hanging around, getting hungry as they wait to be born again?"

Scott knew very little about Buddhism or any other religion but had heard of reincarnation. Ory didn't contradict him but explained that the statuettes and dolls, cheap and tacky though they were, represented the different spirits that dwelt hereabouts. People placed food and drink to appease them, to protect themselves from evil and to bring them…

"Don't tell me!" he interrupted with a mocking laugh. "Luck! You're all obsessed with luck!"

Still, he knew all about luck, particularly bad luck. It was bad luck that the little Chinese virgin he had amused himself with back at UWM couldn't take a joke and had reported him. As for reincarnation, well, it might all be bollocks, but if he had to choose, he'd rather have another chance at life than spend an eternity in hell, or even in heaven. Torture in the one, boredom in the other. What would be the difference?

His musings were interrupted by the shrill barking of a dog erupting somewhere to their right, which caused him to notice a barely visible gravel path he otherwise would have missed. Completely untended, it was almost hidden from sight by unkempt undergrowth, thick bushes, and a clump of trees at its far end, through whose branches he could just make out the tiled roof of another mausoleum. He took a step on to it, whereupon the dog emerged into view a few feet away. It was quite small and pure white apart from some red markings on its tail. It saw him and let out a high-pitched screaming sound like no dog he had ever heard.

"Hey, no. Come back!" Ory backed away.

"What's the matter? You scared of that thing?" Scott picked up a thick length of branch about a metre long from the side of the path.

"That the tomb of very bad man. Everyone knows it very bad luck to go there. The fox warn you to stay away."

Scott sighed and raised his voice. "That bad man, whoever he was, is just a dead man now. Alright? Just dead! As for the dog or fox, whatever it is…"

He swung the branch with all his strength, aiming for the jaws, but the animal leapt to the side, and he caught it in the ribcage. The force of the blow was violent enough to lift the creature into the air. It screamed again as it landed in the dust a few feet away and limped off into the undergrowth, where it stopped and turned. He could still see it, jaw open, panting and staring at him.

Scott breathed heavily.

"See?" he said. "There's nothing here to be afraid of."

But Ory was already running back along the path the way they had come.

"Hey, so you don't want breakfast?" he called after her, sarcasm in his voice. "Ah, fuck off then!" he muttered when she showed no sign of returning. Still breathing hard, he cast his eyes about. There was no one around, and the animal had disappeared. He looked down at his makeshift club and smiled before hurling it into the undergrowth and setting off down the path.

He trod gingerly to avoid the thorny bushes and soon found he needed to remove his sunglasses to see properly. The mausoleum was no more than forty metres from the main path but deep in darkness under the dense shade of the trees, where just a few spangles of sunlight glittered on the terracotta tiles of the roof. Despite the aspect of neglect outside, it looked to have been recently built.

The loud shrieks of a bird sounded in the near distance as Scott approached the glass doors, but what set his nerves alert was the strong feeling, the certainty, that these were the very doors that had featured in his dream. He tried to open them but, as in the dream, they were locked. He touched the glass gingerly with his fingertips, and the sensation penetrated through him like a low current of electricity. When he stared into the gloomy interior, it was so dark he needed to use the torch on his phone, and the beam reflecting off the glass as well as illuminating the objects inside had an uncannily distorting effect on what he could see.

There sat a slim vase on the altar, and Scott noticed with some astonishment that it contained three fresh flowers, purplish-black in colour, with long, white stamens spilling out and over the side, identical to those he'd been given the night before. Behind it was a larger metal urn, the kind used to store the ashes of the dead after cremation.

He tried to steady his hand as he shone the torch on to the wall behind them, lighting up a single framed photograph, the black and white portrait of a middle-aged man with a hard, stern face and cropped fair hair. He looked Northern European and, even through the gloom and distortion—or maybe because of them—he emanated a powerfully unsettling charisma. The eyes, in particular, were hypnotic and held Scott transfixed. Alive, he knew, this man would have been a formidable presence, and he instantly regretted that he had never known him. It took an effort of will to drag his eyes away and shine the beam around the rest of the mausoleum.

On a table in the centre and just on the other side of the door was the wooden statuette of a female dancer, about a foot high, exquisitely carved and painted. Scott noted she was similar to the sculptures he'd been having fun within the temple, the ones he had photographed a few days before—bare-breasted, legs and arms bent at improbable angles, hands and fingers poised in clearly defined gestures. But if those had been angelic presences, the woman here was far from that. There was something distinctly diabolical about her. He knew, because he had seen her dance in his dream, albeit large as life and wickedly sexy. The allure of her gaze and in her smile were just as marked in this carving.

"Come and dance for me again tonight, girl," he chuckled, "and this time let me in!"

He raised the beam of his torch and, at first, was startled to see his own reflection staring back at him from within the glass panels before he was able to look through it and distinguish the portrait hanging from the back wall. And it seemed to Scott that the man in this photograph was smiling at him, too.

January 18th, evening

Land of Smiles Sex forum: Field report on Ory of *Blues Bar*.

Submitted by *Hardman*,

I had been to Blues Bar before. Most of the girls there are right mingas, but Ory had caught my eye. She is a good-looking girl, lovely long hair, nice tits, no older than eighteen, I'd say. I'd seen her looking me over, too, and from the twinkle in her eye, I could tell she liked what she saw. I sat down and called for a beer. She had seen me enter and made sure she was the one to bring me the order. All smiles, she sat down with me. Being the gentleman I am, I bought her a drink, then another as we danced to the excellent music that they play in this place. Soul, soul and more soul! She pressed her body tight against mine and complimented me on my muscular frame. One thing led to another, of course, and back at my place she couldn't get her clothes off (and mine!) fast enough. Her skin is soft and her body firm. I am far too polite to describe everything we got up to. Let's just say neither of us got much sleep and the next morning she was still exhausted! When she asked if I would be seeing her again that night, were those tears in her eyes when I said only, "maybe"? Truth be told, I fancy a turn with another of the girls in that bar, so Ory will have to wait a short while. "Don't be greedy!" I said as I slipped her 1500 baht. She didn't seem interested in the money, just hugged me hard. She is an eight out of ten, boys—but mind you, I have very exacting standards...

Scott put the finishing touches to the report and pressed the submit button before closing his iPad and retreating from his balcony, where the late evening sun had been shining directly into his eyes. James Brown played loudly through his portable speaker, the kind of music that put him in the right mood for a night on the town. After checking the time, he took another beer from his fridge, stripped off his shorts, and placed his sunglasses on the table before grabbing a quick shower. Then, dressed in a Hawaiian shirt and a pair of baggy shorts, he admired his face in the mirror, sliding one hand slowly across his smoothly shaven head while slipping on his shades with the other, all the time moving to the beat and joining in with the chorus, about being a sex machine. Ten minutes later, out on the main strip, he decided to try a new restaurant, the one that all the Russians seemed to favour, but wasn't impressed. He simulated putting his fingers down his throat and vomiting as he paid his bill, then walked up the street to the Blues Bar.

Ory was working again but was evidently making a point of ignoring him.

"Bitch ought to be grateful for that review. Eight out of ten, my arse," he muttered and was glad to see Greg, the older of his two companions from the night before, smoking in a corner on his own.

"Greg!" he called out with a false show of bonhomie as he sat down opposite him. "Just the man I'm looking for! Stub out that foul-smelling stick of crap and I'll buy you a beer."

Greg gave a weak smile and duly complied. In a minute, they both had bottles of Singha in front of them and Scott leant forward towards him.

"You've lived here for how long? Twelve years?"

"Fifteen and then some."

"Then what can you tell me about the fucker whose mausoleum is off to the side of the path that skirts round the Big Buddha temple? Anything?"

Greg took on the look of a man complacent in his role as the fountain of local knowledge.

"You mean Magnusson," he said.

Scott nodded, recalling the Nordic features of the man in the photo. That sounded about right.

"He used to run a club, a very popular one. Music, dancing, drinking, and lots of girls. Nothing unusual about that, of course. But he was particularly choosy about which girls he would hire. They had to be young, they had to be *very* pretty, and they had to be prepared to do anything he asked, which included servicing him whenever and however he wanted."

Greg paused to take a slow drink. From the smug smile on his face, Scott could tell he was enjoying being the centre of attention.

"And what else did he ask of them?"

"The usual, mostly, but a lot more on occasion, depending on how much the clientele were prepared to pay." Another pause, another drink. "Rumour has it he used to put on special nights when all kinds of things went on."

"Did you ever go to one of those?"

Greg shook his head regretfully.

"Beyond my means. I'm no cheap Charlie, as you know," he ignored Scott's guffaw, "but I'm no rich Reggie, either."

At Scott's request, he went on to describe some of the stories he had heard about these special nights. Scott worked hard to maintain his cool and hide his growing excitement.

"So why did the girls put up with this? Why didn't they leave?"

"Control. He controlled them until he had no further use of them."

Scott took a swig of beer and tried to sound calm.

"And how did he manage this control?"

"Through a mixture of rewards and fear, mate, how else? Nice clothes, money to spend, roof over their heads. And sheer terror of his lieutenant."

"He had a lieutenant?" Scott fancied that job. "Who was he, then?"

"She, mate, she." There was a twinkle of amusement in his eye as he observed the shock on Scott's face. "How about another beer, then?"

A few minutes later, beer in hand, he continued.

"She was called Ra. Spelled R-A-T but pronounced 'Ra.' Older than the girls, of course, but not *old*. Very beautiful but in a hard, scary way. And a great dancer. Everyone said so."

"Scary?"

"Yeah, scary. Scared the clientele as well as the girls. If any of the guys got drunk enough to try it on with her, apparently, they sobered up quickly and never tried it again!"

Scott snorted. He didn't believe in scary women. But he recalled the dancer in his dream and her resemblance to the statuette that he could swear smiled at him, a smile of invitation. He was intrigued to know more about this Rat, but Greg couldn't add any further details.

"So, what happened then? To Magnusson, the woman, the club?"

There were going to be no more beers on offer, Greg knew, so before replying, he lit up one of his cheap cigarettes, much to Scott's annoyance.

"Cancer is what happened, about eight years ago." He drew hard on his cigarette, evidently unaware of the irony. "Magnusson died, the woman disappeared, the club was closed down. It's still there, falling apart in disuse. People keep away from it. Just as they keep away from his mausoleum. Bad spirits and all that."

"All that crap, you mean."

Greg gave him a serious look.

"Whichever way you look at it, a lot of very bad things happened to some of the girls who worked in that club. And I don't just mean sex and perversion."

"Nothing bad about that, mate!" Scott forced a laugh, but Greg's smile was rueful.

"People said—and still say—that if they crossed Magnusson in any way, even just the once, that was it for them."

"'It' being...?"

"They'd be found dead in an alley—drug overdose. Or fall out of a window from one of the tall apartment blocks. Again, high on drugs and alcohol. More often than not, they'd simply disappear. Be spirited away."

Images of the statuettes and the food left out to appease the evil spirits sprung into Scott's mind.

"What about the police?"

Another rueful smile.

"Well, what do you think? Magnusson made enough money to grease a few palms. And some of those special nights were laid on free of charge especially for them. And in return…" Greg paused, then added, "He certainly must have made a fortune. But apparently none of it could be traced once he'd died. Spirited away, the locals said. Just like those poor girls."

Scott shook his head and said nothing. He had known as soon as he had seen Magnusson's portrait in the mausoleum that he must have been strong, impressive, a force to be reckoned with. *You cunning, clever bastard*, he thought and then asked, "So what was his club called?"

"Soul Sacrifice," Greg replied and laughed. "Sounds right up your street, hey?"

January 19th, early hours

ORY CONTINUED TO blank Scott, and Yahi never showed up, so some time around midnight he staggered homeward, drunk and frustrated. No flower lady tonight, just the security guard seated behind the reception desk in the foyer.

"Sawadee Khrap!" Scott shouted to him as he entered the foyer, placing great emphasis on the word *khrap*. "You soft twat with very soft job!" he added with a big smile, knowing that he wouldn't be understood. The guard looked briefly in his direction before returning to scrutinise the screens in front of him, each of which displayed images from different parts of the building. "Bloody waste of time!" Scott called out as he clambered noisily into the lift.

SEVEN CURSES

Once in his apartment, Scott turned on his music, stripped off his clothes and dropped them on the floor before throwing open the windows to let in the cool evening air. As he turned to go into his bedroom, his eyes were drawn to the colour of the bat flowers, which, in his drunken state, seemed to glow darkly in what little light was making its way into the room. With a loud belch, he picked one of them out of the vase, noting that their fragrance seemed to have regained all of their pungency, which he breathed in greedily.

He continued to hold the flower to his chest as he let out a huge yawn and lay down on his bed. Early the following morning, he would run up to the temple and do a couple of circuits of the mausoleums for a good energetic work out. Later, he would take a taxi over to Soi Bukhao, one of the town's major sex districts, to have a look for himself at Magnusson's old club—Greg had told him where to find it. Even in his drunken state, Scott couldn't shake off his fascination with Magnusson and what he'd achieved. With images inspired by Greg's descriptions of the club's "special nights" swirling through his head, and the songs of James Brown still playing in the next room, he was soon asleep.

This time the dream, when it came, was more vivid, more detailed than on the previous night. Standing on his balcony in the darkness and looking out to sea, Scott had the sudden sensation of falling, then flying—or rather of being sucked through the air, above the roads, the nighttime traffic and the lights of the streetlamps, over the golden head of the Big Buddha and the temple, and down on to the hidden track, where he landed lightly. Approaching the mausoleum with no fear of the thorny undergrowth, he tried the lock on the doors and felt no surprise as they slid open without effort.

The statuette of the dancer stood on the table before him and, as he gazed at its tempting beauty, in the stillness and silence he became aware of how light his body felt, as if its form were made of something thicker than mist or vapour but much softer, less solid, more emollient than his usual muscle. He tried to pick up the statuette but could only caress it, his hand sliding up and down its form in his attempt to grasp hold of it. In the process, he felt it warm and come to life and, looking on in astonishment, he saw it grow in size and stand upright before him.

The dancer, suddenly as alive as she had been in the previous night's dream, drew his hand to her breast, which was hard and warm beneath the softness of his touch. Clasping her own hand over his, she pressed down on it firmly, the pressure forcing him to squeeze her flesh, which yielded only a little. All the while she stared into his eyes and he sensed her power, which both frightened and excited him. With her other hand, she drew his body closer to her own, forcing him to yield and give way to her solidity. At the same time, he became aware of the portrait of Magnusson on the wall behind her, staring at him over the black flowers, his eyes gleaming red in the glow of the candle that burned before it. The metal urn he had noted on the altar that morning began to emit a glow that throbbed rhythmically in the darkness to a repetitive drumbeat that he was suddenly aware of. The dancer pressed her lips to his ear.

"Come, come dance with me. Give your soul up to the dance," she whispered.

He felt himself weaken as she lifted him from the ground and began to spin and hurl his weightless form about the space of the mausoleum as the drumming grew louder and its rhythm more intense. In a state of delirium over which he had no control, his swirling body smashed into the furniture. The small table upon which the statuette had been standing was sent hurling into one of the doors, shattering its glass panel and sending shards of crystal in all directions, including into his face. He was aware of blood spraying about him, of the amused face of the dancer, of the vase of black flowers being kicked over and sent spinning through the air and then, only gradually, of sharp, loud rapping coming from the direction of the doors.

At this point, the dancer drew his body to hers and, grasping hold of his head and squeezing it tightly, brought it closer to her own. But the loud knocking was too insistent, and her hold began to loosen. With a great effort, Scott drew his head away and turned to look at the door behind them. At first, he could only make out vague, indistinct forms in the darkness; then, with a shock, he saw his own apartment door materialise, not the doors of the mausoleum. Turning back to look at the dancer, he saw that she, too, had disappeared; that he was holding on to nothing more than the shirt he had worn the previous night and that it was stained with blood.

Slowly, the entirety of his apartment materialised around him, as did the pain in his nose from where blood was dripping profusely. The drumming, too, had transformed, or rather become the backing to the jerky rhythms of a James Brown classic, playing at an inordinately high volume, Dumbfounded, Scott noted the mayhem surrounding him—scattered cushions, overturned furniture, shattered glass from the vase which had previously held the flowers, now lying limply in a pool of moisture that had soaked into the shorts he'd discarded a few hours before. All the time, the knocking at his door grew louder.

"Fuck!" was all Scott could manage as he lifted his shirt up to his face in an effort to staunch the flow of blood, then calling out, "Hold on! Hold the fuck on!" as he turned off the music and stepped over the wreckage of his room to open the door of the apartment.

Outside stood a burly Russian, taller and more sturdily built than Scott, whom he had seen once or twice in the lift travelling to the floor below his own. Gesticulating furiously, he pushed Scott aside, strode into the apartment and gazed about him, eventually turning to Scott and shouting in heavily accented English, "What the fuck?"

With somebody else and at some other time, Scott might have flared up in anger. Instead, he smiled meekly, went into his bedroom and re-emerged with an unopened bottle of Johnny Walker red that he held out, gesturing for the Russian to take it as a peace offering.

A minute later, Scott stood at his door watching the Russian step into the lift when he noticed an elderly Thai gentleman staring at him from an open doorway along the corridor. Giving him a threatening look, he shouted, "What the fuck are you staring at, grandad?" whereupon, to his satisfaction, the old man quickly retreated into his room, closing the door behind him.

Slamming his own door shut, Scott leaned against it and gingerly felt the cut on his nose. It was still bleeding, but thankfully, the flow had slowed to a trickle. He looked about him again and couldn't believe the mess he'd made while fast asleep. The Russian had been right. *What the fuck?* What the fuck was happening to him?

January 19th, morning

SCOTT ROSE FEELING the worse for wear early the following morning but was determined to stick to his planned schedule. First, he went into the bathroom and checked the cut on his nose. Seeing that it was covered thickly in dried blood, he bathed it gingerly with iodine before securing a large medical pad in place with two strips of sticking plaster.

"Christ, you look like Jack Nicholson in *Chinatown*!" he muttered before setting off for his run. The room he would sort out later.

His shades protected him from the brightness of the low morning sun as he ran up the hill. Reflecting on the strange events of the previous night, he wondered if, in some way and by some means beyond his comprehension, he had while dreaming been in both his room and the mausoleum simultaneously.

He was breathing hard and sweating heavily when he eventually approached the overgrown path behind the temple that led down to the mausoleum. A man dressed all in black, about his own size and weight, was disappearing around a bend in the main path as he arrived, and Scott hesitated for a second, slowing down to a walking pace to watch him before turning off into the undergrowth. Uncertain of what he was looking for, he was nonetheless clear in his mind that he had no choice but to return here.

The insistent call of a tropical bird grew in intensity and volume as Scott made his way along the path, echoed by an animal scream some distance away—surely that of the fox he had clubbed the day before. The eerie cries gradually became muffled as he walked further beneath the thick canopy of trees that overhung the tiled roof. Once again, he had to remove his sunglasses and use the light from the torch on his phone. As he shone its beam over the glass panels, he noticed with a touch of disappointment there was no sign of any damage to them and no broken glass or overturned furniture inside, where a fresh candle was burning on the altar and everything looked exactly the same as it had in his dream before the dance had begun.

He placed his hands on the sliding doors and saw with some excitement that the padlock was lying open on the ground. His excitement grew as he slid them open, stepped inside and stood alone in the silence and the obscurity, breathing in the scent of the flowers that seemed to be freshly placed on the altar, so strong was their fragrance in this enclosed space. The more he breathed in, the more he became convinced that the dreams were a message of some kind, pointing him towards the dancer and in the direction of Magnusson and his legacy. It struck him that the dance he was engaged in was a dance of destiny, and that it was his destiny to become Magnusson's heir. This thought thrilled him to the point that he felt an erection swelling in his shorts. He turned to the statuette of the dancer and slid his hand lightly up and down her form, as he had done in his dream.

This time he could have grasped her, but he didn't, just caressed her gently, and found himself whispering, "Are you coming back to me tonight? Are we going to finish what we've started?" And as he did so, he felt the wood grow warm and could have sworn that it was softening into flesh beneath his touch.

January 19th, afternoon

The club, when he found it, was rather as Scott had expected. A large, square, single-storey building, it was situated at the far end of an open patch of dusty, stony ground, boarded up and dilapidated but still showing signs of its former, garish splendour—in the broken neon lights that had once flashed out its name, in the flakes of black and purple paint now peeling from the wood and block of the walls, and over which could be seen the ragged remnants of posters in which the smiling faces of scantily clad young Asian women were still identifiable. There were no boarded-up windows, of course, no windows at all in fact; whatever had gone on inside here was always meant to be a secret—and the large steel entrance door was securely barred and locked.

Undaunted by the unwelcoming appearance or by the intense heat of the afternoon sun, Scott walked around to the rear of the building, thinking about what would be needed to restore the club to its former glory and maybe even build upon it. He had no financial means and not even the hint of a strategy, but the sure sense of destiny persisted in its hold on his imagination. When he saw that a small rear door was flapping open, he did not hesitate to step inside to survey what would hopefully one day be his domain.

A short flight of wooden stairs led up to a narrow corridor and into a large, open space, dimly lit by shafts of sunlight that shone through a number of skylights. The remnants of what would once have been the bar were located at the far end, and broken lighting rigs hung dangerously from the ceiling over what would have been the dance floor. Most of the tables and chairs had been removed to expose bare floorboards, stained with damp and dirt. Looking about him, Scott fancied that the thick motes of dust were dancing in the beams of light from the skylights to the faint noise of traffic that issued from the busy soi[8] some distance away, but in his mind he visualised noisy crowds of drunken sex tourists and sexy working girls dancing to the music of soul.

"Who are you, and what do you want?"

The accented voice had come from behind him. Scott turned round, startled. At the top of the staircase, a man stood dressed all in black, the same man he had seen on the path near the mausoleum that morning. He was evidently several years older than Scott and looked and sounded north European. Scott sensed the threat in his eyes, in his voice, in the baseball bat he was holding in one hand and, above all, in the presence of the large black hound being held on a tight leash by the other. In the moments of silence that followed, he realised with some relief that the dog, although staring at him, had not barked and was not even growling. Its nose flared, but it seemed quite content with whatever scent it was detecting. The man studied the dog and frowned. If Scott was relieved by the dog's docility, the man seemed to be puzzled by it.

"Hmm. Doom doesn't know what to make of you. Strange."

Scott let out a short, nervous laugh. "That hound is called Doom? Are you serious?"

This alleviated the tension a little, but the man didn't smile.

"He was a gift as a puppy to his previous owner, from a woman who was very close to him."

"You mean Magnusson, right? And Rat, the woman who worked for him?"

The man looked at Scott sharply. "*With* him rather than *for* him," he said after a brief pause. "She named the puppy Dhumraksha, who was, I am informed, a demon in the tale of the Ramayana. Magnusson shortened the name to Doom."

Scott had never heard of the Ramayana, so remained quiet. The man repeated his initial question, this time with less menace in his voice,

---

8   **soi**: in Thailand, a side-street branching off from a main street.

approaching Scott so that the dog could inspect him. Scott tried not to flinch as it sniffed at his shoes, his trousers, his crotch, before eventually returning to sit at the man's feet, and Scott knew he had passed some kind of test.

"What happened to your nose?" the man asked, stooping to tickle Doom around the ears. "A knife fight?"

Scott scoffed. "An angry Russian."

The man nodded his understanding before asking, "So, what do you know about Magnusson?"

"Some but not enough."

"What do you want to know?"

"As much as you can tell me."

"There is a 7/11 over the road. Come back in ten minutes with beers and cigarettes. Maybe a donut or two. And perhaps I will tell you more than you would rather know."

A quarter of an hour later, the two men sat on two wooden chairs at a dusty table in the middle of the dance floor, positioned to make the most of the light from a skylight. The dog was curled up in a corner in front of the remains of a mess of meat, while the man, who gave his name as Bjorn, ate the cakes greedily before lighting a cigarette and leaning back in his chair with a beer in his hand. Relaxed now, he looked at Scott thoughtfully as he recounted how he had moved to Pattaya ten years before and had come across Magnusson through his contacts with Swedish ex-pats. He had begun working for him almost immediately, as doorman, bouncer, and sometimes-confidante. Before Magnusson died, Rat had approached him and explained that he would be left a secure sum of money, to be paid monthly into his bank account, enough to keep him employed to watch over the club *"until he returns."*

"Until he returns?" Scott repeated, intrigued. "What did she mean by that?"

The man called Bjorn drew heavily on his cigarette before stubbing it out in a battered metal ashtray.

"What a lot of Westerners never understood was that Magnusson was a spiritual person."

"What?" Scott was naturally incredulous, but Bjorn continued, ignoring this interruption.

"My Thai co-workers, particularly the older ones, understood this and explained it to me. Apparently, this hadn't always been the case. When Magnusson first opened the club, there was nothing special about it. Until he met Rat, who, believe me, was no ordinary woman."

Scott recalled the dancer of his dreams and found he could well believe it. "And how did he meet her?"

"After I had been here for about six months, he went off on an extended holiday. Though he didn't call it that. 'A dark pilgrimage,' he said. He had become increasingly interested in the idea of reincarnation or the transference of the soul, as he called it. You know, that when you die…"

"Yeah, I know about that," Scott intervened.

"The night before he left, he spoke to me at length about it. Sitting here, in this very spot, in the early hours before dawn broke. It became clear to me that he was a true believer, that he honestly thought his soul would survive beyond the death of his body. But he was deeply troubled by it."

"Why? Being able to believe that you have another shot at life? Isn't that what he wanted?"

"Not just any life. *This* life. Not the life of an insect or a pig. And not even just any human life. He wanted to be able to choose how he came back so he could repeat a life as perfect as the one he was living now, he said. That's what he told me."

Scott nodded. He could appreciate that.

"Anyway, he told me he had been searching on the dark web—you know of this?"

"Of course."

"Not for weapons or criminal activity, not for videos of sexual practices even more violent and perverse than those he encouraged here. But for wizards, shamen[9], corrupt monks, any practitioner of dark Eastern arts who might help him discover how to access the supernatural assistance needed to grant him that choice."

"Like some local equivalent of selling your soul to the devil, you mean?"

Bjorn shook his head. "A beautiful life followed by an eternity in hell is not exactly appealing. And in Buddhism, your next life will be some kind of retribution for wrongs you have committed in the one you are leaving. No—he was sure that, with the right kind of help, he could avoid all of that. He wanted choice."

"So, what happened?"

"After a few weeks, he returned. And not alone."

"With Rat?"

Bjorn lit another cigarette.

"The woman was beautiful. Maybe beautiful is the wrong word, as there was nothing warm or soft about her. Striking, handsome, perhaps; but harsh and cold as a person. She was never introduced to us, you know. 'Rat' was a name given to her by an elderly Thai woman, one of the cleaners who worked here at the time. Short for Raksasi." He smiled at the blank expression on Scott's face. "They told me that a Raksasi is a mythological figure from these parts; a female demon who can shapeshift and take human form as a seductive dancer, using her powers for evil purposes. She dressed the part too, always appearing in public dressed as a traditional dancer, often bare-breasted. Very large, firm breasts, like the ones ladyboys favour." Scott flinched at the mention of ladyboys. "The girls were immediately as terrified of her as the clients were fascinated. It was after she arrived that the club developed its particular identity and, as a result, its notoriety, a notoriety that soon had the clients, and more importantly their money, flooding in through those doors."

---

9   **shamen:** the plural of "shaman".

Scott was thoughtful.

"And what do you think of all of this?"

Bjorn shrugged.

"It is my experience that a woman doesn't have to be a demon to make you live in hell."

Scott nodded his agreement.

"So, Magnusson gets to grow rich from this partnership, but what did the locals think this devil woman got out of it?"

"Fun, what else? She got to play her dark games with us silly, weak humans."

Scott was silent for a second.

"Okay. But let's go back to my original question. What did she mean by '*when he returns*?'"

Bjorn still didn't answer directly but told him at length about Magnusson's final days, his body wasting away with lung cancer, hidden from sight, seen only by Rat. It was she who had taken on the task of securing a site for his mausoleum near the temple. This was important, apparently, but with Magnusson's reputation being as it was, substantial sums had to be paid to various parties. Even then, she'd had to consent to it being set back from the path, away from the sight of any passing soul who might be visiting the tomb of a family member nearby. When he finally died, he was swiftly cremated and his ashes immediately stored in an urn made from pure or "cold" iron—to keep his spirit securely trapped inside, according to the locals. One of Bjorn's tasks, as directed by Rat, had been to maintain the mausoleum; to sweep it, to ensure that a candle was always lit and that fresh flowers were always on the altar. Always the same flowers, those purple-black bat flowers. Bjorn hated them, particularly their scent, which made him feel nauseous, but he wouldn't ever offend or disobey Rat, even now.

"Besides," he added, "she is there watching me every time I visit, isn't she?"

"The statuette," Scott added.

"It appeared the day she left. I don't know who carved it, but I'm always struck by what a perfect likeness it is." He gazed at the dying light at the end of his cigarette before stubbing it out. "I'd never go there after dark, believe me. Anyway," he continued, "the day before she walked out of this club for the last time, she assured me in no uncertain terms that Magnusson would indeed return. Not his wasted body, but his soul, reborn anew in a healthy body. Of course, this would take several years, she said, but one day he would walk back through those doors, and I would know him when he did."

"So, when did he die, exactly?"

"Eight years ago." Bjorn smiled. "So I reckon I've got another seven years at least before he has grown from baby to child to wicked youth, old enough to reclaim his kingdom once again. Meanwhile, I take it easy and live off the money." He looked about him. "Plenty of time for me to clean this place up, hey?"

Scott followed his gaze and inspected once more the filth, the wreckage, the ruins of the once great club. He was angry but didn't show it, suddenly certain of what his new role would be. He would take control of the place, throw this bloodsucking Swede out on his arse, and restore the club to its former glory. When Magnusson returned—and Scott was sure he would recognise him if and when he did—everything would be as it had been. Until that day, if it ever arrived, Scott would be in charge and have the time of his life. He sat back in his chair, relishing the thought.

"Now I'm going to ask *you* a question," said Bjorn. "It's very dark in here yet you haven't removed your sunglasses once. Do you ever take them off?"

"Only to sleep."

"My mother used to say that the eyes are the windows of the soul. And from where I am sitting, your soul is as black as night."

Scott smiled. He liked this. He liked it very much.

SEVEN CURSES

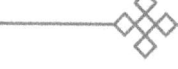

January 19th, evening

THE LETTER OF dismissal lay crumpled in the wastepaper basket.

"Khun Lyle, Khun Lyle!" the receptionist had called out to him when he'd returned from the club in the late afternoon. "A letter for you!"

Until a few days ago, Scott had been dreading its arrival. If it was dismissal, what would he do next? Where would he go? But tonight, once in his apartment, he had opened it almost carelessly. Yes, as he had suspected, there it was. "...*after due consideration of all the facts*...blah blah... *Having carefully examined the nature of the offence and past complaints and warnings*...blah fucking blah... *of a similar*...drone on...*the disciplinary committee has agreed unanimously it has no alternative but to terminate*..."

Scott had read no further. He'd screwed it up and shouted "Gerrin!" as it landed in the basket on his first throw. What the fuck did he care now? He wouldn't have gone back to work in that fucking hole, anyway. This was where he belonged; he was certain of it. Finally, he'd found his true calling. He danced joyfully about his room to Stevie Wonder's "For Once in My Life," a song that captured his mood perfectly. Dismissal? It was more like a letter of release.

Later that evening, still in an upbeat mood, he made his way up to the Blues Bar, devouring a takeaway pizza en route. He was pleased to find a fair crowd for a weeknight and even happier to hear Isaac Hayes playing at just the right volume; *Hot Buttered Soul*, his finest album. No sign of Greg or the fat man, no sign of Ory either, but Yahi was sitting at the bar alone, looking quite bored. Things were truly working out well for him today.

At his invitation, she joined him at the table near the entrance, adjacent to the street, where he had been sitting a few evenings before with his two comrades. He ordered a beer for himself and, on request, a Campari and lemonade for her. She wasn't going to be cheap then, he thought, and studied what was on offer before him. She was slimmer, more petite than Ory, with finer features and even longer hair, which she'd dyed with purple streaks. Scott wasn't sure if he liked it or not but told her that he loved it in a vain attempt to get her to smile. What he didn't like was the ring through her nose; a stud he could take, but a nose ring always made him think of a bogey. Putting that aside, he tried to continue with his charm offensive.

"How would you like to come and work for me, then? In a much better club than this one."

Her face lost its look of boredom for the first time.

"You own a club?" she asked incredulously. "Then why you here?"

"Not yet, but I will soon. More central than here. Soi Bukhao."

She immediately lost interest. She'd heard such offers before, no doubt from cheap Charlies with their pipe dreams and piss poor prospects.

"No, no, I'm serious," he began. "It's… Aaahhhh!"

His face lit up, his words fading into silence as one of his favourite tracks began to play, a slow, silky romantic number called "One Woman," in which Isaac Hayes sang of his dilemma, being torn between two women, his wife and another who was "making him do wrong." Yahi's face registered some amusement as he began to sing along to the chorus, directing the lyrics at her. When the song finished, she was even more amused to see him remove his sunglasses and wipe tears from his eyes.

"Why you crying?" she giggled.

Scott was more than a little disappointed with her reaction.

"Because Isaac Hayes gets it so right, *so* right in this song when he makes it clear that it's a woman making him do wrong. It's her fault, the bitch, not his."

She was looking at him now with some confusion.

"Look," he explained heatedly. "When it comes to sex, there are only three types of women in the world: bitches, virgins, and whores. And they all make men do wrong in different ways."

She said nothing, so he continued.

"Bitches flaunt themselves. The way they dress, the way they walk, the way they look at you. They lead you on. You think they might be interested in you, so you buy them drinks, you say nice things, you're polite and pretend you're interested in them as a person rather than just a fuck." Scott was looking into the distance, as though reliving a memory. "When they leave without saying goodbye, you have to follow them as they shouldn't have done that. You wait until the street is dark, until the time is right, and you're alone with her. Then you creep up silently from behind. Grabbing her, you spin her round, pull down your zip and force her head down close to what you know she wants. When she screams, you slap her…"

Scott stopped talking, his eyes clearing. Yahi was looking at him with curiosity. "And the virgins?" she asked.

He continued.

"The virgins are worse. All sweet and innocent, forced smiles and nervous laughter until you compliment their figure, or their legs, or ask them bluntly if they've ever had sex with a man, saying at their age they really, really should have. Then they freeze up, all embarrassed. So, you have to push it. I mean, she needs educating, doesn't she? You're doing her a service. You get her against a wall and stroke her tits, you slide your hand down to her pussy. You're sure she's getting damp… But then she spits in your face and starts shouting in Chinese or whatever fucking language it is until a door opens and two weedy Asian students come out shouting, too, and shining a torch in your face…"

Scott was wrapped up in his own story and didn't notice the disdain on Yahi's face. "And the whores? How do whores make you do wrong?"

Scott focused his eyes on her.

"Because you make me pay for it, and I shouldn't have to."

Yahi laughed derisively.

"Why you shouldn't have to? You not my boyfriend." She paused and pointed to his nose. "And you have ugly scar! You not handsome like my boyfriend." She leaned forward provocatively. "I bet you not make me come like him."

Scott recalled the fat young man who had been fawning over her. Involuntarily, he fingered the cut on his nose before stretching his hand over to Yahi and stroking her face. "Come on now, be nice to me, hey." He smiled at her, then grabbed her nose ring and gave it a sharp yank.

It ripped through the flesh, and he held it for a second before dropping it onto the floor in disgust. Blood was now spurting over the table, onto Yahi's clothes, into her drink. She jumped up, howling, her face twisted in pain as she covered her nose with a hand, where more blood was seeping in thick trickles through her fingers. By now people on other tables had turned to look, and bar staff were making their way over. One girl already had her arms around Yahi and was shouting at Scott, "You! You go fuck somewhere else!"

Scott stood up, raising his hands in the air. "It was an accident!" he said. "Just an accident. Here." He pulled a thousand baht note from his wallet, then a second, and threw them onto the table, saying, "This should cover it." He turned and left. No one followed him. But he knew they knew who he was.

January 19th - 20th, night

ALTHOUGH THEY KNEW who he was, only Ory knew where he lived. But she wasn't working tonight, and no one had followed him. Anyway, he didn't give a fuck. Soon he would be away from here and besides, much worse things happened to girls every night in Pattaya. Magnusson had made a successful business out of precisely that.

Back in his apartment, he poured himself a scotch, took off his sunglasses, picked up a writing pad and pen, and settled down onto his settee. It was time to make plans. He would find out who Magnusson's legal agent was—Bjorn's money had to be coming from somewhere. And there must be lots more of it. This agent would know where it was hidden and how to access it. Scott would make him a proposition from which they would both greatly benefit financially. He would take over the club, rebranding it as Scott's Soul Sacrifice. He wrote this down on the pad in large, ornate lettering and read it aloud. He liked the sound of it very much.

But his musings were interrupted by another sound. Someone was rapping on the glass of his balcony doors.

He looked up. The curtains had been drawn earlier to keep out the heat of the afternoon sun, so he could see nothing. Had he been mistaken?

There it came again, though, this time more insistently, in a rhythm he recognised as that of the drumming from his dream the night before. He put down the pad on the sofa, walked cautiously across the room and drew back the curtains.

She stood large as life, just a foot or so away from him on the other side of the glass, her dark skin glistening, illuminated by the pale moonlight and the green lights of the shrimp boats moored far out at sea. But she seemed, too, to be radiating her own light as she drew open the doors and stepped inside, where she stood still, looking at him as she spoke.

"You invited me, so here I am." Her voice had a feminine lilt to it but was remarkably deep.

Scott thought he must have dozed off on the settee. He rubbed his eyes and slapped his cheek.

"Will I wake up in a minute or two?" he asked aloud.

At this the Raksasi laughed.

"Oh, no. Soon you won't have to wake up ever again, as you will never be asleep."

She approached him and caressed his face.

"Imagine that," she said. "Always, always to be awake. Never, never to be at rest."

Before Scott could respond, she grabbed him roughly, pressing her body into his and forcing her lips against his mouth. Her breasts felt unnaturally firm, her kiss unnaturally savage.

In his dreams, Scott had felt excitement tinged with fear when in contact with this woman, but now he felt only fear. As in his dream, his form seemed to dissolve into hers. More frighteningly, her kiss was no kiss at all but an act of physical violence. He struggled to loosen her grip, but she was far too strong for him and all the time he felt her sucking the air from his lungs, the consciousness from his mind, the very life from his being. The feeling was one of being caught in a vortex within his own body, in an explosive rush of air that was drawing his essence out from the materiality of that body. He had the sudden terrifying revelation that he was going to die and that he could do nothing about it but wait for the blackness, the emptiness of eternity, to engulf him.

Then…there came a sense of release, of letting go, and though he could neither see nor hear anything, he felt the sudden euphoria of being one with another being, followed by a sensation of falling, then of floating, then of flying away…

BELOW AT THE reception desk, the security guard was enduring another empty night of boredom in front of the screens, gazing absently up from his phone on occasion to scrutinise the images on display from the security cameras. Earlier, he'd had to clear the pool area and suffer the verbal abuse of a French couple in the process, fortunately in a language that he did not at all understand. Later, he would make his patrol around the apartment block and the public spaces surrounding it, but until then, he had to stay seated in front of these screens. His employers insisted on this ever since a tragic incident had happened in a neighbouring condo the year before, when a bar girl had been thrown off the roof garden by a drunken tourist from Birmingham, England. The inquest had concluded that better supervision by the night watchman could have prevented the tragedy. He took a sip from his bottle of water and glanced up casually at the screens, whereupon he gave a sudden start.

What had he just seen?

Swallowing hard, he wound back the recording to look again.

Yes, there it was. The body of a woman in the air, falling gracefully from a balcony. He jumped up from his desk and ran as fast as he could through the main entrance and round to the rear of the building, horrified by what he imagined he would find on the ground there.

With a mixture of astonishment and relief, he found nothing.

He shone his torch in the flower beds, the bushes, over the fence into the car park beyond, but nothing. Bewildered, he returned to his desk and spent some time studying the image over and over again. There was no doubting what he could see there, and he knew that he needed to determine whose balcony the woman had fallen from so he could investigate and record the incident. Finally, he was certain; it was the apartment rented by that rude, arrogant Englishman, Lyle. He wouldn't be at all surprised if he was violent, too. What had he done to this woman?

The guard took the lift to the thirteenth floor and knocked on the apartment door. A deep voice—not Lyle's—shouted "Just a minute!" in Thai. When the door opened, the guard was shocked to see standing before him a woman dressed like a dancer from one of the old movies his mother used to like; and was doubly shocked to see that she closely resembled the woman he'd seen—or thought he'd seen—falling from the balcony. She looked at him inquisitively with something like amusement in her eyes.

"Are you…is everything all right with you?" he stammered, gazing past her into the room where he could see a man who looked like Lyle lying on the sofa, apparently sleeping.

"I am absolutely fine. And him? He is fine, too." She leant towards him and whispered, "His body has had a nasty shock. He just needs me to kiss him better, that's all." As if to demonstrate, she pursed her lips, curling her tongue between them, and with her eyes flashing in mischief, she began to let out a long, rasping breath, a seemingly endless breath that grew in intensity rather than showing any sign of easing off. She stopped suddenly and laughed, slamming the door in his face.

Bewildered, the guard returned to his desk and deleted the recording.

Thirty minutes later, he set out to patrol the same corridor, passing the same apartment on his nightly tour. The light was still showing from underneath the door, and he could see moving shadows passing across it. He paused outside for a moment and heard the rustle of paper and the sound of a voice which he recognised as Lyle's. The woman's kiss, strange as it was, had evidently worked its magic on him. He heard Lyle pronounce his own name—Scott—followed by a short phrase in English. Then the sound of laughter from two voices—loud, unpleasant, mocking laughter—that echoed along the corridor as he quickly continued on his rounds.

January 20th, late morning

IT WAS THE dog that reacted first. From his lazy, forlorn state on the filthy blanket in the corner of the huge, empty room, Doom suddenly pricked up his ears, then tensed and lifted his head, alert, his tail beginning to wag in anticipation. Bjorn noted this with surprise but shrugged and turned his attention back to the cheap second-hand paperback he'd picked up the day before. It was a collection of English ghost stories, old-fashioned and antiquated in their style but still fun to read.

When the dog barked and ran over to the rear entrance, he put the book down, picked up the baseball bat he always kept at hand and stood, ready to act tough if necessary. He heard the door swing open and saw the dog, suddenly ecstatic in its excitement, jumping up, barking, licking the figure who had just entered.

"Doom, Doom, look at you! Calm down, now, calm down. Did you miss me that much, old fellah?"

He recognised the voice but was puzzled on two counts. Why was the dog so happy to see this man again? And why hadn't the Englishman told him he could speak Swedish?

He put the bat down and walked over as he saw him come further into view at the top of the staircase, just as he'd done the day before.

"You again, so soon. And full of surprises! Doom has evidently decided you are his best friend! What magic do you possess, I wonder?"

He had spoken in Swedish and couldn't be certain whether the Englishman understood him or not. He seemed to be ignoring him, just looking around the space and studying it, as though for the first time. Finally, when he turned his gaze towards Bjorn, although he couldn't see behind the sunglasses, he could register the fury in his voice and in the contortion of his face.

"You fucking lazy bastard," he said in Swedish. "You bloodsucking, useless, lazy cunt. And to think I trusted you enough to leave you in charge."

At this, the Englishman took off his sunglasses and, for the first time, Bjorn saw his eyes. He blanched and felt his stomach churn. How could this be?

These were the eyes of Magnusson. There was no doubt about this.

But how, *how*? How had he not recognised him the day before? What game had he been playing with him?

"I… I… But I never expected… She told me it would be years, *years* more before you returned." The words faded to silence, but Bjorn's desperation only increased when he saw *her*, Rat, walk out of the shadows and look at him. He recognised that look. He'd seen it many times before when directed at some unfortunate girl who had displeased her. An unfortunate girl who would soon disappear inexplicably.

Piss began to run down his legs as she came towards him.

Any date, any time

If Scott had been able to smell, he would have smelled the fading scent of the purplish-black bat flowers that he liked so well, mingling with acrid smoke drifting from the candle on the altar, now snuffed out for the first time in eight years. If he had been able to see, he would have seen the mausoleum lit by moonlight, much as he had seen it during his dream visits; but he would also have noticed that the statuette was no longer on its small table, and the frame which had once enclosed the portrait of Magnusson was now curiously empty. If he had been able to hear, he would have heard the insistent cry of a tropical bird, growing louder, then fainter, as it drifted from tree to tree above him. And the excited barking of a fox, somewhere close by. If he had been able to touch, he would have felt the cold iron that now enclosed him in its tiny space. He might have speculated that the very same urn which had once contained the soul of Magnusson now entrapped his own.

The transference had been initially exhilarating. Being one with the spirit of the Raksasi, riding within the body of a supernatural being, was something akin to being on a roller coaster. But when the ride came to a halt, the sensation had abruptly changed from exhilaration to the extreme anxiety of rejection. In a sudden stormy chaos, he had become conscious of another being passing near and then through him, leaving an icy sensation in its wake.

This was at least better than the loneliness that ensued when the storm had ceased, when his host and her new guest had drifted away, to leave only this sense of nothingness behind, a nothingness which held him trapped in absolute darkness and in absolute silence. He tried to shout, to scream, but he lacked the tongue, the lips, the lungs, the vocal cords, the physicality to do anything at all.

He recalled the words of the Raksasi before she delivered her fatal kiss, that he would be awake forever. It made sense to him now. The body tires, the soul does not. When the body sleeps, the soul dreams. But even the forgetful release of sleep would be denied to him now.

Suddenly he longed to die but knew immediately that he was dead already, that this was what remained of him after death.

Could it be destroyed? Would he ever be granted that luxury?

Ever?

It was agonising to realise that annihilation was his only hope, preferable to remaining trapped for eternity in a void of unceasing recrimination and endless regret.

And in death, as in life, mistakenly, he blamed it all on a woman.

CURSE THREE
PEONY

Let number three, who stole from me,

Be crushed by scorn and mockery...

Those who recall the academic career of Associate Professor Charles Towne fall very much into two opposing camps: his admirers, who saw him as a charismatic teacher with strong rhetorical gifts; and his detractors, who remember him as a self-promoting showman rather than a proper academic and who demonstrated only a superficial understanding of the concepts he espoused. They also point disapprovingly to the numerous sexual encounters he was rumoured to have had with impressionable young female students, both in his own university and as a visiting academic overseas. Unfortunately, he left very little in the way of writings through which we might properly judge his intellectual legacy, which in any case remains indelibly tainted by the unexpectedly abrupt way his career terminated.

Although the circumstances that led to his withdrawal from academia were admittedly more acutely embarrassing than properly scandalous, he quickly sank into obscurity (although many would argue that his light was never very bright), re-emerging only briefly some two years later to teach drama in an undistinguished international school in Shenzhen. Here he caused some upset when, in the first and only play he directed, he insisted that the leading actress paint her lips bright crimson and her teeth ebony black, offering no explanation for this curious decision. Soon after, he met a swift and lonely fate at the relatively young age of fifty-five, after contracting COVID-19 for which he had apparently never been vaccinated.

The academic profile of Charles Towne is still available to anyone who follows the outdated links on the website of the University of West Midlands. His key intellectual influences were, we are playfully informed, BBC: Brecht and Beckett in the theatre and Camus for his politics, philosophy, and general approach to life. His profile photograph is accompanied by a caption that places him in a Parisian café on the left bank of the Seine. There he sits at a table in a black leather jacket, with coffee, cognac and a packet of Gitanes[10] on display in front of him. His collar is turned up and smoke is curling from his cigarette, his face a picture of serious concentration and intellectual intent as he studies a text that could well be in French. The image suggests that, on a good day, he might pass for Jeremy Irons' chubbier cousin.

The same photo was included under his name in the programme for the conference that took place in an ancient but minor university town not far from Kyoto, where the unfortunate breakdown in his mental health occurred. The soulful elegance of the image was matched by the notes that accompanied it, where he writes that his constant concern as an academic has always been to "bring theatre to the people and not simply to the elite." We are informed of his "love" for Japan, its people and its culture, and of the humility he feels to be invited to introduce his very own "intercultural performance practice as innovative adult pedagogy" through the Japanese stories and theatrical traditions he admires so much.

And so, we find him on the first day of the conference in a spacious room that was to serve as his drama studio for the morning, this after a long flight, a very late arrival and a restless night spent in the nearby Best Western hotel, a fifteen-minute taxi ride away. Universities are one of the many modern institutional settings (among which we might include hospitals, airports, hotels, and shopping malls) that differ little from country to country, continent to continent.

---

10   **Gitanes:** A French brand of cigarettes.

So, despite the unexplored charms of the local town, the many appealing sights, fragrances, and tastes it had to offer for a new visitor from the occident, it was with a sense of dull familiarity that Towne cast his eyes about the space and began to organise it for his teaching session.

He placed his bag on a desk at one end of the room, arranging the chairs into the usual circle and then walked to the far end of the room. As he drew back the curtains that covered two large floor-to-ceiling windows, he saw with some surprise that they overlooked a traditional Zen garden, the kind he had seen recently when searching for "Japan and its culture" on the internet. He looked at his watch. He still had plenty of time, and the cool winter sun cast an aura of charm over the garden. Feeling a sudden desire to explore it, he opened the fire door and stepped outside, shivering slightly in the fresh, cold air as he looked about him.

Small in its dimensions and surrounded by a fence of bamboo, the garden displayed a pattern of gravel paths, rocky corners and overhanging ferns and mosses within an arrangement of topiaries, dwarf conifers, and azalea bushes, all quite delightful to the eye. In a far corner, Towne spotted a small bridge over a water feature that led to what appeared to be a crimson-coloured pagoda or traditional temple of some kind.

He decided to take a closer look but paused on his way in front of a circle of stones that could have been an ancient well, next to which was a rosebush with just one white blossom in flower. A closer inspection revealed a thin red stripe running through each of the petals. Far more striking, however, was the peony bush in full flower alongside it, with blooms of flaming crimson, matching almost exactly the colour of the pagoda, apart from just two flowers that stood out from the rest—one pink, the other with petals a delicate shade of purple. An illustrated placard to the side described these as specially cultivated winter peonies. He lingered, inhaling the subtle scent that reminded him of citrus—or was it spice, or rose, perhaps? A small notice next to the bush explained in English the special role played by peony flowers during the Japanese

SEVEN CURSES

Festival of Returning Souls—what they call the Bon—adorning lanterns whose light will guide the spirits of the dead as they return to visit their loved ones.

Towne made a mental note of this tradition, thinking that a timely reference to it might impress, and made his way to the temple. This proved to be a disappointment, being nothing more than a shell with a line of uncomfortable looking wooden benches running along the inside of its walls. As he turned to leave, he noticed a glass casing positioned by the entrance to the left of the sliding door, within which sat an illustrated account, written both in English and Japanese, entitled *The Legend of the Peony Lantern*. Towne began to read it.

This classic tale, set in this very town, relates how a young Samurai named Hagiwara, while playing with friends some distance from his home, hits a shuttlecock over a bamboo fence and into a private garden. While searching for it, he meets the beautiful Lady O'Tsuyu ('Morning Dew') and her pretty young maid, O'Yone. The Samurai and the Lady fall in love and, as Hagiwara leaves the next morning, she tells him he must return to her every night, or she will surely die. But, once home, the young Samurai resents being forced to make such a promise and does not return until several months have passed.

By that time, he finds the house and garden in ruins and is informed by an old servant that the Lady and her maid have died. Full of regret for his lost love, he returns home and commemorates her passing in the traditional way during the Bon, the Festival of Returning Souls. Sitting sorrowfully in his own garden, he is astonished to hear and then see the two women approach him under the light of a peony lantern carried by the maid. He of course gives them permission to stay for the night and to return on future nights, during which the Samurai and his Lady make passionate love together.

However, during the daytime, Hagiwara grows increasingly weak, much to the consternation of his servant, who detects the mark of death upon him. Spotting a light in his master's room one night, the servant peers through the window and, to his horror, sees his master in the embrace of a skeletal corpse. Unable to convince Hagiwara that he is suffering a dangerous illusion, the servant tries to ward off the spirits of the dead women through the use of religious charms; but the two are too cunning and finally manage to claim the spirit of Hagiwara, whose dead body is discovered the following morning. (Find the full tale related in English in the works of Lafcardio Hearn.)

Towne was unimpressed by this account, judging it to be stilted and badly written. He had never heard of Lafcardio Hearn and was, besides, not at all interested in ghost stories, dismissing them as trivial nonsense.

He did, however, find himself gazing at the illustration, a line drawing executed in vivid colours, of the lady and her maid walking together under the light of the peony lantern. Their faces were left, blank, but their shapely bodies were suggestively beautiful and the artist's impression of the mysterious yellow glow of the lantern, draped as it was by two peonies—one purple, one pink—was strikingly effective. Studying it, he became lost in a reverie of exotic, beautiful women and passionate lovemaking. It was only gradually that he began to realise he was being hailed by name from somewhere in the near distance, whereupon he shook his head as if dazed and left the temple, flushed and distracted.

Inside the open fire door stood a young Japanese woman. Even from this distance, Towne could tell she was singularly unattractive, and his disappointment increased as she approached him and introduced herself by name as his assistant and interpreter for the morning. She asked him in detail about his flight, his hotel, his room, even his breakfast and said how delighted she was to be working with him this morning. Her English was good, but he found her naïve enthusiasm and fussiness irritating and realised that he had already forgotten her name.

"I see you were admiring the garden of our Lady of the Morning Dew," she said with a broad smile. "You were captive to the beauty of the peonies, I believe. Such striking colours. Such deep and delicate shades. You know the symbolic meaning of such colours in our culture, of course?"

Towne wasn't sure if this was a question or not. Blood, passion, vengeance came immediately to mind, but he held his tongue.

"Romantic love, faithfulness. Also, modesty." She sounded as though she were reciting a memorised text, Towne thought. "And sacrifice. Did you read the story in the temple? Yes? Ah, so moving! Some versions of the legend propose that her lover did not remain with her, even after their spirits were united in death, leaving her lost in sorrow and eternally dreaming of revenge."

A breeze blowing in from the garden through the partially open door ruffled Towne's hair, bringing with it a scent of peonies, spicy and sweet, as it caressed his face seductively like a scarf of perfumed silk.

He inquired if it was usual for such a garden to be located within the grounds of a university. His assistant replied that it was not so unusual.

"A small place to find a few moments of peace, calm, and beauty. After all, the endless quest for new knowledge can be exhausting, can it not? You must know that?"

Towne didn't answer, and she continued, regardless. "Some say that this garden is identical to one more ancient, hidden somewhere in the old town, in which…"

She stopped and they both turned, startled by a sudden loud crash. A pile of chairs had tumbled into Towne's desk, knocking his bag onto the floor. He picked it up and examined it, showing no interest in what the assistant had been about to tell him, and she began to re-stack the chairs.

Eventually she said, changing the subject, "That is a very charming bag, if I may say so. Is it real leather?"

There was more than a hint of condescension in Towne's smile.

"Of course. It's a Gucci bag. It used to be called a hobo bag." He caressed it. "You know, a certain Sam used to have one just like this."

"A certain samurai??"

Towne laughed heartily.

"Sam Beckett, the famous Irish playwright."

She blinked nervously. Surely, she had heard of Samuel Beckett!

"Well, it's a lovely bag," she said, evidently embarrassed.

"Gucci have since renamed it, you know. It's now an Aphrodite. So, Sam had a hobo on his arm, but Charles has Aphrodite on his." He smiled again. "It's very expensive. Maybe your boyfriend might buy you one…?"

That was cruel, he knew, but before he could enjoy her deepening embarrassment, the first of the workshop participants chose that moment to arrive and sit compliantly in the chairs Towne had previously arranged for them. Ignoring his assistant, he gathered the notes, props, and materials he needed and turned his full attention to the imminence of the next three hours.

OF THE WORKSHOP itself, we need say only a few words. It was quite well attended and, despite some moments of disconnect, seems to have been fairly well appreciated. Towne professed his admiration for the traditional comic theatre tradition known as Kyogen, which he said was "of the people" even though nowadays—wrongly, in his opinion—it was seen as remote and elitist. As an introductory activity, he attempted to demonstrate how its conventions could be adapted to appeal to modern sensibilities, but this fell rather flat with the Japanese students and academics in attendance.

Some smiles were exchanged, however, when he solemnly introduced a game he called "Noh Play with the Master." In this, a mask was passed around and across the circle, a mask that was said to contain the Master's very soul. The aim, therefore, was never to touch the mask itself, only ever to hold it by a string threaded through its apex, and then only between thumb and forefinger. When asked from where he derived the inspiration for such games, Towne repeated the words he had written for the programme notes: "For me, inspiration comes first and foremost from love. In this case my love for Japan—the country, its people, and its culture." His assistant beamed as she translated his comment, but reactions among the participants were more mixed, some nodding their appreciation, others remaining inscrutable.

Two further incidents within the workshop are worth reporting in a little more detail, given the specific nature of subsequent events. During a Q and A session, participants were invited playfully to introduce themselves using a famous name they identified with, and a specialist in Classical Japanese Literature introduced herself as Associate Professor Marusaki. There were some amused laughs of recognition before she spoke. Declining Towne's invitation to address him as Charles (she pronounced his name as "Professor Tan") she asked if he might explain what he'd meant earlier when he had said—here she consulted her notes—"Theatre is illusion but through illusion we can discover important truths." In particular, she wondered what kind of truths he had in mind.

Towne thanked her for this excellent question and, putting on his most thoughtful expression, he answered slowly and quietly, in a tone of soulful solemnity. "The deepest truths," he said. "Truths about society, truths about culture, above all truths about ourselves." He paused meaningfully before adding, "I sometimes like to say that Theatre is an illusion, and illusion is the handmaiden of Truth." The silence that greeted this response was tangible, the meaning behind it perhaps less so.

The second incident pertains to the theatre game with which Towne chose to end the workshop, a game he called "The Maid of Genji." Participants were asked to stand in a circle as he withdrew from his folder a thin paper cut, pink in colour, that resembled in its shape a Japanese woman wearing something like a traditional kimono. The aim of this game was to keep the figure in the air once it was launched. Whoever in the circle was closest to her was to time their breath so as to blow her to someone else.

Of course, this was very difficult. The poor maid kept fluttering helplessly to the floor, and the game had to be restarted several times.

On each occasion, Towne would approach a different participant, look her in the eyes (it was inevitably a female, always a young and pretty one) and quietly say, "We succeed as two if we breathe as one." At this point, they were to stand almost cheek to cheek as he launched the figure and both would blow it together to a neighbouring participant, amid much giggling and embarrassed laughter.

The game came to an abrupt if rather dramatic conclusion, however, when a sudden gust of wind blew the fire exit door completely open and the hapless maid flew out into the garden, up into the air and out of sight, to much clapping and a mixture of laughter and shouts of wonder. Towne at first looked confused but then bowed in mock appreciation, joking that he had, of course, planned this finale all along.

As the participants were exiting the studio, he brusquely dismissed his assistant before leaving to retrieve the errant maid from the garden, where he searched for several minutes. It could not be seen anywhere on the path, and he wondered if it had been caught in any of the bushes. He approached several and scanned them carefully, noticing in the process that the single rose had disappeared. He frowned at the thought that someone from his workshop might be responsible for this. Would it reflect badly on him? Reluctantly re-entering the studio empty-handed, he registered the shock of its silence, a silence disturbed only by the echo of his footsteps as he walked to his desk. As he was about to gather his belongings together, he heard a voice speak his name.

"Professor Towne?"

For the second time that morning, a young female had caught him unawares. This time, however, the surprise was altogether more pleasurable. She was standing just inside the fire door, framed by the sunlit garden behind her, wearing a smart white dress. A wide silk belt, red in colour, emphasised the slimness of her waist and the swell of her breasts. He watched as she came towards him. Her footsteps made no sound, such was the elegance of her movement, which also contained something seductively animal-like in the way she swayed her hips. She looked young and typified that petite, demure, Asian prettiness he found so appealing. There was something about her that he thought he recognised, but, certain that she had not been in his workshop, he was intrigued as well as excited by her sudden appearance. He gave her his most charming smile, and she approached him, holding up the pink paper cut he had been searching for.

"Well, this is a pleasant surprise, and a relief, to be sure," he said, reaching out to take it, but she withdrew her hand before he could. His expression became one of curiosity. "And you are...?"

Instead of answering, she took a step closer to him and, with her free hand, drew a small, purple envelope from her belt.

"I have something else for you. An invitation. Someone, a woman, wants you to visit her in her chamber tonight."

Tonight. Things were happening faster than he could have hoped for and taking shape just as he had fantasised. Not even the euphemism of "this evening," or "for dinner" or "for coffee." And in her *chamber*! It sounded as if all preliminary games were to be dispensed with. His excitement mounted.

"And this woman... Is she as pretty as you?"

The young woman did not acknowledge this attempt at flattery.

"Not pretty, no. But beautiful. Far, far more beautiful than me."

"Oh, surely that's im—"

"Please," she interrupted. "If you take the invite, you must, in exchange, let me keep the maid of Genji."

"The maid of...? You mean my paper cut?"

"Yes. But..." She paused before continuing. "I think maybe you should refuse this invitation."

Towne was puzzled, able to see neither sense nor purpose in either request. That she was urging him to refuse the invite was less puzzling, perhaps; she was probably jealous and would prefer to spend the night with him herself. Pretty as she was, however, in no way did he wish to endanger what would surely prove to be an unusually interesting tryst. He told her she could keep the paper cut, which she slipped into a small pocket and, giving him a curiously knowing look, handed over the purple envelope.

"This woman. Do I know her? Have we met?"

She shook her head and, for the first time, showed the hint of a smile. A very charming smile, Towne thought.

"Then why does she want to meet me this way?" he asked, slipping his finger under the seal of the envelope.

"Oh… Let us say she has heard of you and is interested in your work."

He began to draw out the card, also purple. "What? But how or when did she…?"

He never completed the sentence. A powerful fragrance had been released, a heady perfume that Towne did not recognise but that immediately made him feel pleasurably dizzy. As he brought the card closer to his face, the sensation was even more intoxicating. He glanced at the image on the front, which was indeed curious. An exquisite drawing of what must have been an ancient arch or gateway framed a small mirror upon which was painted a tiny but beautifully executed purple peony flower that only partially obscured the reflection of his face. The sight of himself looking old and tired in the midst of such delicate beauty distressed him, so he quickly opened the card to examine the inside, which proved to be even more curious. On the left was drawn the reverse of the mirror—or was it the reverse? For inside its frame was a macabre drawing of two skeletons in what looked like a lover's embrace, while on the opposite side, where he expected to read a message of invitation, was the following cryptic rhyme, written in English:

SEVEN CURSES

This looking glass, this glacial lake,
Where women bathe their beauty's sin,
Adrift beneath its silvering,
How many phantoms float within?

Bewildered, he looked at the back of the card, which consisted of a set of complicated directions, also written in English. His lingering puzzlement was disturbed by the young woman, who was turning to leave.

"The lady is expecting you after dark. The directions are clear. You will need to follow them on foot, so give yourself plenty of time."

He watched as she left through the fire door and walked silently into the garden but then lost sight of her, distracted as he was by the intoxication of the perfume and the very strangeness of this unanticipated turn of events. He placed the card carefully back in the envelope and gradually his head cleared. A wind had started to blow in chilly gusts outside and he felt the draft through the still open door. Grabbing the mask of the Master with both hands, he stuffed it into his bag along with the invitation and left the studio without re-stacking the chairs.

THE REST OF the day was spent in a state of restless expectation which surprised Towne with its intensity. He avoided the research and discussion groups he was supposed to attend, ensconcing himself instead in a corner of the conference canteen and surrendering to a compulsion repeatedly to handle the mysterious invitation, to savour again and again its heady perfume, the effect of which grew progressively stronger as the afternoon passed. At one point, it seemed to take on the material form of a thin, purple mist that dimmed his vision and overpowered his senses, whereupon, in an attempt to clear his head, he decided to revisit the garden. Here he walked along the paths between the bushes, passing over the bridge and into what he called the temple. He lingered by the peony bush and noted that the bloom he had earlier thought to be missing from the neighbouring rose bush was still in place. He shook his head in puzzlement, unable to comprehend how he'd previously missed seeing it.

Towne dined back at his hotel early on a plate of fruit and a glass of sake, followed by two glasses of cognac. By 5:15, he'd showered and dressed in his best smart casuals—pale blue Ralph Lauren trousers, a beige Cucinelli cashmere coat draped neatly across a hanger and set aside on a coat hook—when he was suddenly overcome by a wave of fatigue.

It was still light outside, so he lay on his bed to relax for a few minutes. The invite card sat perched on the bedside cabinet, where he had earlier placed it. His attention was drawn to it when a shaft of low sunlight suddenly caught the mirror. He picked it up and admired once again the miniature peony that seemed to grow in size and float on its glacial lake before his sleepy eyes.

With a sudden start, he awoke to find his room in darkness. Checking his watch, he was shocked to discover he'd dozed off and slept for over two hours.

The directions on the card were many and complicated, quickly leading him away from the busy roads and thoroughfares into a network of small side streets and dimly lit alleys where fewer and fewer people were to be seen. At one point, he approached a large wooden archway, astonished to see that its shape and design were identical to the frame of the mirror on his card. Surmising that it must have provided the model for the drawing, he walked through it into what seemed to be the picturesque old town. Here the wind felt colder, and he was grateful for his warm coat, no longer just a fashion item. He stopped to huddle himself inside it, noticing that in this part of town there was no sign of any living inhabitants apart, perhaps, from the dim light being cast by the differently designed lanterns adorning the walls of the tiny houses that fronted straight on to the narrow streets. It occurred to Towne that he was walking back through time as well as forward towards an exciting sexual liaison; and it was only thoughts of this latter that displaced any fearfulness he otherwise might have felt.

By now, he was using the torch from his mobile phone to read the instructions and feeling as much relief as excitement as he drew closer to his destination. Finally, he came to a halt outside a gap in a bamboo fence, as instructed. He stood there in almost total darkness for no longer than a minute or two when a dim light became visible through the gap, swinging lightly as it approached.

As it came into view, he could distinguish the yellow light of a lantern tied to the end of a wooden pole and adorned by two peony flowers, one purple, the other pink. It stopped just on the other side of the fence, its light surprisingly bright, bright enough for Towne to see the bearer, beguilingly clad in what he judged to be a traditional kimono with a light pink floral pattern and pale horizontal stripes. It lacked the usual girdle, he noticed, and so hung loosely around her small but shapely body. Her face, however, initially alarmed him. Covered in thick white face paint, it reflected the light from the lantern so brightly that it almost dazzled his eyes. The contrast with the crimson lines of her lips and the jet-black thickness of her hair could not have been sharper. The hair itself had been arranged neatly above and around her ears with pins of silver and brooches of coral. She was pretty, to be sure, but not the woman of staggering beauty he'd expected to find waiting for him.

She stopped and looked at him, saying nothing.

"Well, here I am!" Towne's words broke the silence. He tried to sound casual and vaguely amused. "I must admit, I wasn't expecting to find myself in the middle of a costume drama," he added with a laugh.

Finally, she spoke. "Do you have your invitation?"

He held out the purple card, and she took it from him.

"I am O'Yone," she continued, "handmaiden to O'Tsuyu, the Lady of the Morning Dew." Her voice was soft, musical, and entirely serious. "My lady awaits your presence." To his surprise, she then handed him the pink paper cut he had previously exchanged for the invitation. "Throw the maid into the air and she will guide Prince Genji to his Lady."

"This is like one of my games," said Towne and, after a brief pause, did as he was asked with gusto. O'Yone paused for an instant, then let out a breath that was surprisingly powerful, and he watched in wonder as the maid sailed into the air to be caught in a sudden gust of wind that sounded as though it were blowing through what might have been reeds, or perhaps canes of bamboo, carrying with it the vague and distant sound of a wooden flute whose notes rose and fell, grew and faded in a tune impossible to identify but dream-like in its appeal.

"Follow, follow her quickly," urged O'Yone.

Spots of rain were now falling and could be seen as well as felt, their speckled patterns dancing in the wind, backlit by the lantern's glow. Towne clambered through the gap, imagining himself indeed as Prince Genji, the famous lover from Japanese literature whom he'd recently read about and whose bedroom antics he yearned to emulate.

Once in the garden, it was as if he had stepped into a different, more ancient world. O'Yone and the peony lantern had vanished, dreamlike, from his presence. Instead, the whole garden was illuminated by bright moonlight, bathing pathways in rosy hues of pink, crimson, and purple. The design and layout were greatly reminiscent of the garden on the university grounds. Similar, yes, but far more luxuriant, and Towne wondered if he'd been brought to that ancient garden his assistant had briefly referred to. He looked up into the sky to see the maid of Genji being buffeted from one gust of wind to the other, but nonetheless guiding him at a walking pace across the garden towards the temple.

As he made his way, he searched for evidence of a lighting rig of some kind but could see no sign of one. Instead, he was captivated by the sight of white blossoms drifting through the air and falling languidly into the well on his right, and onto the water of the pond up ahead. He noted that the gentle *splish* they made as they landed was much quieter than the sound of the raindrops, but more resonant. He noted, too, the *splash* of a single koi carp, orange and white, that twice leapt from the pond as he passed it. Meanwhile, from one of the bushes, a single cicada played a shrill accompaniment to the music of the flute, which grew louder as Towne approached the peony bush. Then a cloud drifted across the moon, greatly dimming its light for a few seconds. When it passed, the maid of Genji had disappeared. But it did not matter, for there, by the bridge over the pond, sat the other maid, of flesh and blood.

O'Yone was effortlessly fingering, effortlessly conjuring notes that harmonised with the natural sounds around her, creating a soundscape of beauty to match the visual perfection of the garden itself.

Her face expressionless, O'Yone watched Towne as he passed her and crossed over the bridge. The peony lantern still hung from its pole but was now suspended above the door of the temple, which was open just a crack.

"Shoes!" called out the maid. "Remove your shoes!"

Towne did so, along with his woollen socks, feeling the chill on his feet. The music of the flute resumed. With the tips of his fingers, he slid open the door with ease before taking a breath and stepping inside.

The impact on his senses was immediate and immense. The warmth in the air, the soft touch of the woven silk carpet on the soles of his bare feet, the semi-darkness in which subtle shades of dark colour—purple, indigo, violet and green—covered the walls and partitioned the room, curtains, and screens of damask and silk so thin they were transparent. Above all, the perfume of citrus and rose, the same sweet, spicy, sensual fragrance that had so overpowered him for the entire afternoon and which now drifted around him in thin swirls of mist that spiralled from jars arranged on the wooden benches that stretched along the walls. The charm and beauty of the garden was forgotten; the allure of this temple was of an altogether more erotic intensity.

At the room's far end was a white screen, patterned with pictures of flowers and leaves and backlit by a lantern whose dim glow cast a shadow before it. Suddenly it was pulled aside, and the shadow became the figure of a woman, shimmering and fluid in the flickering half-light. Her hair flowed in thick, black tresses the length of the robe that hung loosely about her shoulders, and whose sleeves were billowing and blowing as if caught by the breath of some ghostly wind. Most striking of all was her face. It glowed like a bright white flower around the glistening crimson of her lips. When the screen was drawn again, Towne was left transfixed and utterly bewildered. The image had lasted for just a few seconds, but he knew that it would linger in his memory for the rest of his life. He stood still, waiting in breathless silence. When at last the woman spoke to him, her voice was mellifluous, a slow whisper in the darkness.

"Pull back the screen and step inside."

His hands trembling, Towne entered what appeared to be a private chamber. Cushions and pillows lay scattered across a large futon mattress at his feet. Across from him, shading what little light there was, sat the woman.

"Do you know who I am?" she asked

"O'Tsuyu, the Lady of the Morning Dew, I assume."

To his surprise, he detected no irony in the tone of his answer.

"You looked at me. What did you see?" she asked.

"The most beautiful of women."

"I am certain you have said this before."

"But this is the first time I've meant it."

"Not even to your wife?"

"I'm divorced."

"Where is she now?"

"In Paris. She is French." And he added, without knowing why, "She used to call me "Shar-le.'" He emphasised the two syllables and let out a short, nervous laugh.

"'Shar-le,'" repeated the woman. "I think it suits you." She paused, then added, "Men are so faithless, so inconstant, I have always found. Don't you agree?"

He said nothing. The conversation, though unanticipated, did not seem strange to him.

"What do you know of Genji? You spoke of it this morning."

He wondered how she could know this.

"It's a famous work of Japanese literature. About a young, handsome prince. A great but cruel lover."

"So, you have read it?"

He found it impossible to lie to this woman.

"Er… No. I had a doctoral student once who loved Japanese literature."

"Was she beautiful, this student?"

"Not especially."

"What about her mind?"

He frowned. "She was clever, passionate about her work. Too outspoken, too forthright."

"Too forthright. And too generous?"

He said nothing.

"She gave you ideas that you have taken and used."

He still said nothing.

"You stole a paper she wrote for you and claimed to have written it yourself."

"She made an official complaint, but the university dismissed it. Look, how do you know all this? Why have you led me here?"

O'Tsuyu continued as if he hadn't spoken.

"These were ideas you do not understand."

Before he could respond, she stood up slowly, stepping into the half-light and slipped open her robe. Towne began to perspire.

"The pattern and colour of my junihitoe[11]. Do you understand this?"

"Erm, yes, yes. The purple of the peony flower. Faithfulness." He struggled to recall the words of his assistant from the morning. "Romantic love."

"And honesty. And sacrifice," she added. "Sacrifice, above all else. Sacrifice in the service of truth."

The faint music from the flute suddenly stopped.

"Take off your coat and lie down."

It was a command, not a request, and Towne obeyed. The floor was soft, the cushions were of silk.

The woman stood over him, her face glowing in the semidarkness.

"You want to love me, do you not?" she asked, a direct question that shot through Towne like a jolt of electricity.

"More than anything," he whispered.

"But do you understand what that means?"

"I want to find out."

O'Yone entered from behind the curtain and stood watching them both.

"And O'Yone. Will you reward her if I command it?"

"Yes." His throat was dry, and his heart was thumping.

The woman glanced at the maid and knelt beside him, caressing him gently across the chest.

"To love me, you must give yourself over to me, body and mind."

At this, she stroked his cheek, then placed her hand on his forehead and leant her face over his.

"And you will find that truth, like love, as well as being beautiful, can often be cruel."

And as she opened her mouth to kiss him, she pulled back her lips, and he saw her teeth were as black as ebony and her eyes bright with a passion that was furious in its intensity.

---

11 **junihitoe:** A twelve-layered kimono; first worn in the Heian period by noble women and ladies-in-waiting of the Japanese Imperial Court.

SEVEN CURSES

Towne awoke in his room, early morning light shining through narrow gaps between the curtains. He was still in his clothes, the coat draped over a hanger behind the door, just as it had been on the previous evening. He had the invitation card clutched against his chest, even though he could recall handing it to the woman who had called herself O'Yone.

Examining it, he was astonished to find that, apart from the front image, the card was not at all as he recalled it and, if anything, was even more macabre. Instead of two embracing skeletons within the frame of the mirror, there was just the one, clutching what appeared to be a purple peony flower against its skull. And instead of the rhyme he recalled reading earlier, there was a single line of Japanese script, with its English translation underneath. In utter bewilderment, he read it out loud.

"If I should die beneath a peony flower, will I still be charming as a ghost?"

His headache was as intense as his astonishment, which intensified further when he saw that the back of the card, from which he had followed the instructions, was blank.

He could not recall a single detail about his return to the hotel, his last clear memory being of ebony black teeth as the woman bent over him. Had she indeed kissed him? Erotic images of lovemaking, of lying with the woman and her maid naked on the bed, swirled through his mind—but they had the elusive quality of fantasy about them. More akin to dreams than memories, they left him with feelings of emptiness rather than satisfaction, frustration rather than elation.

His inquiries at the hotel reception desk only compounded his confusion. The night staff were about to finish their shift, but none could recall having seen him on his return. This was not in itself strange as their shift had been unusually busy, with many other conference participants returning late and in high spirits from various haunts in the centre of the town.

Turning away from the desk, he spotted a small group of women who had been in his workshop the previous morning. He ran across the lobby, calling after them. They stopped, their faces registering some alarm. He excused himself and asked if they'd seen anything of a young woman dressed in a white dress with a belt of red silk who might have attended his workshop. None of them recognised her from the description he gave them.

Towne was supposed to be chairing a panel later in the morning but excused himself, pleading illness. Instead, he returned to his hotel room to try to make sense of what had happened.

He was used to one-night stands, of course. In fact, their non-committal nature was what he liked about sexual liaisons at conferences, and he often cited Albert Camus' writings in praise of Don Juan as a philosophical justification for male promiscuity. But the elaborately staged nature of the whole encounter and the many mysteries that surrounded it made this one very different.

Firstly, there was the matter of the identities of the woman and of her maid, not to mention the girl who had appeared so mysteriously from the garden to hand him his invite. Then there was the convoluted nature of the directions he'd had to follow and the strange ritual of having to swap the paper cut for the invite and vice-verse on his arrival at the garden. Not to mention the wonder of the garden itself, enchanting and gorgeous in its other-worldliness.

But above all there was the woman, this lady of extraordinary beauty, who had summoned him to make love to her. The first time he had caught sight of her, when she had drawn back the screen and revealed herself to him, was indelibly printed on his memory. So, too, was the image of her face as she had leaned over to kiss him, an image that was simultaneously both chilling and erotic, and all the more exciting for that.

SEVEN CURSES

He'd recently heard stories about fox fairies, spiritual entities who took on the form of beautiful women and sapped the energies from the men they slept with, and legends of imperial courtesans of immense beauty. But O'Tsuyu, he felt, had more of the power and intensity of a goddess about her. He thought of Aphrodite and how she would, in Greek mythology, lust on occasion after a mortal man and take on human form in order to seduce him.

This idea appealed to him; that he, Charles Towne, had been desired and chosen by a *goddess*.

He laughed as he thought of the quip he so often used about his bag, a joke that now seemed to have real truth to it. The rational part of his mind tried to dismiss such musings, of course. The overpowering fragrance on the paper and the densely perfumed mist in the temple that had shared the same scent—surely it was more reasonable to conclude he'd been the victim of some powerful, hallucinatory drug. But for what possible purpose he could not fathom. Instead, he gave himself over to fantasies about his goddess, dwelling only on the experience and not on any possible explanation for it. In doing so, he felt a growing and overwhelming desire to see and make love to her one more time on this, the final evening of the conference.

He slipped on his coat and took the elevator down to the lobby, determined to retrace his steps of the previous evening. But try as he might, as soon as he turned away from the main street, it proved impossible.

Every time he thought he was headed in the right direction, it was never the case. Sometimes he would find himself back on a main road, other times trapped in a narrow cul-de-sac. Once, he even found himself treading through what appeared to be a derelict cemetery. He wondered if anyone could direct him to the old wooden archway that he'd thought to be the gateway to the old town. But very few of the people he came across could speak English, and the few that did shook their heads in confusion. They had never heard of such an archway. And besides, they told him, the old part of town was far away from there, by no means as close as his questions implied. To his great dismay, Towne had to accept that it would be impossible to return to the garden after all.

By now he was completely lost but fortunately was able to hail a taxi that took him back to his hotel, a journey that turned out to be much shorter than he'd anticipated. Once again, he wondered about the directions he'd been asked to follow and, in a sudden revelation, a cold fist gripped his heart; for whatever reason, everything had been arranged so he could never find his way back to the garden. The crazy instructions, that he'd had to hand back the invitation on which they had been written, that it had evidently been later replaced by another with the directions erased. He'd been led to paradise and then immediately ejected from it. It had all been a cruel joke, whose purpose and intention he could not fathom.

As he walked in through the entrance into the hotel lobby, for the third time in two days, he heard a female voice hailing him by name. He looked up to see two young women, both participants in his workshop, smiling at him. He recalled having chosen them both as partners when playing The Maid of Genji.

They walked up to him and expressed some disappointment at not having seen him in the conference since the workshop and were very insistent that he attend the farewell drinks reception at 6:30 that evening. He thought them both rather pretty and their flirtatious manner lightened his spirits. He asked to be reminded where it was being held, whereupon they both giggled, sharing an amused look with each other. Why, in the room where he had held his workshop, they informed him, and in the garden outside. He pursed his lips and forced a smile. The irony was not lost on him. Yes, he told them, he would be more than happy to spend an evening in the delightful company of such charming young women. They giggled again and walked off, chattering excitedly to one another—

like two silly teenagers, he thought. Nevertheless, one—or even both—could prove to be a pleasurable distraction for his final night.

That evening he dressed in loose white linen—trousers, shirt, and jacket—and, for effect, draped the Aphrodite bag over his shoulder. As he walked past the reception desk, the receptionist informed him that a package had been left for him, and he was handed a small, white box, hardly any weight at all, labelled "Fragile." It had been left by a young woman, evidently a conference participant.

Towne was used to receiving gifts from admirers of his work, particularly in Asia, and usually left them in his hotel room when he checked out. Doubtless, this would prove to be another unwanted bauble or cheap cultural artefact. He tossed it into his bag and joined a group of colleagues waiting for the minibus. He was glad when it arrived almost immediately; he so needed a drink.

Once at the reception, he helped himself to a bottle of Asahi beer and looked about the room for the two silly girls who'd been so looking forward to seeing him again. Unsurprisingly, with free alcohol on offer, it was a noisy and rather crowded affair, but Towne spotted them standing at a table over by the window. They waved a greeting as he pushed his way towards them. It was now dark outside and, although the fire exit door was open, no one had yet made their way into the garden. Unsurprising, as there was a distinct chill in the air and the atmosphere in the room was warm and vibrant enough.

Towne commented on how nice they both looked this evening. They, in turn, commented on how taken they were with his smart leather bag. He repeated his story about Sam Beckett and Aphrodite and, at their request, placed it on the table for them to admire. As he did so, it tipped over and the package fell out. The girls were very curious to know what was inside, so he opened it.

He broke the seal and recognised the fragrance at once. For their part, the girls gasped in admiration at the beautiful purple peony flower and asked who'd left him such a lovely gift. He didn't hear them at first, just gazed in astonishment, wondering what it might mean. Then, before he could answer, he looked over at the table where the drinks were being served and was certain that he caught sight of a young woman in a white dress with a wide red belt about her waist. It was she who had undoubtedly left the gift in the hotel, and she who could and would explain this whole mystery to him.

He elbowed his way through the now thickening crowd, only to find that once he reached the table, she had disappeared. Frantically, he looked about the room. He could not see her—but he did see something else. The flowing purple robe, the long, billowing sleeves, the thick, ebony black tresses down her back as she stepped through the fire door and into the darkness of the garden…

O'Tsuyu herself.

Thoughts of everything and everyone else were forgotten as he pushed his way to the door, not caring whose drink he caused to spill in his desperation to reach her.

Towne ignored the two girls who were now calling after him and paid no attention to those colleagues who were braving the chill of the garden, drinking and talking in the pale light that spilled out from the room. A shadow was visible some distance away along the path that led past the peony bush, the well, the pond, up to the temple, hidden now in the far corner of the garden. He knew this was where she was leading him.

When he eventually stumbled into it, he stopped, breathless. He had not expected it to be transformed into the sumptuously erotic chamber where he'd been summoned the previous evening and nor had it been. The dark, empty interior was as he remembered it from his first visit, but this hardly registered on his consciousness, for there in the corner, standing in a pool of moonlight streaming through an adjacent window, was the woman. His goddess. Although her face was in shadow, he could see that she was facing him with open arms.

As he watched, she let slip her robe and stood there, gloriously naked, her skin bathed in silvery shades of violet, the strange but alluring effect of the moonlight. She took a step forward and he could see her face, ghostly white, shining brighter than the moonlight. The red lips spread into a smile, her teeth of the blackest ebony moist, glinting and glistening. Surely, she was inviting him to approach her. He did so, with neither thought nor hesitation, stripping off his clothes and casting them aside, before grasping her hand tightly in his as she eased him onto the floor.

THE TWO "SILLY girls," to use Towne's pejorative description, had been calling after him for a reason. Although the white package still sat on the table where he'd left it, along with his bag and unfinished beer, the peony itself had inexplicably disappeared. They wanted not only to inform him of this but to assure him they had never for one second left it unattended. How and where it had vanished to was a complete mystery to them. The glazed look they'd seen in the professor's eyes as he had pushed his way out of the door had alarmed them, as had the fact that he'd evidently heard but chosen to ignore their cries.

After a few anxious minutes, they decided to seek him out to explain what had happened. Not wanting to leave such an expensive bag unguarded, one of the girls carried it carefully under her arm while the other picked up his beer. Together they made their way into the garden, where several groups were now gathered haphazardly in varying states of alcohol-fuelled merriment. The girls inquired politely but at first could find no one with any idea who Towne was. After several attempts, they eventually approached a particularly rowdy group of Australian academics who were able to help them.

"He disappeared that way, up that path." The portly, middle-aged man's voice was unnecessarily loud. "We called after him to come and join us. 'Hey, Towney, you won't have to buy a round, you stingy bastard.'" His friends laughed. "Anyway, he ignored us—he usually does."

The girls listened to all of this with forced smiles, thanking the men, but pleased when they closed back into their circle and began to ignore their presence. Soon they were passing the barren rose bush and the bush of winter peonies, and the girl carrying the bag noticed how the flowers all shared the same darkly coloured petals, apart from the pink one. However, they paid little attention to any of the garden's charms, intent as they were on finding their esteemed professor.

They reached the bridge over the pond and were making their way across it when they stopped and shared a look of alarm. The faint sound of a man moaning appeared to be coming from the wooden building in front of them. Was this their professor? Had he been taken ill? A young Asian woman in a white dress and wide, red belt stood nearby, smiling as she looked intently at the phone she was directing through the open door into the interior of the pagoda. The moans grew louder and more intense as the girls approached the door and, without pausing, stepped through it, wanting to lend their assistance in any way they could.

The scene that confronted them was so bizarre, so shocking, that they could, for some time, make no sense of it. There, on his back, entirely naked in a bright shaft of moonlight, lay Professor Towne, his expensive clothes strewn untidily about him. A look of ecstasy on his face, he held the purple peony flower in one hand while vigorously masturbating with the other. The girls stood watching, agape, unable to take their eyes from such a grotesque spectacle as he pressed the peony into his face, thrusting his tongue into its petals and its petals into his mouth. When jets of jism began to pump from his penis, they both uttered gasps of horror. Bag and bottle dropped noisily to the floor and beer began to drain in gentle spurts into the soft leather interior of Towne's prized possession.

The noise seemed to have an effect on Towne. His eyes gradually cleared, and the girls could see him slowly begin to register his surroundings, as if for the first time. They watched as he looked at them both, evidently puzzled by their presence and by the horrified expressions on their faces. They saw him switch his gaze to the woman in the white dress with the red silk belt, who'd entered behind them, and his eyes grew wider. He finally turned his attention to the peony, still clutched in his hand. Incomprehension became astonishment, then shock, as something deeper and more intensely painful seemed to now possess him—fear, perhaps, or shame, or abject terror, or all of these at once.

The girls screamed as he let out a strangled cry and hurled the peony flower into a shadowy corner, where it disappeared from sight. Frightened now, they flinched as he jerked himself up into a sitting position, clutched his hands about his knees, and began shaking his head from side to side, shivering in the cold that only now his body seemed to react to. They looked on as the woman in the white dress picked up the coat that lay in a muddle on the floor and approached them with it, speaking in English.

"Here," she said, handing it to one of them. "Perhaps you should drape it over his shoulders so he doesn't catch a chill."

The girl promptly did this as the young woman turned and left the temple. Towne stared after her, dumbfounded, then began to shake his head again, muttering incoherently before peering into the corner where he had thrown the peony. The two girls could barely identify what he was mumbling to himself beyond the words *truth* and *cruel*, which he repeated again and again. In an attempt to be helpful, one of them pulled her mobile phone from her pocket and shone its torch into the shadows, evidently searching for the peony; but shine where she might, it could not be seen anywhere.

When she finally switched off the beam, what sounded like the sinister, ghostly strains of a woman's laughter echoed from the corner. The professor went rigid while the two girls gazed wide-eyed at one another, listening intently as the sound faded into the distance. They remained in stillness and silence once it had vanished, a silence broken only when others began to arrive on the scene, curious to discover the source of the commotion that could be heard outside.

The young Chinese woman was no longer anywhere to be seen.

THERE WAS ONLY one subject of conversation, speculation, rumour, concern, and jocularity for the rest of the evening. Groups of academics, students, and bar staff alike looked on, stunned, as they watched Towne being led out of the garden to a warm, secluded room, where he could await the ambulance that would take him to a local hospital.

Those who knew him spoke later of their great shock at his appearance, of how haggard he looked, as if touched by death, in such sharp contrast to the dapper individual with the charming smile they were used to. More than this, there were, it was generally agreed, signs of madness in his overall comportment, in the stumbling and the shivering, in the twitching of his face muscles, in the vacancy of his eyes, as though all sense of reality had been drained from them. They'd been especially alarmed when, on passing the peony bush, he'd pointed to it and broken into hysterical laughter, screaming, "These violent delights have violent ends and in their triumph die!"

Several recognised the quote from *Romeo and Juliet*, but no one had the remotest idea what had provoked his outburst.

Towne did gradually recover, inasmuch as he was well enough to be discharged from the hospital after several days of sedation and monitoring, but he was never the same man again. The charm, the self-confidence, the charisma, the self-assurance had disappeared.

Looking many years older, he returned to his university only to hand in his resignation after a term's sick leave. This came as a relief to senior management, who had for a long time been unhappy with the poor quality of his research and the rumours about his personal life.

What had made his position untenable, however, was the anonymous release on social media of a video taken through the doors of the temple building in which the whole sorry scene of his sexual encounter with a peony flower had been made available for all to see. By the time it'd been removed, the damage had been done. Students from the university had recognised him and overnight turned him into a figure of derision, subject to cruel jokes that circulated the campus, from graffiti on toilet doors to cartoons left anonymously on notice boards, to obscene memes posted on Facebook and Instagram. Towne no longer had the energy or the will necessary to combat such extensive ridicule and instead chose a life of obscurity and relative anonymity, which, alas, did not prove to be a lengthy one.

ONE FINAL EPISODE is worth including as a footnote to this account. A few weeks after the conference, a departmental secretary was disturbed in her office by one of the university's gardeners asking to speak with her. She could tell he was somewhat shaken, so she invited him to enter and sit down, whereupon he explained that he'd been detailed that morning to the nearby Zen garden to mend a gap in the bamboo fence and carry out some general maintenance work.

While pruning the peony bush, he'd discovered a thin paper cut lodged between two blooms, one pink, one purple, whose beauty had impressed him but also made him feel strangely uneasy. At this point, the gardener carefully withdrew the paper from his wallet and held it out to the secretary. She noted that it was pink in colour, in the shape of what looked to her like a geisha, and gave off a faint fragrance of citrus, maybe spice. Puzzled, she asked if this is what had disturbed him. He shook his head and described how the paper had suddenly and inexplicably fluttered out of his hand and across his face before he'd managed to catch hold of it again. She saw him shiver as he recalled the sensation of its touch on his cheek and on his lips.

"It was as if the hands of a ghost had caressed me," he explained, "as if the lips of a ghost had kissed me." He paused, a haunted look in his eyes. "And I cannot bear it."

CURSE FOUR
USELESS PASTRY

Four is the foolish poisoner;

My curse will ruin his sole pleasure...

Tuesday, November 21st, morning
(two months ago)

THE FOX HAD been scavenging through his rubbish bin again. For the third time in as many weeks, Terence raised the blinds and peered through the window of his kitchenette into the pale morning light of early November, only to glimpse debris scattered about his garden lawn. With a sigh of annoyance, he tightened the belt on his dressing gown, took from a drawer a black bin liner and a pair of rubber gloves (items supplied by the university to all resident tutors) and pulled open the back door.

The weather was mild for this time of year, but puddles on the concrete path signalled that it'd been raining during the night. He grabbed a hat, twisted his feet into the pair of green wellington boots he kept in a cardboard box in a corner, stepped outside and, with a red rubber glove on his right hand and a green bucket hat on his head, set about gathering the various items of food waste from the sodden grass.

Not for the first time, he wondered what attracted this particular fox to his bin as it never seemed to eat anything it found in it. Scraps of meat, fish, rice, pasta, bread, cheese, fruit, and vegetables cooked and raw, lay spread across the unkempt garden on either side of the path. And pastry crusts, above all else, evidence of his fondness for pasties and pies of all kinds. The fox always paid its visits on the night before the bin was due to be emptied, as if it had purposely built this particular inconvenience into its routine. There were also items of detritus Terence didn't recognise as his own; a bunch of rotten grapes, an entire bag of onions, an empty bottle of wine vinegar. Where had these come from? More than once, he suspected students of secretly dropping their own mess into his bin, though why they would want to do this or found it amusing was beyond him. As were, in fact, many things about the students who resided in Laurel Hall.

Terence had only caught sight of the fox once, after its first assault on his rubbish bin. He'd raised the blinds and seen it standing calmly on the wall at the far end of the garden, drops of dew on its white fur glistening like jewellery in the dim early light. It turned its head lazily and looked straight at him, holding his gaze for several seconds, its calm demeanour contrasting sharply with his astonishment, an astonishment that intensified once he noticed the weekly food waste littered across his lawn. Only then did the animal quietly jump off the wall and disappear, as if satisfied to be identified as the creator of this particular scene of chaos.

As on the previous two occasions, the mess of rubbish Terence collected almost completely filled the extra bin bag. Although he was no mathematician, he knew enough about volume and capacity to be puzzled by the fact that contents that had previously filled only one bin bag had now swelled in size to fill two. Foxes had the reputation for cunning, not for conjuring, he mused. One plus nought should not equal two in any universe, not even a fox's.

Back in the kitchenette, while boiling a kettle for the first of his three morning cups of earl grey tea, he searched, "what do foxes like to eat?"

"Virtually anything!" he read—cooked and raw meat, fried bread, cheese, fruit, cooked vegetables...the list went on. Not his fox, though. His fox didn't appear to eat a thing; it just liked making a mess.

He then searched, "what do foxes *not* like to eat?" To his surprise, grapes and onions were registered at the top of the list, with chilli and wine vinegar noted as especially repellent. Apparently, these would all make the fox ill. Terence shook his head, completely baffled. Modern life for him was puzzling enough. Only his strict routines kept him sane. This was no way to start a day when a difficult meeting with Madeleine lay ahead of him. As he sipped his tea, his mind drifted back to a particularly difficult morning earlier that year, although he also recalled it as the day when Madeleine Lim had been ushered into his life.

Friday, January 20th, morning
(twelve months ago)

"So, Dr. Usgood. Tell us in your own words what happened."

Terence had been called to attend a formal hearing before a panel led by the head of student accommodation services in order to respond in person to a complaint that could lead to the loss of his position as resident tutor of Laurel Hall.

"Well, it was all rather unfortunate, really. I was simply acting on a university directive that urged all residential staff to make sure that those overseas students unable to return home would feel welcome over the holiday period. My hall—that is, Laurel Hall—has—rather, *had*—two such students, both from China, who shared the small flat at the far end of the building, the one especially reserved for postgraduates."

The three committee members stared at him stony-faced, so Terence continued.

"I would be staying in my flat for the entire holiday period, so I thought I might invite them for a meal one evening and that New Year's Eve would be suitable. This was the first suggestion on the list presented in the directive. I went to their flat. The complainant wasn't in at the time, but her flatmate responded positively to my invitation. I suggested Italian food, this being my own favourite, and she said yes, that she herself was particularly fond of fillet steak cooked with onions in a red wine sauce. So that is what I ordered, for three, even though it was the most expensive meal on the menu." He paused to let this sink in. "I also bought two bottles of Chianti from Tesco."

"Dr. Usgood," a severe-looking woman with silvery grey hair spoke, "do you often welcome dinner guests dressed as a Roman centurion?"

"Well, the university directive said I should expect some students to respond to such an invitation by dressing formally in their traditional costume. And the meal was Italian, so I thought the costume appropriate on both counts. It is entirely authentic, by the way. I shall be wearing it again at the Wroxeter ancient arts festival in two weeks' time."

A serious-looking gentleman with a beard now spoke. "Dr. Usgood, when did Rose, the complainant, take ill?"

"Just as I was about to serve the tiramisu for dessert. It had been on offer at a reduced price in Tesco when I bought the wine." He blinked as he scanned the faces in front of him. "I can recommend it. It's very nice."

"She informed us she felt painful stomach cramps and began vomiting violently, and that you reacted in an inconsiderate manner."

"I only repeated that, as myself and her flatmate were perfectly well, it must have been something she'd eaten earlier. One of those awful Chinese snacks they are so fond of."

"You actually used that word, awful?"

"Well, yes, they are awful. Have you never tasted one? Anyway, I called a taxi to take her to A and E."

"Which she had to pay for."

"I mean... I had already spent a great deal of money entertaining her."

"She says you sent her off alone with a plastic Tesco bag on her knee."

"Yes, in case she was sick again."

"You didn't consider it appropriate to accompany her?" the grey-haired woman asked.

"Well, I was still dressed as a Roman centurion. I hadn't had time to change."

"So, you didn't offer her support or sympathy?"

"Would that have stopped her vomiting?"

"And you didn't think it appropriate to visit her the next day? Or to call the hospital?"

"But those options weren't listed anywhere in the university's directives."

The panel eventually dismissed Terence, and he was asked to remove himself from the room. Thirty minutes later they called him back in and told him that, although the complainant's adverse reaction to the food was a mystery and could not be blamed on any apparent negligence on his part, his subsequent responses had displayed a distinct lack of sensitivity and care. He would not be asked to resign his position as hall tutor but would, however, be required to attend the university's next Sensitivity and Empathy staff training course. He was also advised to refrain from wearing his centurion costume in response to any future university directives.

With some relief, Terence cycled away at speed. He checked his watch. With any luck, he might just have enough time for his 11:00 a.m. coffee and pastry at the departmental café before his second meeting of the morning.

"Ah, Dr. Usgood, do come in."

The head of the department was seated behind his desk, where the untidy mess of papers scattered across it made Terence feel uncomfortable; but he resisted the urge to approach and sort them into neat piles. "Please, take a seat."

Terence duly did so, sitting stiffly and in silence in front of this balding, pink faced, sixty-year-old man whom he seldom had any dealings with. Being the sole classics scholar in the university, he'd been attached to the department of anthropology as a research fellow purely out of convenience.

"I saw you cycling in earlier," the head commented in a hearty voice. "Goodness, that bicycle of yours looks rather ancient. You didn't unearth it on one of your Roman digs, did you?" He was known for his genial demeanour and quirky sense of humour.

"No. It's a 1950 Sunbeam Gents special tourist model WR3," replied Terence.

"Yes, yes, quite." The head let out a sigh and continued in a more serious tone. "Anyway, much as I would enjoy sharing a friendly chat with you, I'm afraid that I've asked to see you about a pressing departmental problem that I need your help with."

Terence felt a headache coming on.

"You know we're short-staffed and your research grant, generous as it is, doesn't quite cover your salary—well done for getting it, by the way. I'd never heard of the Lucius Quintilian Trust before. So, to get straight to the point, we have a new master's research student, only with us for a year, a young woman from Singapore. She comes with the highest recommendations and also a full scholarship. She was going to be supervised by Dot Sweeney but, as you probably heard, she took bad last week. Yes, what she had initially thought to be a bout of severe indigestion turned out to be a serious heart attack. Dreadful business, very sad. In short, I need *you* to be her supervisor." The head was still scrutinising the references. "Goodness... I wouldn't worry, Terence, it looks to me she's bright enough to supervise herself!"

Terence was stunned. "But is she a classics scholar?"

"Oh, ha, no, no. Her topic is very Asian. But quite up your street, I would say." He began rifling through some papers on his desk. "Yes, here we are. You are researching..." he read from one of them, "The Shifts in the Domestic Culture of the Augustinian Period as Evoked in the Works of Ten Minor Poets from Different Outposts of the Roman Empire." He paused. "Fascinating, I'm sure. Well, it's the word 'domestic' that connects you both. Her proposed topic is…" He picked up another paper, "'Patterns and Paradigms of the Tiger Mother in the Chinese Community of Singapore.' You see? Motherhood. You can't get more domestic than mothers, can you? Not so sure about the tiger, mind. Unless it's the kind that comes to tea, hey?"

Terence's expression remained blank.

"Anyway," continued the head, "it's the process as much as content that matters, isn't it? Getting the research question right, finding the appropriate methodology, all that kind of stuff, blah blah. No, Dr. Usgood, it's all been decided, and Ms. Lim has been informed. You are to meet her for her first supervisory session on Monday at 10:00 a.m. She is very keen to get started, I hear."

Terence left the office feeling most unhappy. He had little experience of supervising students and had always found them a burden, an unwanted distraction from his research. He sighed. It seemed his life was being plagued by young Asian women.

Monday, January 23rd, morning
(twelve months ago)

TERENCE DRIPPED ALONG the corridor, only removing his yellow sou'wester and matching cycle cape once in the staff toilet, where he hung them on the two coat pegs at the back of the door. His dress sense was legendary, although he didn't know it. Jacket too small, tie too narrow, shirt collar too tight, trousers too short, coloured socks too bright, suede shoes too scuffed; he was often the subject of amused banter between the departmental secretaries during their tea break. Today, both the fox and the rain had delayed him, and his new student was already waiting outside his office door when he emerged from the toilet.

SEVEN CURSES

At 10:00 a.m. promptly, Madeleine Lim sat down in his office. Terence looked at her. She was small and slim and could have been any age between fifteen and thirty-five. She wore one of those puffy anoraks and a colourful woollen hat, which she removed to reveal short, neatly trimmed black hair that fell over her ears and forehead. Her face was quite pretty, especially her eyes, which had a sharp intelligence about them.

Terence welcomed her in a not very welcoming voice, asked if she was settling in without listening to her reply, then read aloud through the details written on her application form, including the summary of her proposed research project. She sat impassively throughout, her eyes focused keenly on Terence as he began to talk about his own specialism, explaining with no great enthusiasm why she'd been allocated to him for supervision.

"But I do have to be quite frank with you," he concluded. "I know nothing about mothers. I never knew mine. I didn't grow up with one."

There was a pause. "Lucky you," said Madeleine.

"I'm sorry?"

She had spoken softly, and Terence wondered if he'd heard her correctly. Typically, whenever he gave any details of his difficult, lonely childhood, people would mutter their condolences or shake their head and utter the usual platitudes of how terrible it all must have been for him.

"You are lucky," Madeleine repeated, this time more loudly. "I often wished that I never had a mother."

Terence recalled the deep sense of absence he'd often felt when, as a small boy in boarding school, his classmates had spoken fondly of their own mothers.

"Even when you were very young?" he asked.

"Especially when I was very young."

Madeleine's voice was strong without being strident and she spoke with only a slight accent, in a rhythmic, almost musical tone. Her English was excellent. Terence was not surprised by this, knowing that English was the language of schooling in Singapore; but he was surprised by what she was telling him.

"But your thesis, your research, it's all about mothers!"

"It's all about *Tiger Mothers*," she replied. "And I'm an expert, having been raised by one, you see."

She paused and cast an admiring glance at the bookshelves that lined an entire wall of his office. "So many books!" she exclaimed. "How wonderful to be able to escape into a world of books!"

Terence was both very proud and very fond of his books, many of which were either in Latin or ancient Greek. All the great classics were there, both in the original and in translation, some of the most famous in several translations. One of his ways of relaxing was to compare the merits and demerits of different translations of the same poem, selections from the Roman poet Ovid being a particular favourite for this little game of his.

Madeleine continued. "I want to escape for a year. This study, for me, will have therapeutic value. I see it as a kind of holiday."

Terence wasn't sure about any of this, so he ignored it all.

"I'd never heard of a Tiger Mother before I saw the title of your research," he said. "My first image, I must tell you, was of a mother fiercely protective of her child." Madeleine gave no reaction. "But perhaps that's not entirely accurate?"

For the first time, Madeleine smiled slightly. "Fierce, yes. Fiercely critical, fiercely demanding, fiercely punitive if the child in any way steps out of line. Many ambitious Chinese mothers are Tiger Women. They put a lot of pressure on their children to succeed. And the pressure is relentless."

"It must feel unreasonable at times, I suppose. Though, surely, she must always have had your best interest at heart?"

Madeleine made no direct response to this. Instead, she told Terence a story.

SEVEN CURSES

"When I was six years old, Mother made Father buy me a violin and pay for me to have lessons. She'd become very irritated when listening to a neighbour boasting about her son's great musical talent. He was the same age as me, you see, and she told me I had to learn to play better than this obnoxious little boy. But I struggled. I am not very musically inclined.

"After two months, when I still couldn't play a simple tune, she lost her temper, snatched the bow from my hand, and began to beat me about the legs with it. I dropped the violin and tried to run away, but she chased me round the apartment, screaming what a lazy, ungrateful girl I was, landing blow after blow so forcefully that the bow finally broke. This made her even more angry. She had been a good woman all her life, she screamed, so why had she been punished this way, afflicted with such a wicked daughter? She actually began to weep tears of rage." Madeleine paused. "Until the doorbell suddenly rang. I was now cowering behind a table leg but could hear and see mother when she answered it, suddenly all smiles, chatting and laughing as though nothing had happened to upset her. I took the opportunity to slip out and disappear." She sat back in her chair, visibly relaxing a little. "That was the first time that she called me a 'useless pastry.'"

"A what?" exclaimed Terence. "I rather like pastries, personally." The word triggered him to check his watch. It was almost 10:45. There were still fifteen minutes until coffee and pastry time.

"Oh, it's just an expression we have in Chinese. Some think it comes from the time a dowager empress had an enormous pastry baked for display, in the shape and colour of a pink peach. No one was allowed to eat it, of course, and so it went stale and eventually had to be thrown away. A pastry is useless if you can't eat it. To call someone a 'useless pastry' is to imply that they are good for nothing."

Madeleine took a drink from a small flask of water she'd brought with her.

"You know, Mother makes delicious pastries, both sweet and savoury. When I was ten, Father bought me a pet rabbit for me to keep in a cage in my bedroom. Mother hated it, saying its smell affected her breathing. One evening, she threatened to cook it the following day while I was at school. I had learned to take Mother's threats seriously, so that night, while everyone slept, I carried the cage out of the apartment and down the stairs—all eight flights—and set the rabbit free. I was very sad, but at least I had saved it from being baked in a pie."

Terence had a thought. "Were you never really naughty, then?"

Madeleine laughed, and there was mischief in her eyes. "Once I stumbled across a discarded cigarette lighter while playing in the open area underneath our apartment block. All apartment blocks in Singapore are designed like this, with outdoor tables and plastic chairs for people to get together communally, well-sheltered from the sun and rain. I was still very young, about six or seven. I found the lighter underneath one of the tables. I'd seen these, of course, the old men and women using them to light their cigarettes and pipes as they played checkers or mahjong. I'd always been desperate to get my hands on one. Now I had, I lit and extinguished the flame at will for what must have been several minutes, thrilling at the dangerous power suddenly in my possession.

"Looking around me, I wondered what I could test this power on. There was a cable running horizontally across a wall, about two metres up from the ground. If I stood on one of the chairs, I thought I could reach it, so I dragged one over to the wall—they were very light—and stood on my tiptoes. I stretched my arm up as high as I could, lit the flame and watched fascinated as the wire above me visibly went soft, buckled, and partially melted. When I had seen enough, I put the chair and lighter back where I had found them. No one had seen me, I was sure."

Terence was quite taken with this tale. "It sounds like you got away with that particular prank. What was the cable, by the way?"

"Later that day, a neighbour came to the door and started shouting about how some 'son of a turtle' had burnt through the apartment's telephone cable. This was over twenty years ago, you see, and not many of us had cell phones then. Mother instantly turned her gaze on me." Madeleine let out a short breath. "It was her fiercest gaze, the one that can pierce right through you and pin you to the wall. I looked away, I began to shake, I must have blushed. Mother knew straight away that the son of a turtle was me."

Terence frowned. "Did she beat you again?"

"Worse," said Madeleine. "Mother sat me down and made me write a letter of apology, admitting that I was the culprit. Twenty-one copies, handwritten, one for each of our neighbours. It took me an entire weekend, and I had blisters on my fingers by the time I finished. She dragged me round each in turn. I had to hand over the letters in person while mother wept and complained about her wicked daughter." Madeleine took a sip from her water bottle. "The neighbours all expressed great sympathy for her. I can still remember the harsh looks they gave me for weeks afterwards."

Terence let out a sigh and shook his head.

"My. Was she like that all the time?"

"Oh yes," replied Madeleine. "She still is."

"Then you must have left home as soon as you could."

Madeleine shook her head slowly. "No. I still live at home. With Mother."

Terence was astonished. "Why? Is it money? You don't earn enough to be financially independent?"

"That's not really it," replied Madeleine. "It's much deeper than that. You see, once the tiger gets its claws into you, it's very, very hard to escape from its clutches."

The image this created in Terence's mind was vivid, broken only when he glanced at his watch again to see that it was already 10:57. He immediately rose from his chair, picked up his bag, and dismissed Madeleine, telling her to come back and see him in exactly a fortnight's time.

"Monday will be our day, 10:00 a.m., our time," he said. In the meantime, she was to become acquainted with the library resources and search for research papers relevant to her study.

"No emails," he insisted. "Avoid emails if you possibly can. Just report to me, same time every fortnight."

He hurried away to the café, leaving her in the corridor outside his office door.

OVER THE NEXT few months, Terence felt he got to know Madeleine's mother as much as he got to know Madeleine. He learned the young woman had initially completed a law degree and now had a rather lowly, ill-paid position in the Community Mediation Unit, a department in Singapore's Ministry of Law. But he knew more about her mother's constant complaints about her poor salary and lack of promotion than he did about the nature of her work there.

Initially, he had argued with Madeleine about the ethics of her research. How could she place her own mother at its centre and hope to justify it in objective terms? But Madeleine was stubborn and could quote enough feminist theory and narrative methodological references to silence him. Terence was still extremely doubtful but, somewhat to his surprise, he found he didn't really care about her theory or her methodology, or indeed the ethics of it all. What interested him were the many stories Madeleine had to tell. In the end, he let her continue because he wanted to read more tales about her dreadful mother.

One day, about two months into their acquaintance, a thought struck him.

"Your mother. From everything you have told me and have so far written about her, I cannot believe that she approves of your research topic. Didn't she try to prevent you from coming here?"

"Well, she couldn't exactly stop me," Madeleine said, with a slight smile. "I got that scholarship, after all, and have my own money, a bank account into which I have been filtering part of my salary for the past ten years. And as for the subject…" Her eyes twinkled a little. "I wasn't entirely honest with her. She thinks my aim is to educate readers about the Asian virtues of motherhood that she personifies. She doesn't think of herself as a Tiger Mother, you see, and I haven't told her anything about what I am *actually* writing. Besides, she has told me she may well visit me when I least expect it."

"You mean she will fly over to see you? Will I get the chance to meet her?" Terence paused. "I'm not sure I want to, actually…"

"No, no. She means that she will send her ghost to check over me, to make sure I am behaving properly."

Terence let out a laugh but then went silent. "Sometimes I am never quite sure whether you're being serious or not."

She didn't answer him directly. "There are stories in our culture in which people are visited by the ghost of a living relative while their body sleeps. Mother sleeps between the hours of 11:00 p.m. and 6:00 a.m. every night. That's 3:00 p.m. to 10:00 p.m. British time. I am always very alert during those hours." She leant closer to him, her voice conspiratorial. "That is why I will only ever meet with you in the morning and why I am often seen keeping very late hours in the library. It is also why I'm writing an alternative thesis alongside the true one."

"What?" Terence was speechless.

"I leave it out in my bedroom, in case she visits there while I'm out at college. It is called 'In Praise of a Devoted Mother.'" She drank from her water. "Let's just say that the stories are told very differently and Mother will be happy with them. Much, much happier than she would with this version."

"But most students have trouble writing just the one thesis!"

"Oh, they fuss and worry so much. It isn't that hard, really. I still have time to do lots of travelling, as you know."

Terence knew because she often told him stories about these trips, always playful, witty, and keenly observed. She occasionally told him about other aspects of her life in England, too; about her landlady, for example, who insisted on calling her Maddie even though Madeleine had told her this sounded like a terrible swear word in Chinese, one that would greatly upset her mother. But her best stories were always about her home life in Singapore. They began meeting in the café for some tutorials, and Terence noted that whenever she began one of these tales, students on neighbouring tables would often look away from their cell phones and stare surreptitiously in her direction, gripped by her charismatic storytelling.

Once she had asked about Terence's bicycle and, on learning that he had inherited it from his grandfather, embarked on one of her tales. She always told them with great vocal dexterity, full of expression and convincing characterisation.

"Oh, grandfathers. Mine became very difficult once he got older, especially after Grandmother died. He claimed he was unable to look after himself and advertised for a live-in nurse. Mother was furious. She said he was perfectly fit but just wanted a pretty, young woman to fuss over him. 'You just wait!' she told me. 'When he finally employs one, she will be young, pretty, and a hopeless nurse.' As it turned out, mother was only partly right. She was much younger than Grandfather, from Indonesia, and was indeed quite pretty, but she did care for him very well. But Mother was still very unhappy. 'I'm telling you, I don't trust that woman. She is only being nice to Grandfather to get her hands on his money. He is such a fool, and so vain. Next thing he will be telling us he has fallen in love and wants to marry her. And what will happen to our inheritance then? That wicked woman will run off with everything that should be coming to us!' I was fifteen years old at the time. 'Go round and offer to run errands for him,' she would tell me and would send me there regularly with treats. 'Here, take these pastries,' she would say. 'They are his favourite, I know. And you,' she would add, accusingly, 'why aren't you buying him presents? We must do everything we can to steer him away from that evil witch.'"

From what Terence could gather, the plan seemed to have worked but only partially. Grandfather was still alive but apparently had a younger, even prettier nurse looking after him now.

As Terence got to know Madeleine, he grew increasingly fond of her. Not in any sexual way, just a feeling of human affection that was strangely pleasurable to him. He looked forward to their fortnightly time together, without ever wishing it to develop into anything more intimate.

Then, one day in early November, when she had been his student for just over nine months, she told him about her illness.

Monday, November 21st, late morning (two months ago)

MADELEINE WAS SITTING in the same chair she always sat in, and Terence was struck by how pale and thin she looked. She'd been suffering from headaches and tiredness for a few weeks now. Dissatisfied with the attention she'd been receiving from the NHS, she was about to fly back to Singapore the following day, where her mother had fixed an appointment with a specialist for three days' time. She would inform Terence of the prognosis by email as soon as she knew it.

Terence felt awkward, not knowing what to say. He nodded at the bulging ring binder that lay on the small round coffee table, beside which Madeleine had placed her day bag.

"Well, you've nearly got the whole thing finished. Well done for that. I'll have plenty to read while you're away. I say, this is the true and not fictional version, isn't it?" He picked up the folder and flicked through its pages before putting it on his desk with an expression of relief.

"Oh yes, I double-checked," she replied. "The only paper version I have packed is the one for my mother to see. I intend to return in January or February to submit the thesis in person. As soon as this is all cleared up." She gestured vaguely with her right hand towards her eyes and her forehead. "Of course, Mother is convinced that it is serious, that my life is in danger and that I will never be coming back here."

"Your mother…" Terence began, then stopped. There was an awkward silence.

Madeleine abruptly stood up and took a small package from her day bag. "I need to go now and finish packing, but this is for you." Placing it on the coffee table, she said, "Thank you for everything, Dr. Usgood," and gave him a brief smile before turning to leave the office without looking back.

Terence picked up the package. A book, obviously. He unwrapped it and smiled in appreciation. A copy of Charles Martin's 2004 translation of Ovid's *Metamorphoses*, a version he had often thought of buying for himself. He caressed the cover, then opened it carefully and saw she had written a brief dedication on the inside page.

"To my professor, with thanks for being the perfect audience, Madeleine."

On reading this, Terence felt strangely emotional.

A WEEK LATER, Madeleine sent a short email telling him she needed a minor operation. This was carried out very quickly and successfully, after which she informed him in a second email that she was about to move temporarily into her grandfather's apartment, where the live-in nurse could help with her rest and recuperation. This surprised him, and he wondered what her mother had to say about the arrangement. But, in fact, he heard nothing more from her.

Throughout December and January, Terence never quite got used to Madeleine's absence. He would pick up her thesis every other Monday at 10:00 a.m. precisely and write some small suggestions for improvement in the margins. Later, he would email them to her. She never responded, but he was not inadvertently worried by her silence as, at his insistence, they had never used email much, even for sending work. He had always asked her to bring a hard copy for him to read. At 10:57, he would pick up the file and make his way to the departmental café, buy his coffee and pastry, and settle down to re-read stories of Madeleine's mother.

Monday, January 29th, late morning (present day)

ONE MONDAY IN late January, Terence was considering how the mother's tiger-like qualities might have changed but certainly hadn't mellowed as Madeleine had grown into adulthood. He turned to the tale entitled *Fifty Buns*.

The office where I work in the Ministry of Law is tightly run by a woman who used to be a judge. If you saw her, you might think that I'd been lured into the lair of another tiger woman—small, wiry, grey-haired with a thin face, a pointed jaw and sharp eyes. But, although a demanding employer, she is rather a kind lady who cares for the welfare of her staff. Last year, before we broke up to celebrate the Spring Festival, she instructed the canteen to prepare fifty steamed buns for each member of the department as a gift for them and their families.

They were very nice buns, too—white, light, very tasty, ideal for breakfast—but they were bulky, packed into five boxes and difficult for me to carry home, especially as I had no car and was travelling by public transport. Everywhere on the sidewalks, people were rushing—always, it seemed, in the opposite direction to me—and there were never any seats available on the metro or the bus. When I finally reached our apartment building, I was exhausted. With no little relief, I pressed the elevator button, only to find that it was out of action. We live on the eighth floor...

At last, my legs and arms aching, I staggered into the apartment and dropped the boxes onto the kitchen table. Mother looked at them inquisitively while

I explained how kind my boss lady had been. This was evidently the wrong thing to say. Mother hesitated, then asked if everyone had collected their quota. I replied that I didn't know, at which point she became furious. "What? You didn't ask?" she shouted. "So instead of just fifty buns, we could easily have had a hundred! But because you are so thoughtless and never consider the needs of others in your family, we have to be satisfied with half that many. Why didn't you think just for once in your ungrateful life? What about your grandfather, hmm?"

This thought seemed to make her even more animated.

"Haven't I told you we need to be nice to him? Don't you think he would have been grateful for fifty buns?"

I interrupted her to remind her that I had only recently, at her suggestion, bought him a robotic hoover to clean his floor. "One thing for which he won't need to be grateful to that bitch of a nurse," as she had put it. But this didn't pacify Mother.

"Oh, it's easy to spend money, isn't it? I'm talking about being genuinely thoughtful here, something you never, ever are!"

I suggested that I could easily take Grandfather one or two of the five boxes, but this made mother even more angry.

"Giving him our share? Depriving your immediate family of food just so you won't feel guilty? Oh, why was I afflicted with such a thoughtless daughter!"

It is pointless arguing with Mother.

In the event, Grandfather never got any of the buns. The five boxes were all stuffed into the fridge. After six days, when we had only finished two of them, Father called me over and told me, quietly, that the others had gone stale. With fear in his eyes, he asked if I would throw them away before Mother noticed. I knew that he was too frightened to get rid of them himself.

Terence shook his head and sighed, marvelling at the mother's selfishness and vindictiveness. Not for the first time, he thought how fortunate his own position was, with no living parents and no relatives to discomfort his life or disturb his routines. He turned to another of the tales, which also involved excessive amounts of food, the one entitled *The Sweetest of Sweet Potatoes*.

Mother returned home very excited one evening after having had dinner with a friend. "Potatoes," she said. "She served us sweet potatoes, and they were delicious. My friend has them delivered straight from the farm to her door. They tasted so fresh!" But it wasn't the meal that had so animated her. Mother has relatives who own a small farm holding out of town and she was certain, of course, that their crop would be even better than her friend's. She was excited because she could already envisage everybody exclaiming how her sweet potatoes were the best they'd ever tasted.

Rather than deliver them directly to us, her cousin told Mother to meet him at a point in town through which he would be travelling en route to his regular deliveries. The taxi journey took about half an hour, and we stood, Mother and I, waiting by the side of the road for another twenty minutes. Finally, a truck drew up, and we watched in shock as a huge, filthy sack was dumped on the ground in front of us. In her excitement to impress, Mother had ordered far too many—a hundred kilos, to be precise. Her cousin drove off with hardly a word, leaving us gaping in astonishment and wondering how on earth we could get this dirty baggage home. Neither Mother nor I had appreciated how big and heavy—nor, indeed, how dirty—a sack of one hundred kilos of sweet potatoes would be.

As usual, Mother found a way to blame me. "If you had only passed your driving test and got yourself a car, we wouldn't be in this mess now," she complained. It is true I had avoided learning to drive, but this isn't rare in Singapore, where obtaining a driving licence is extremely expensive. I reminded Mother of this. "So why don't you finally get yourself a wealthy husband, then?" she replied. "God knows, I've tried to help you find one!"

None of this was helping us solve the immediate problem. We tried hailing a taxi but, as soon as a driver saw the size and filthy state of the sack at our feet, he would shake his head and drive off. In the end, we had to drag it between us to a bus stop a few hundred metres away. The bus driver wasn't pleased, but he had no choice other than to let us heave it on board.

Fortunately, we didn't have to change buses, and he eventually stopped relatively close to our apartment building.

We couldn't possibly store all of these potatoes in our kitchen; it simply wasn't big enough.

"Thank God for my foresight!" exclaimed Mother as we dragged the bag over the paving stones towards the row of garages that served our apartment block. "At least I had the wisdom to rent a garage, even though you were too lazy to learn to drive!"

Later that day, still exhausted by the morning's ordeal, Mother and I divided the potatoes into several large portions, one each for friends and relatives, and I helped her deliver them to those who lived close by. The others she telephoned, urging them to come and collect their portion from her while the potatoes were still fresh. "They have the sweetest, the freshest taste," she assured everyone with great enthusiasm, even though she hadn't tried any herself yet. "Mine are so much better than anything you can buy in a shop or supermarket."

And, truth to tell, she wasn't wrong—or at least at first she wasn't.

You see, we still had half the sack full stored in the garage. So, for a month, we had nothing but sweet potatoes for dinner—boiled, baked, fried, roasted, cubed, mashed or chipped. I began to miss rice as well as put on weight. And every time she served them, Mother would comment on how they had the fullest, freshest flavour of any sweet potatoes we had ever had, daring either my father or myself to disagree. Which, of course, we never did. Eventually the potatoes went spongy and began to rot, but still Mother refused to give in until each and every one had been cooked and eaten. This process took over a month.

Needless to say, we have never had a sweet potato in the apartment since, and I have never since been tempted to eat a potato in any form, sweet or otherwise. I am one of the few Asian girls I have met during my time in England who can truthfully say that not a single chip or French fry or potato wedge has ever passed her lips. As a result, it has been far easier for me to remain slim. And, as I am sure Mother would say, I have her to thank for that.

SEVEN CURSES

There was something of the appeal of the horror story in these tales. As a child, images of being lured into a gingerbread house and being force fed by a witch had occasionally haunted Terence's dreams, but this had not stopped him from returning, enthralled, to tales such as *Hansel and Gretel* and *The Juniper Tree* again and again. As an adult and a scholar, Ovid's *Metamorphoses* had exerted a similar fascination over his imagination—these tales of humans transformed into animals, or of men and women being subjected to hideously excessive punishments because they had, often inadvertently, upset the gods in some way. Madeleine's tales were having a similar effect on his dreams. Indeed, a few nights before, he had dreamt of being a child again, a smiling, evil-eyed old woman standing over him to make sure he ate up huge quantities of mashed potato and sickly cream buns. All the following day, his stomach felt bloated.

Terence decided to escape from the subject of food and instead turned to a story that particularly enraged him, the one entitled *All Men Have Affairs*.

Since I graduated from university, Mother has become increasingly unhappy with my unmarried state. "Not only do you not have a fiancé, you do not even have a boyfriend! How can you ever expect to find a decent husband?"

I could, of course, point to the fact that she has always appeared to be entirely dissatisfied with her own marriage and has often complained that she could have been one of Singapore's leading pastry chefs, if only her life hadn't been ruined by her "stupid husband and wicked daughter." But silence is often the best form of defence when Mother begins one of her tirades.

Just the once she managed to persuade a friend of hers to act as matchmaker and fix me a meeting with a potential husband. The young man in question was a neurologist. "What an excellent prospect!" exclaimed Mother. "And already on a very good salary! All the neighbours will be so envious when they hear of this." I agreed unenthusiastically to meet him one evening outside the entrance of the hospital where he worked, at the end of his shift.

It was already dark when I arrived, and it was raining. The reception area was far too brightly lit and too public for such a meeting, I thought. On the opposite side of the road, I spotted two cafés. I chose the most comfortable looking of these and, sitting at a secluded table, sent him a text to inform him where I was. Before I could even order a drink, I received a reply that read: "Too expensive. Meet me in the one next door. I will have an Americano." This café was much shabbier, as well as cheaper, but I duly complied.

Fifteen minutes later he was lounging rather than sitting opposite me, sipping at his coffee, a slightly overweight young man, reasonably good-looking but no Tony Leung. He remained silent for a while, scrutinising my appearance before giving a small nod with a brief smile that I interpreted as one of modest approval. Then, stirring an extra lump of sugar into his drink, he began to speak.

"So, Madeleine, here we are. I am pressed for time, so I think it best that I get straight to the point. I've looked over your profile, the one your mother's friend sent. You are well-educated and have a decent job. There is nothing improper in your personal history as far as I can tell. Your family, too, has certain financial resources. Now that I have met you, I see that you are passably pretty. So, there is every chance that this marriage can go ahead."

He paused to sip at his coffee.

"This is great news for you, of course. I am the youngest qualified neurologist in the hospital with excellent prospects ahead of me. I am well-respected and well-liked. My salary is already good and will increase substantially. So, congratulations, Madeleine. I am quite a catch!"

When I failed to smile at this quip, his tone changed.

"You do need to understand what being married to a top neurologist like me will be like, however. For one thing, I will have affairs. That will be inevitable. It is part of the culture of working in a hospital. A handsome young doctor like me will have pretty, young nurses chasing him all the time. But don't worry," another sip at his coffee, "I won't ever bring that part of my work home with me." He laughed at his little joke but then straightened up and adopted a more serious tone. "This won't mean that I will allow you to have affairs, mind. I have my professional reputation to think of, after all.

Anyway, I can tell from your appearance that you aren't the type of woman that attracts the attention of that kind of man."

He paused, doubtless waiting for a response from me, but none came.

"First things first, then. Your mother has already invited me to dinner next Sunday. You can tell her that I accept. After all, it is never too soon to discuss important financial matters. Like how much your family can put down for a mortgage. We will need a decent apartment, of course, and I'm afraid my parents won't be able to help. Their mortgage is huge, and their lifestyle lavish. Here's to them, though! They know how to live!"

He looked at his watch.

"Okay, time for me to go," he said, standing up. Seeing the expression on my face, he must have realised that I was rather less impressed than he'd anticipated. "Look, Madeleine, you aren't going to find a better prospect than me," he said in a petulant tone. "I'm sure you realise that. After all," he looked me up and down, "you aren't getting any younger. And you won't be getting any prettier."

With that, he left the café without a backward glance, leaving me to pay the bill. Of course, I was astonished, insulted, infuriated, and never wanted to cast eyes on this rude, conceited idiot ever again. I returned home to find Mother chopping up vegetables with one of her sharpest knives. I had calmed down by then but told her forcefully that there was no chance of me ever marrying this appalling man. "He had the gall to inform me that he will have all the affairs he wants and that I must accept this!"

Mother carried on slicing and shook her head impatiently. "Don't you understand anything?" she said. "All men have affairs. They can't help it. And you are ignoring the advantages of marrying a man who works locally," she added, rather cryptically.

"What do you mean by that?" I asked.

"Well, you are such a difficult, inconsiderate person. Why do you think I had to beat you so often when you were younger? Anyway, if he ever starts beating you, as I am sure he will, it will be easy for you to come and stay with us for a few days until he calms down."

Thus began a blazing row; Mother agreeing with everything the young doctor had said. Well, almost everything. I tried to focus her attention on his expectation of financial support, but she persistently remained deaf to this, instead throwing her usual litany of insults at me: I was ungrateful, I was stupid, I was wicked, I was obstinate, no man would ever want to marry such a woman, and so on. At one point, she became so furious she pointed the knife straight at me. "Is this the only way you are ever going to be forced to see sense?" she screamed, "by having a knife held at your throat?"

I stomped out of the flat, slamming the door behind me.

He didn't come to dinner the following Sunday, and I never saw him again, but that hasn't been the end of the matter. Mother's frenzy might have abated somewhat, but she still hasn't forgiven me. She frequently recalls my obstinacy at ruining such a good prospect and weeps, looking heavenward, asking aloud if anyone will ever deliver her of her burdensome daughter.

Terence could never read this without being both astonished and outraged—at the arrogant, conceited neurologist, of course, but, in particular, at the inconsiderateness, and above all the barely hidden menace in the words of the mother. He was still feeling indignant when, on arriving back in his office, he noted with surprise and with pleasure that he had finally received an email from Singapore. The pleasure was short-lived. On opening it, he saw that it was from Madeleine's mother.

In two short sentences, she informed him that her daughter had died the previous day.

Wednesday, January 31st, evening (present day)

TERENCE HADN'T SLEPT well for two nights and had barely been able to work. The news of Madeleine's death had come as such a shock that he hadn't yet been able to process it. The fact that it happened so remotely, at the far side of the globe, made it all the more difficult for him to appreciate its finality. For the last two months, Madeleine had lived in his imagination through her writing, through the bulky ring binder that still awaited him on his desk, each time he entered his office. It was hard for him to grasp that the vibrant, playful person who had written it no longer existed.

During these difficult hours, his routines were more important to him than ever. Today was Wednesday. On Wednesday afternoons, he always did his shopping and took it home before returning to his office for a further hour of administrative chores.

Given the shortness of the days at this time of year, it was already growing dark by the time he unlocked his office door that evening. In the dim light that issued in through the single window, he groped his way to his desk, where he switched on the lamp and, to his great surprise, saw a package, square and quite deep, positioned tidily alongside it. Puzzled by what it might be, he pulled off the plain wrapping paper to uncover a tin, deep red in colour, decorated with Chinese characters. He prised open the lid, immediately releasing a rich, buttery, savoury aroma. Holding the tin under the lamp, he saw that it contained a number of home-made pastries.

How had the package got here? Someone must have left it with one of the secretaries while he'd been out that afternoon. Everywhere had been dark and empty along the corridor when he'd returned just now. She would most probably have brought it into his office before going home. But there was no message or card of any kind to indicate who this *someone* might have been.

The delicious smell of pastry made him hungry. Though rigorously keeping to his usual mealtimes, he hadn't been eating much at all over the past two days. He took out one of the pastries and examined it. It was thick and square-shaped and felt quite heavy in his hand, delicately patterned around the edges. He bit into it. The pastry itself was light, flaky, and delicious, and inside the filling was of meat—pork, most likely, but the most exquisite pork he'd ever tasted. He devoured it greedily, uttering appreciative sounds of delight after every mouthful. Immediately he picked out another and bit into it—the same delectable flavour, the same mouthwatering filling.

"I'm pleased that you find them to your taste."

Terence let out a shriek, the pastry dropping from his hand and landing with a mild thud on top of Madeleine's folder. The words had come from out of the gloom that completely obscured the far corner of his office. He swivelled round in his chair as a small figure emerged silently from the shadows into the dim border of the light cast by his desk lamp. He scarcely felt reassured when he saw that it was an old woman dressed in black. She was very thin, with silvery grey hair knotted tightly at the back of her head in the traditional manner favoured by many Asian women. From her features, even in this dim light, he could spot the family resemblance.

"M…Mrs. Lim?" he stammered.

She bowed slightly.

"Forgive me. I didn't see you there. Who, who let you in?"

Instead of answering his question, she nodded in the direction of his coffee table, where two copies of Ovid's *Metamorphoses* lay open, the original and the translation Madeleine had bought for him.

"Such interesting books you have," she said. Terence remembered Madeleine saying something similar on her first visit to his office all those months ago and felt a sudden pang of sadness.

"I was sorry, so sorry to read about your loss," he said.

She acknowledged this with a slight tilt of her head.

"But you have come all this way. I don't understand. Won't you take a seat?"

"No, thank you. I won't be staying." Her English was very good, although her accent was far more pronounced than her daughter's had been. "I just wanted to make sure you got this gift. A final memento of my daughter, so to speak." She paused. "And I wanted to talk to you."

SEVEN CURSES

She took a step closer and pointed to the pastries.

"I baked those myself. Did Madeleine tell you I was one of Singapore's most sought-after pastry chefs?"

Terence was still in shock and now in some confusion.

"Yes... Well, erm, not exactly. She said you thought you could have been if you hadn't got married..." His voice grew quieter as he spoke. The way she was staring unremittingly at him was unsettling, to say the least.

The old lady shook her head sadly.

"Such a wicked girl! She was such a liar, you know. God rest her soul. My reputation is such that I can call on the finest bakery in Singapore any time I have prepared a batch of special, savoury fillings for them." She indicated to the pastries again. "But these I baked especially for you. They are very fine, don't you think? Go on, eat the one you dropped. Don't let it lose any of its flavour."

Terence did as she bade him, feeling he had no choice but to obey. She then told him to eat a third and watched in silent satisfaction as he did so. But then, quite suddenly, her facial expression hardened.

"I found her thesis, you know, the true one, the one she had been hiding from me. Not the one she had written for my eyes only."

She took a step closer to him, and Terence flinched, instinctively recoiling from the fierce look in her eyes.

"Oh, she is quite the storyteller, isn't she? And you believed every word she wrote! Didn't you ever think to question their truthfulness?" She paused to let this sink in. "Or to consider the hurt they would bring to the heart of her poor mother?" She spoke more quietly now, in the voice of an old woman who had been grievously wronged.

Terence tried to justify himself. "You were never supposed to read them." He realised how pathetic an argument this was and went silent. She ignored him.

"As I read, tears flowed from my eyes," she said mournfully. "Her words brought to my mind an old Chinese saying: 'Even if I gave her my heart to eat, she wouldn't appreciate the flavour.'"

Terence was still trying to digest the meaning of this when she changed her tone once again, this time to one of painful resignation.

"Well, I suppose I must forgive her. Bitterness will not help me endure a lonely old age, bereft of the comfort and support of a daughter, even one as wicked as my own."

She sighed and began to make her way towards the door. Once there, she stopped and turned to face him again.

"She was wrong about her rabbit, you know."

"I'm sorry?"

"Her rabbit, the one she set free." The old woman bent forward and whispered, "I found it!" Her eyes gleamed with malevolence. "I found it and cooked it and fed it to her in a pie and she never, ever knew." The memory seemed to lift her spirits.

Then, to Terence's alarm, she began to let out a long, loud exhalation. He could see her breath like a jet of steam make its way towards the coffee table. He pushed his chair away and watched in horror as the pages of both books began to flutter and turn, flutter and turn, simultaneously coming to rest at one. Terence stared at the old woman, dumbstruck, as she stood upright, a look of triumph on her face.

"I did have to punish her, you see. One final penance. There are some things that just cannot be forgiven." She paused. "And you had to be punished too; you do realise that. For encouraging her wickedness."

"Punish me?" blurted Terence, genuinely scared. "How?"

The old woman smiled her malevolent smile. "Oh, her punishment has become your punishment." She glanced at the books on the coffee table and added, even more cryptically, "For the one you are missing is inside."

Fearfully, Terence followed her gaze towards the books, noting with some surprise that the pages of both volumes had come to rest at the same tale. But when he looked up again in the direction of the old woman, remarkably, she had disappeared, and he hadn't even heard the door open or close. He ran into the corridor, but in both directions, it was gloomy, silent, and entirely empty of life.

What had she meant by that parting comment? It reminded him of something…something he had read quite recently. Shaken by the strangeness of the whole encounter, he picked up the books and sat down at his desk, placing them both directly under the lamplight.

The old woman had managed to blow the pages of both books from the story of King Midas to that of Philomela and Procne and the terrible punishment they meted out on Tereus. With a mounting sense of dread, Terence flicked through the pages until he found the line he was looking for. Tereus calls for Procne, his wife, to bring him their son, Itys, and in Martin's translation she answers, "The one you are seeking is inside," meaning…

Terence dropped the book at the sudden awful realisation of the enormity of the old woman's crime. Wide-eyed, he stared in blank terror at the wall in front of him. Madeleine hadn't died unexpectedly. The old witch had murdered her in a fit of fury.

And then she had, she had…

Oh, God.

That cryptic line about giving her a heart to eat, the story of the rabbit, and finally this, this conjuring trick of hers. The misty breath, the sudden vanishing act. She was much more evil, much more dangerous than he had ever dreamed.

That wasn't pork he'd been eating. It was…

His stomach began to heave. He ran out of his office, along to the toilet, and just made it to the basin in time. Pieces of barely digested pie, a mess of pastry and pork—no, not pork, minced human flesh, Madeleine's flesh—spewed forth from his stomach into the bowl, spattering the white enamel with its yellow brown mess, the acrid smell of bile mingling with the savoury smell of pastry, making the stench of his vomit all the more sickly. He flushed the disgusting mess away and tried to stand, but his stomach heaved again. This time he spent longer leaning over the bowl, torturing himself with horrific images of mutilated flesh being stirred into the pies, of his own lips and tongue chewing it into a messy pulp that mixed with his own saliva. His stomach heaved and heaved over and over again, desperately trying to empty itself of the last vestiges of this terrible meal.

He flushed the toilet again, staggered over to the washbowl, rinsed the bitter taste from his mouth and stared at his pale, red-eyed reflection in the mirror. He knew he hadn't done enough. He needed to make sure that every last bit of those obscene pastries was flushed out of his system.

He ran back to his office, grabbed his coat, and sped recklessly along the corridor, past the departmental café, now closed, out of the door and into the bracing cold. He pulled his coat on as he ran, ignoring the small bands of students who were drinking, smoking, chatting or just making their way across the campus as he raced like a frightened animal in the direction of the students' union building. He charged through the entrance, elbowing past any student in his path, bellowing for them to get out of his way as he did so. They stopped in their tracks, their mouths agape, as he ran into the pharmacy, straight up to the counter, pushing all and sundry aside and screaming out his demand for their most powerful emetic.

"I need to vomit!" he screamed. "Now! I need to vomit!"

On seeing only a pale look of fright on the face of the assistant, "I've been poisoned!" he yelled. "If I don't get it out of my system now, this minute I will… I will…"

As if to support this lie, his stomach went into involuntary convulsions. In terror and utter astonishment, the girl behind the counter ran over to a shelf and came back with a bottle in her hand.

"Syrup of ipecac," she stammered. "Take it once every—"

Terence grabbed it. "I can read! Get me another. ANOTHER!" Seizing the second bottle, he threw a twenty-pound note over the counter. Not waiting for any change, he spun round and hurled himself out of the shop in the same demented fashion that he'd entered.

A small crowd had gathered and watched in fascination.

"Salt water," a voice called after him.

"Hot water and mustard," called another

"Ginger, lots of ginger," shouted an Asian girl.

Terence heard them and noted their advice without pause or thanks as he blundered his way blindly back to his office building. Breathless and panting, he unlocked his bicycle and pedalled furiously back to his flat, drawing strength from the sheer force of his terror. Two grinning students approached him as he fumbled with his keys, trying to open his front door. He caught sight of them as he struggled to haul the bicycle into his entrance hall.

"Not now!" he screamed whereupon, shocked and bewildered by the sight of this dishevelled madman who was staring at them wild-eyed and terrifying from under the glare of his hall light they backed away, open-mouthed and speechless, before turning and fleeing at speed away from his flat, away from the hall altogether.

That night Terence drank one and a half bottles of the syrup, two tumblers of salted water, and a whole pot of hot ginger tea. He spent most of the night doubled up, retching over the toilet bowl, eventually bringing up nothing but dribbles of pure bile. At one point as he raised his head, an image from over a year earlier, of a Chinese student being sick on this very spot, sprung into his mind. But eventually, totally exhausted, he did finally fall asleep. And he dreamed.

He dreamed the tale of Ovid: of Procne, the wife of Tereus, and of Itys, their son; of Procne discovering that her sister, Philomela, had been imprisoned, raped, and mutilated by her husband; of the two sisters slaughtering the boy Itys and serving him up to be eaten by his father, cooked in a stew; of how, on discovering the truth, Tereus had chased the two sisters, who both escaped from him by being transformed into nightingales while he himself was transformed into a more savage looking bird, a hoopoe.

But in his dream, Tereus became Terence and didn't transform into a bird but into a rabbit. And instead of being the pursuer, he became the pursued, chased by a fox, his fox, round and about his garden. The fox was gradually closing in on him, was about to pounce when Terence awoke with a start, sweating and terrified and ready to be sick once again.

Thursday, February 1st, morning (present day)

EXHAUSTED AND BLEARY-EYED, his stomach wracked with cramps, Terence nonetheless stuck to his precious routine and made it over to his office by 9:30 a.m. But before he could even unlock the door, he had to run to the toilet, where he spent ten minutes doubled up, retching, still haunted by horrific, cannibalistic images but unable to bring anything up from his stomach. Finally, he rinsed his mouth and his face and staggered out of the toilet, only to see Madeleine waiting for him outside his office door, whereupon he collapsed in a dead faint.

TERENCE SIPPED AT the cup of hot camomile tea that one of the secretaries had made for him. She'd also called for an ambulance but had been told that the waiting time might be over twelve hours; so, once he regained consciousness, she and a colleague had helped him through the door of his office and into the comfortable armchair, the one that Madeleine had always sat in. There was a bruise on his forehead and his appearance was ghastly but, although weak and in shock, he was evidently not in any physical distress. On catching sight of the still open tin of pastries on his desk, however, he had screamed and gone into convulsions, whereupon the secretary had, at his urgent request, removed them from the office, leaving him alone with Madeleine.

He looked at her nervously. "Let me… Let me touch you to check you aren't a…ghost."

She held out her hand, and he pressed his own into it, squeezing it gently.

"You're real. You're really here. You're alive, after all." And he smiled with evident relief.

Slowly and in broken sentences, Terence managed to explain what had happened—the lie about her death, the uncanny visit of her mother, his subsequent panic and its terrible aftermath. Madeleine listened in silence with downcast eyes, her lips pursed. When he finished, she let out a sigh and shook her head sadly.

"It was her ghost, wasn't it?" Terence said eventually, his voice still hoarse. "She sent her ghost to punish me. But the pastries, how…?"

"I brought them myself yesterday," said Madeleine, her voice much softer than usual. "I know your routines. I knew you would be out. I left them with the secretary. I thought they would be a nice surprise for you. But I left them with a note, saying I would see you at the usual time this morning. What happened to the note?"

Terence closed his eyes. "Try the wastepaper basket," he said.

Madeleine duly found it there and looked at him, an inquisitive frown on her face.

"She blew the note into the bin before I returned. Just like she blew the pages of the book."

Madeleine nodded her understanding. "The ghost has no material essence other than air, which it can channel through its breath."

Terence was recovering very slowly. "How did she know about the story, about Ovid?"

"She saw me with the Ted Hughes version that I'd been reading on the plane." Madeleine's tone was apologetic. "She questioned me about it, and I told her you always had copies of different translations on your desk. That I'd bought you one." She paused. "She must have read it when I was staying at Grandfather's. That's when she would have made her plan. After she discovered the other version of my thesis, the one for your eyes, not hers."

Madeleine sat in Terence's chair and began to tell him what she knew. According to her father, while she was in hospital, her mother had spent hours in her bedroom going through all her notebooks and diaries until she finally located the password for her laptop. She'd then searched through all of her folders until she located what she had suspected she would find all along.

"I don't think she ever trusted you," her father had told Madeleine weakly. Apparently, Mother had read it in one sitting while father could hear her curses and shouts echoing around the apartment. Increasingly fearful of her growing fury, he'd left to stay at a friend's apartment for a few days. He'd been relieved on his return to find mother very calm, though with a gleam in her eye that made him wary.

"She must have already made her plan by then," Madeleine explained. "I should have realised something was amiss, you know," she continued. "She was strangely calm while I was recuperating and unnervingly sweet for the whole of last week, before I flew back here. She told me not to worry, that she would inform you of my return. And she insisted on me bringing you the pastries, which I knew were her finest, baked to her most special recipe." She paused. "Mother never gives presents unless she has a very special reason for doing so."

There were a few moments of silence.

"Well," said Terence eventually. "The important thing is that you are very much alive and weren't put in a p… Well…you know…" He nodded at the two bound volumes she'd had under her arm in the corridor and that were now on the coffee table. "And, just as important, you've completed your thesis. I never did hear back from you about the few comments I sent you." He paused. "I suppose you weren't reading your emails. Doctor's advice?" He looked puzzled for a moment. "But then how…?"

"Oh, Grandfather's nurse helped me. She is very kind and extremely capable. She would print pages out and then type in my amendments. I was fine working on paper, you see, it was just the glare of the computer screen…" She let out a deep breath. "No, I didn't reply to your comments because…I felt a little embarrassed."

Terence frowned. "Whatever for?"

Madeleine indicated to the bound theses. "Take a look," she said, a glint of mischief in her eyes.

Still frowning, Terence reached over and picked up one of them. Placing it on his knee, he began to turn the pages but halted when he read the title page: *"Like a Tiger: A Mother's Resistance to Patriarchy in Present Day Singapore."*

"You've made a mistake, surely," he said. "This is the alternative version. Where's the true account?"

Madeleine nodded to the ring binder still on the desk. "It will stay with you." She sighed. "I loved writing it, I really did. But I came to realise as I went to classes and seminars that the examiners at this university wouldn't like it at all." She pointed to the volume, which he still held in his lap. "With that version, however, the title alone should guarantee me a pass." She gave a wicked smile. "You have to know your audience, after all. I'll see you at the graduation ceremony in June, won't I?" She stood up.

"Will your mother be there?"

"I imagine she will be. Mother is happy enough with this version. I don't think you will be having any more visits from her."

Madeleine picked up the two bound copies, then she paused.

"You know, I am still very puzzled. Mother isn't a great reader, and I have never known her to come up with such a wickedly cunning plan before. That ghost of yours… What did she look like?"

"Like, just like I imagined your mother would look. I could see the resemblance. It was very noticeable."

Madeleine still had that puzzled look on her face. "But everyone says I take after father…" She paused. "She sounds more like a fox fairy than Mother."

"A fox fairy?" Terence felt uneasy at the mention of the word 'fox.' "What on earth is a fox fairy?"

"A female spirit. Very powerful, very cunning, very cruel. And mischievous. I've always loved them," she added. "I'll send you a book of stories so you can read all about them."

She stood there, frowning for a few more seconds.

"By the way, whoever she was, ghost or fox fairy, she lied about the rabbit. For two weeks, it was seen running around the community grounds before it was found dead in the road, killed by a passing motorist. I buried it myself. So, she never baked it in a pie." She smiled ever so slightly. "You shouldn't believe every story you are told, Terence." Her smile faded quickly as she noticed he had gone pale at the mention of the pie. "Do you need me to stay a while longer?"

"Oh no, no. You can leave me." He let out a stoical sigh. "And please tell the secretary to cancel that ambulance. I'll be fine once I've got over the shock."

BUT TERENCE NEVER did get over the shock. Like a man who has stumbled into a nest of termites or was once chased by a swarm of wasps, he has been left traumatised. The very sight of a pasty now brings him out in a rash; his guts spasm violently if he sees a hot meat pie; bile will surge from his stomach to his throat if he ever smells a warm croissant or a fresh pain au raisin. Not only has he had to forgo forever his favourite mid-morning snacks and midweek suppers, he's also been forced to change his work patterns and shopping habits. He can no longer walk past the departmental café, as the wafting aromas he had once found so tempting now physically nauseate him.

Instead, he has had to find a distant side entrance, far from any offending sights or smells. Of course, the kind of coffee breaks he once enjoyed are now a thing of the past, as there is no café free of pastries anywhere on the campus. Nowadays he brews his own coffee at home every morning and will later sip it from a flask in the dreary, soulless common room of the anthropology department, where he sits mournfully, regretting his lost routines.

While shopping, he has learned to wear a thick black face mask to protect him from unexpected smells of freshly baked pastry dough. These days he tends to shop only in supermarkets where he knows which aisles need to be avoided. If ever displays are re-organised without due warning and he unexpectedly turns a corner to be confronted by the horror of a shelf full of Ginsters' pasties or a stack of Holland's meat pies, an urgent rush to the store toilet is quickly followed by a heated exchange with the store manager.

Of the fox, however, there has been no further sighting. Not since the morning immediately following the fearful, life-changing visit from what he still believes to be the ghost of Madeleine's mother; when, in the early hours of daylight, he had stumbled from his bedroom into the kitchenette and raised the blinds as he always did. Images from his nightmare were still swirling around his head when he saw it standing there, on the wall of his garden, its slender head turned in his direction, as though the creature had just jumped out of his dream and been waiting for him to appear. Terence let out a groan, but then he noticed to his surprise that the garden was clear and his bin unmolested.

The fox still had its eyes fixed on him when it suddenly let out a sharp, high-pitched bark that echoed around the empty campus in the cold morning air. Dumbstruck, he watched and listened as it let out another, then another, before it jumped from the wall and disappeared from his sight for the very last time. The sharp echo of the bark, however, lingered in the air for several seconds and it sounded, to Terence's ears, like laughter. Like victory.

CURSE FIVE
GABRIEL

Five is the blind and childless wife;

May cruel delusions wreck her life...

JASMINE IN THE morning—how she loved that smell!

In late spring and throughout the summer, she would slip out of bed and into her tracksuit as soon as it was light. Outside in the communal garden, she would lean against the south-facing wall where the plant grew and thrived, its tiny star-shaped flowers not yet reached by the early morning sunlight. There she would inhale its sweet perfume as she sipped at her tea, emptying her mind of all thoughts, relishing for these few minutes the feelings of serenity and well-being that were so precious to her.

Jasmine had been the English name she'd originally chosen for herself as a teenager in Taiwan, having read that it represented a mother's unconditional love and nurturing care, "the fragrant and delicate white petals symbolising the milk that flowed generously from the maternal breast." These words had greatly moved her.

It was later, at college, when she had changed her name to Serena, to comply with her fiancé's wish that they remain always together but never have children. She often recalled the smile on his face—a face so handsome that all the girls had envied her—when he'd proposed the name to her, gently stroking her cheek as he did so, saying softly how it suited completely the serenity they had found in their love for one another. The memory often brought warm tears to her eyes.

On winter mornings such as this, she substituted the smell of the flower for the scent of her favourite perfume, Christian Dior Jasmin des

Anges. Standing in front of the bathroom mirror, she would unscrew the dark brown top from the tall, slim bottle and breathe in the summery fragrance, her eyes closed to maximise the sensation. Then she would open them to gaze at her reflection as she recalled her mother doing when she was a little girl. But whereas her mother would study her face for wrinkles and other signs of ageing or spend hours making herself beautiful for lunches and dinners with her many friends and admirers, Serena would simply smile and remind herself of her good fortune.

"Mirror, mirror on the wall...

Who is the luckiest of them all?"

She had the ideal husband, she would tell herself, hundreds of friends and followers on social media, and a place as a doctoral student in a prestigious university where she was able to devote herself to her passion, the study and care of children.

Her morning run always followed the same route apart from Wednesdays, when it took her only as far as the school where she worked this one day a week. Today was Tuesday. She sat at the table, a small pot of jasmine tea brewing in front of her. Her current flatmate was away until the weekend and Serena was enjoying having the place to herself as she checked her Facebook account, listening to *Prayer For the Day* on the radio.

> *"Oh Lord, unseal unseeing eyes.*
> *Help me find truth where there are lies.*
> *Let me bring warmth where there is cold,*
> *And make me wise ere I grow old."*

As a Christian, she smiled at these sentiments. Her smile broadened on seeing how many more likes and comments her latest post had received overnight from friends in Asia. The short article attached to it had been published in a national newspaper the previous weekend, the first time she'd gained recognition beyond social media. Later, she would read it aloud and record it on her YouTube channel, providing the Mandarin subtitles herself. Her English was perfect as she'd been learning it from early childhood, first in Hong Kong and later in Taiwan, to where she had moved with her mother after her parents' divorce. Her speech and grammar were, in fact, so impeccable that people she met at WMU often assumed that she was a citizen of the U.S. or had at least been educated there.

It was beginning to get light when she stepped outside, bracing herself against the biting northerly wind. *"Let me bring warmth where there is cold."*

An apt wish for today, she thought.

Snow was predicted over the next few days, and puddles left by an earlier rain shower had turned to ice. Careful of her footing, Serena nonetheless quickly found her rhythm and pace and had soon left the campus behind as she followed a dirt track that stretched for just over a mile, past the building site on her left and onto the main Stratford Road. Here she turned right, hugging the fences and hedgerows that bordered the huge gardens of the large, detached houses behind them.

Traffic was already heavy as she ran past the Henry Pottinger school, where she would be working the following day, and directly into the large, open green space of Monks Common—*such a wonderful outlook for these lucky children*, she always thought. A few dog walkers and joggers were dotted sporadically around the various paths that criss-crossed the field and circled the long, narrow lake at its centre, but Serena headed off, as always, in a different direction, towards the mediaeval Church of the Holy Innocents that loomed dark, grim, and sturdy beneath the dense winter clouds. Alongside it, an old wooden lichgate led into an ancient graveyard.

The gate creaked as she opened it, the only sound to be heard at such an early hour in this empty, lonely enclosure. Snowdrops gathered in large clusters beside the gravel path beyond which the gravestones, worn with age, rose haphazardly and at different angles above a thin carpet of mist.

She slowed to a trot and turned off the path, making her way gingerly among the stones, noting how the steam from her breath seemed to match the density and substance of the mist hovering over the graves. She'd looked at these often, never failing to be moved by how young some of the children had been when they died. At the far end, an ancient yew tree stood in front of a crumbling corner of a sandstone wall.

She halted and scrambled into the tiny clearing behind it where she stooped to uncover a small, flat stone that lay hidden beneath a patch of tall, coarse grass. Kneeling there, she withdrew the perfume bottle from her tracksuit pocket and let a droplet fall on to the tip of her forefinger, which she then traced over a Chinese character that had been roughly carved onto the surface of the stone. Bringing the finger to her lips, she kissed it gently, remaining there for some time, her eyes moist as she offered a prayer for all the lost children and for the mothers who mourned them.

… I had paused as I often do to spend a brief moment gazing at the joyful sight of mothers and children playing together, entranced by their laughter and captivated by the joy on their faces; for although not a mother myself, young children are my career. They are where I find purpose and fulfilment in my life, and I often point out to my fellow students that the word 'care' is embedded in the word 'career,' just as 'care' is at the 'core' of my practice as a professional.

As I turned away, however, I noticed one little girl, isolated in a corner of the park, hidden and apart from the happy crowd of others, her own face contorted in spasms of uncontrolled sobbing. No one other than I seemed to be paying her any attention. My heart immediately leapt out to her. I recognised the sense of abandonment in those tears, the loneliness, the feeling that no one cares for or recognises your basic need. The need, of course, for loving attention.

"Hey, little girl," I called out over the fence that separated us. "Have you lost your mommy? She loves you, you know!" But her desperation was so intense, her sobbing so relentless, that I could tell she was impervious to any words of comfort I could offer. I had to show her I understood that the fences that isolate us from the affection we need can be breached; that it just takes someone to reach out.

I'm an athletic person, so I found it very easy to leap over that fence, whereupon I approached the little girl cautiously, talking in my most gentle voice, and stooping down very close to her to show I was no threat, no threat at all. Still sobbing, she turned to me. I could see how pretty she was behind those tears. She recognised in my eyes, I'm certain, the genuine care and concern that I felt for her at that moment. She opened her little arms wide, and I knew she was begging me to hold her tight. She needed to feel at that moment the warmth of a mother's love. For the next minute, I was that mother, consoling her, soothing her, calming her…

Serena finished the recording and took a deep breath. Her mother, she knew, would have spent hours in front of a mirror, making up her face and practising her reading to ensure that her voice and facial expressions conveyed just the right tone of warmth and sincerity. By contrast, she told herself she had simply opened her heart to deeply felt emotions and had let them flow naturally into her speech. The result was one of genuine authenticity, something recognised by her followers, who often commented precisely on these qualities of warmth and sincerity that she so prided herself on.

Nevertheless, there were details she omitted from her broadcast. How the father, a burly young man with a shaven head, had eventually shown up and given her a hostile look as he had grabbed the girl from her, uttering a racist slur rather than offering the words of thanks her actions merited; and how she had felt, as she often did, that some parents didn't deserve the children they'd been blessed with. The emotional impact of these details lingered still and, reflecting on them now, she inevitably began to suffer once more the painful memories of the child she never had.

IT HAD BEEN midway through her first year of study, and she and Ernest had been away from each other for several months. He needed to continue his work in Kaohsiung, not only to further his own career but, more immediately, to help fund the study that their savings barely covered. She was due to fly back for a month's holiday in the summer, but this had seemed an age away. Their weekly video calls and regular texting were emotional lifelines, but they were no real substitute for the warmth of his body pressed against her own. Recalling this sensation not only brought warm tears to her eyes, but it also often took the form of a physical ache.

She had male friends over here, of course, and it was only natural that she should enjoy their attention and flirt with the more attractive among them. There was never intended to be anything serious in this, just some innocent distraction from the deep sense of loneliness that sometimes tormented her.

Parties were dangerous, however, and alcohol was never a good idea. It made her weak and giddy and overly affectionate. Leonardo had told her he was from Florence—*Firenze*, as he called it, in a pronounced Italian accent whose jovial musicality had charmed her. He was handsome, too, with classic Italian looks—slim, tanned skin, thick black hair that flowed in waves down to his shoulders and the most beautiful brown eyes. She'd been particularly vulnerable that evening and had got very drunk, dancing close to him as slow, romantic music filled the room and, later, willingly surrendering to his advances.

But waking the following morning to feel his body next to hers had immediately aroused sharp pangs of guilt and self-disgust. Leonardo had seemed to understand and left with no fuss, but she'd remained wracked with anguish for several days, desperately wanting to tell Ernest but unable to do so for fear of how he—so honest, so faithful—might react to her betrayal.

Much worse was her resultant pregnancy. It reawoke all the yearning for her own child that she'd suppressed for so many years, a tragic longing because the choice before her now was such a dreadful one—have the child or save her marriage. She couldn't discuss her situation with anyone, unable to talk to Ernest for more than a few minutes at a time, unable to make a choice whether to have the child or not. When the foetus had aborted naturally, the huge relief she'd felt was tempered with profound feelings of regret, an emotional confusion she suffered from still, despite the fact that two years had passed since the terrible event.

The ping from her computer snapped her out of her melancholic reverie. An email had arrived from the school asking if she could work the three days up to the weekend. A small group of refugee children had arrived earlier than had been anticipated and, to add to the staffing pressures, the teacher she usually assisted had taken ill.

"Of course. I am always happy to help," she replied and was about to get up from her chair when the ping sounded again. Expecting a simple confirmation of her reply, she frowned in puzzlement at what she actually read. The address was one she didn't recognise on FoxMail, and the subject line was curious: "*Announcing the coming of Gabriel.*" When she opened the message, a musical score appeared and a few bars of gentle piano music began to play, repeating over and over again until she closed it. She'd heard the melody before but at first could not place it.

Only after she'd phoned the school and found they were as puzzled by this email as she was did she recall where she'd heard the music and the discomforting memory she associated with it.

ON A WARM and sunny July morning six months earlier, Serena had taken the short walk from the university library to the arts centre café, enjoying how the fine weather lifted her spirits. As she entered the building, she was struck by the beauty of a melody whose gentle notes floated through the open door of one of the rehearsal rooms leading off from the side of the foyer. She paused to listen. How lovely it was! Unlike the romantic ballads she liked to sing to herself, perhaps, but gorgeous nonetheless, so much so that it brought tears to her eyes.

She approached the door and peeped inside. The piano stood at the far end of the small room, and the pianist sat behind it with only the top of their head visible. It was a female head, she could tell, with short black hair. Suddenly it lifted to reveal a face fixed in concentration, as if in a trance, looking unseeingly in her direction. Serena let out a gasp of recognition and immediately her pleasure evaporated. The music stopped abruptly as the two young women looked at one another. Serena took a step forward and spoke first, conversing in Mandarin.

"I'm sorry, the door was open. I didn't realise it was you."

"Oh, I'm surprised to see you. I thought you'd still be rehearsing in front of that mirror of yours."

The muscles around Serena's mouth tightened, but she said nothing.

"He will be joining me soon," Xie Fei continued, flicking through the music score. "His train was due about twenty minutes ago. I said I'd leave the door ajar so he could easily find me here."

She had mentioned her boyfriend would be visiting this weekend, and Serena had insisted that he obey university regulations and book separate accommodation. This had increased the usual tension between the two flatmates, who shared very little in common.

Their disagreements and mutual hostility had nothing to do with politics. Whereas Serena saw herself as warm-hearted and openly sentimental, Xie Fei, she felt, was cold and misanthropic. She could be sarcastic and cruel in her comments and intolerant of what she called people's stupidity, whereas Serena preached tolerance and forgiveness. As a result, the two seldom talked and avoided each other as much as possible. Xie Fei had even insisted that Serena remove her perfume from the bathroom, complaining that its smell made her feel nauseous. In response, Serena had taken down a print of Xie Fei's from the kitchen wall and replaced it with a crucifix. She had never liked that picture, anyway. The dark colours were threatening, and the circle of white foxes surrounding the bare trees that eerily dominated the foreground sometimes sent shivers down her spine. Apparently, it had been a present from that Japanese boyfriend of hers. Such strange taste in art, she had mused.

"The music was…nice," Serena said after an awkward pause.

"Thank you."

"But a little cold, perhaps?"

"Cold?"

"Your face. It showed no emotion while you played."

Xie Fei scoffed and gave a tiny shake of her head, but then her gaze shifted beyond Serena, her eyes brightening as a broad smile lit up her face. Serena turned to see a young man, evidently the boyfriend, standing in the doorway. She was shocked by how handsome he was, slim and athletic looking, but with a face whose features were delicate, almost feminine, and whose eyes were focused entirely on Xie Fei, as if he hadn't noticed Serena at all.

He moved gracefully past her and, feeling awkward and ignored, she slipped out of the room to leave the couple alone. As she sat in a corner of the café several minutes later, they settled some distance from her, chatting and laughing and holding hands like a pair of silly teenagers. She and Ernest had never behaved so foolishly in public, even in the early days of their relationship. The Japanese boy briefly met her gaze, acknowledging it with a slight wave of his hand and a smile of recognition. He was certainly very handsome, and she wondered what on earth he saw in Xie Fei, whom she had always considered to be rather plain.

Later, as she passed the rehearsal room on her way back to the library, the door was ajar still, and she heard the piano being played much louder than before in lively, complex cadences. The pair were obviously playing a piece together. In a burst of laughter, the music came to an abrupt and chaotic conclusion.

"It's too soon for Mozart," she heard the boy say in English, his voice quivering in amusement. Then, in a tone of pretend solemnity: "Here! Let us graze more gently and go back to Bach!" They laughed once more. After a few seconds of silence, they resumed their playing, this time much more softly; the beautiful melody she had heard earlier was now enriched by the delicacy of the boy's accompaniment. Serena left the building, a knot of envy in her stomach.

A few weeks later and quite by chance, she stumbled upon a video on YouTube of a man and woman playing Mozart's sonata K521 for four hands, which she recognised as the piece that Xie Fei and her boyfriend had been attempting together.

But it was the opening bars of the music by Bach that were unnerving her now, on this cold afternoon in February; for this was the music that had been repeating so eerily in the mysterious email sent from the address on FoxMail.

… I feel so privileged to be working in the Henry Pottinger Preparatory School, honoured and humbled to be part of such a brilliant team of professionals. The head, Charlene Wilson, is an amazing woman, incredibly efficient, always busy, impeccably dressed, too. I don't know how she manages it!

… I love the school buildings, converted from two very large houses typical of those in the surrounding area. It is privately run, of course, and brilliantly resourced due to the generosity of the parents and the many endowments it has been granted from those pupils who have had very successful careers later in life. I also love the fact that music and art are seen as so important here. How many schools can boast a piano and guitar in every classroom?

But most of all, of course, I love the children, and I thrive on the affection they show me in return.

… We are excited to be soon welcoming a small number of refugee children from war-torn Eastern Europe. It is our privilege to reach out and provide them with the care and support they need to settle and thrive in this, their new home.

"… So, your day shouldn't be disrupted too much, Serena."

The lower school had its own entrance, where teachers had gathered to offer their usual smiles and words of endearment to the children as they bade their daily goodbyes to parents. The new arrivals would have been easy to spot, even if they'd been wearing the standard school uniform. Their faces were frightened, some of them tearful, clinging to their mothers who encouraged them in soft Slavic tones to enter this strange building for the first time.

Charlene indicated to them with a tilt of her head. "We're expecting a couple more this afternoon, but none for you. You know your class very well, so I'll leave you to get on. I'm sure I'll be busy enough elsewhere!"

Serena forced a smile then asked hesitantly. "Erm… Is there a Gabriel among them?"

"Gabriel? Umm…" The head looked surprised. She consulted the list pinned to the clipboard in her hand. "No. No Gabriel listed here. Why do you ask? Never mind, you can tell me later. Better get to your class now." And then she breezed off along the corridor toward her office as Serena frowned in unanticipated disappointment.

Her own classroom was rather isolated, a large, well-insulated wooden structure, quite modern, several yards away from the main building and surrounded by a well-resourced play area. As the head had predicted, the morning passed smoothly and calmly enough. There were only twelve children in her class of five- and six-year-olds and they settled quickly, readily following their usual routines. They were a lovely group, she reflected, happy and well-behaved, as indeed were the children in the kindergarten where she had worked back in Kaohsiung. More good fortune she should remind herself of as she looked in the mirror each morning.

She spent lunch break on duty in the outdoor play area, checking that everyone was properly wrapped up against the bitter cold and holding a variety of small hands as she walked about, smiling and observing the children's play, while trying her best to keep herself warm. She never had the chance to tell the head about the email.

SEVEN CURSES

Back in the classroom, she took the afternoon register and, after accompanying the children on the guitar as they sang some of their favourite songs, she introduced the weekly session of "show and tell" that she had instigated earlier in the term.

This week, the three children from the Robins table had been asked to bring in something that had once belonged to a grandparent. One little boy, Peter, proudly passed around a cricketing cap that had been awarded to his grandfather, who once played for England against India. He was followed by a little girl named Simone who held up a delicately embroidered silk handbag, a gift to her grandmother from her husband who'd been in the diplomatic service, stationed in Hong Kong. As many of the children didn't know where that was, Serena explained how she'd been born there and led the children over to the large map of the world displayed on one of the walls, so old that she was surprised it wasn't covered in the red of the old British Empire. After this short interlude, they returned to the carpet and a little girl called Maria, a particular favourite of Serena's, came to the front of the class clutching a bejewelled musical box in her hands. It looked very old and expensive, and the children spontaneously voiced their admiration.

"This was given to my grandmother by her mother," the little girl proclaimed proudly. "My mother says the tune is about sheep eating grass in a big field. And I think it's very pretty."

With that, she opened the lid and soon everyone was in thrall to the lovely tune it released. Everyone apart from Serena, who stared at the box, scarcely able to breathe, until brought to her senses by a sudden chill from behind her and a cry of "Look!" from one of the children.

A boy stood in the doorway, taller than the tallest child in the room. Perhaps he belonged to a class of older children. But, oh, how angelic he looked, especially with this gentle music playing in the background. His dark hair was pushed back from his high forehead and fell in thick curls down past his neck. The skin of his lovely face was tanned to a shade of gold, and his piercing brown eyes were staring at her, or rather, *through* her. He wore only a grey, ill-fitting, collarless shirt, threadbare and open at the neck, and black trousers stained with mud and ripped at the knees. His boots looked as if they might be too big for him and were scuffed and tied with string rather than laces. He had no coat, no hat, no scarf, not even a jumper. Serena's heart went out to him. No wonder he was cold. And she had no doubt at all who he was.

"Children, this is Gabriel," she announced to the class. "Let's all say, 'Hello Gabriel' and make him feel welcome this afternoon." The music box was still playing, so she took it gently from Maria's hands and closed the lid. In the sudden silence, she turned to the boy. "Gabriel, come and join your new friends." She gave him her warmest of smiles. When he didn't move, she leant over to Maria. "Gabriel must be very cold," she said. "Why don't you take him over to the radiator in the corner so he can get warm? He can join your group for painting later."

The little girl smiled and walked confidently towards the boy, who fixed his gaze on her as she approached. She began to slow down, then turned suddenly and hurried back to her teacher, a frown of consternation on her face.

"Maria, what's wrong?"

"Miss, I don't like the way he's looking at me."

"Oh, Maria, look, he has no coat! He's cold and unhappy. We must welcome him, mustn't we?"

Maria still wouldn't move.

"Nevermind. Children, go to your tables now. Maria, you get out the paper and paints for the Robins. I'll bring Gabriel over myself."

When Serena took Gabriel by the hand, she was shocked at how cold it felt and surprised he wasn't shivering. He offered no resistance as she led him to a seat at the table in the warmest part of the room where Maria and the other two Robins were already arranging things, placing a vase of flowers in its centre, and gathering water, paint, brushes, and mixing palettes. Their usual teacher, Miss Meredith, was an art specialist and had the children very well-trained. Serena handed each child a large sheet of paper.

"Now you all know how to look carefully at these wonderful flowers, then mix the colours and paint only what you see, don't you? And aren't the colours lovely? Those gorgeous shades of red and yellow? Can you get them just right? I'm going to work at the Wrens table, but I'll come over later to see how well you've done. I know how helpful you are to one another, so can we all help Gabriel this afternoon? Talk to him and show him what to do?"

The Wrens were working on their number bonds and demanded all of Serena's attention for the next twenty minutes. Occasionally, she looked up to check the other groups of children. Everything seemed fine, although the three Robins were sitting as far away from Gabriel as possible. However, she did spot Peter talking with him and fetching him extra paint. Gabriel seemed to be concentrating, applying vigorous strokes with the thickest of the brushes. She smiled, happy to see him fitting in like this.

Later, she toured around the different tables to look at their work. The flowers painted by the three Robins were lovely, although Maria's was by far the best. Gabriel's painting was colourful enough but looked nothing like a vase of flowers.

She bent down next to him. "What's this, Gabriel?" she asked sweetly. "I can see you have the colours right, all those lovely reds and yellows, and oranges, too. But I can't see the flowers. Are they hiding?" She smiled at him, but Gabriel didn't answer and kept staring at his painting.

It was Peter who spoke. "Miss, he says it's a fire."

"Ah, so you do speak, Gabriel."

"Miss, only a few words," Peter ventured as Gabriel remained silent.

"Well, it looks like a lovely fire, Gabriel. One to sit by and get warm, hey?"

Then it occurred to her that his family, too, might have fled from a war zone, maybe in Syria or North Africa, given his Mediterranean features; and that it probably wasn't a fire to sit by and get warm at all. She felt ashamed of her insensitivity and asked quietly, "Gabriel, where is your home? Can you tell me?"

The boy didn't move for a moment, then he pointed to one of the tall windows that overlooked Monks Common. She could see the tower of the Church of the Holy Innocents peeking through trees in the distance. Did he mean that his family were staying somewhere on the other side of the green? Or was he pointing to somewhere on the large map of the world, hung alongside the window, that the class had looked at earlier?

A sudden crisis at the Bluebirds table made her abandon any attempt at further questioning. By the time the problem had been sorted, children were already clearing away their work and gathering on the carpet for story time. Gabriel, however, remained in his corner, a paintbrush in his hand. Serena decided to leave him there, occasionally glancing in his direction. He didn't appear to be listening to the story, which was unsurprising, as he was unlikely to be able to understand the language very well. It was only when she closed the book and told children to pack for home time that she noticed he'd disappeared.

"Gabriel!" she called out. "Did anyone see Gabriel leave?"

The children remained silent. She went and looked outside the classroom, but there was no sign of him.

"Miss, look at this!"

It was Peter. He was over at his table, staring at Gabriel's painting. The other children were gathering around to look, too, and Serena had to gently push her way through them. When she laid eyes on the painting, she saw Gabriel had added to it. Flecks of white paint had been spattered above and around the fire, like ash. There was also a figure outlined crudely in black from the waist up, the arms raised, the face contorted, the mouth wide open in what might have been laughter but was more likely a scream, given that it was standing in the middle of the fire.

"Look at the hair, miss. And the dress," said Peter excitedly.

The hair was long and black, combed to one side, as her own was today. The dress was blue and, quite remarkably, the same shade of blue as the one she was wearing. Flames were emerging from it.

"I don't think Gabriel likes you, Miss," said Maria, a look of concern clouding her little face.

SERENA TRIED TO see the head after school but was informed that she was in a meeting and would be detained for some time. So, she changed into her running gear and set off, pausing to look over Monks Common, wondering again where exactly Gabriel had been pointing and still feeling guilty about the business of the fire. Her insensitivity must have really hurt him. Why else would he have drawn that figure in the fire?

Later that evening, she felt the need to call Ernest and talk to him about the strange little boy. But she couldn't, of course. The time in Taiwan was eight hours ahead of the UK and it'd been past midnight there when she arrived home from work. She would send him a text in the morning and ask him to fix a time.

Feeling lonely and a little anguished, she searched for comfort in some of her old broadcasts on YouTube. She found one she'd recorded the previous July and started to watch it.

"People sometimes ask me about Ernest—about his name, about his personality, about why I think he is the perfect husband. Well, he chose the name Ernest because his favourite writer is Ernest Hemingway. He loves the direct nature of his prose, the honesty of his style, the seriousness of his themes, the truthfulness of what he writes. That is Ernest—serious, direct, honest, truthful. I know I can trust him always and in everything." She gives a little laugh. *"But please, I don't want you thinking that he has no sense of fun! For instance, I love to sing romantic songs as I do the*

housework, and he will often join in and sing along with me, even though he knows he's pretty tone deaf. Sometimes he'll take some of my favourites and change the lyrics. Instead of Joanna or Maria, he will sing Serena—" She sings, *"'Serena, we walked the summer hand in hand,' 'Serena, I love you, you're the one for me,' 'Serena, I'll never stop saying Serena.' To hear him honour our love in this way brings warm tears to my eyes. They say that beauty is in the eye of the beholder. I believe that in the case of music, true beauty lies in the flow of emotion from the heart of the musician to the ear of the listener. To me, Ernest's singing will always be beautiful. And as for being the ideal husband..."*

The ping of an email interrupted the broadcast. Serena paused to read the message from Charlene, in which she stated how pleased she'd been to hear only positive comments about the new arrivals— *"And thank goodness we've had no signs of trauma!"*

Halting the video, Serena wrote a response about Gabriel and how she felt that he might, indeed, be traumatised and was certainly in need of a great deal of care and attention.

Try as she might, the message kept bouncing back.

In the end, she gave up. She would try to have a chat with the head before school the following morning. Checking her watch, she saw it was later than she thought and was about to shut down her laptop when another ping sounded.

She read the subject line, *"And he shall come again to suffer little children..."* and, puzzled, opened the message. Out came the same piano melody as yesterday, again playing on loop.

Serena snapped the lid shut, a shiver running down her spine. What did it all mean? She wondered if it was from Gabriel's mother, that perhaps *she* was suffering from trauma and these bizarre messages were a religious manifestation of it. And, she realised with a slight shock, that this was the first time she had given a thought to the mother—or rather, her absence—all day.

SEVEN CURSES

Serena sat in the back of a taxi in Kaohsiung, looking at Ernest alongside her. She knew it was Ernest, although he seemed older and fatter. Heavily pregnant, she was telling him about the baby and about Leonardo, but he ignored her completely as if he couldn't see or hear her. Instead, he was complaining to the driver about the sickeningly sweet smell in the cab, the smell of jasmine, one he recognised as it always made him nauseous. Serena was saying no, no, it's me, it's your wife, it's my perfume, what do you mean? Ernest, still apparently unaware of her presence, told the driver to pull over and let him out. Serena was saying no, no, don't, listen to me, and she leant forward to ask the driver to carry on. It was only then that she noticed his hair, the long dark curls that cascaded down the back of his head. He turned his head to speak to Ernest, and it was then that she woke up and spent the rest of the night unable to sleep.

Her eyes were tired and her face drawn as she gazed in the mirror the following morning. She loved this mirror, having bought it to replace the one smashed to pieces by Xie Fei that terrible day she disappeared. The mirror had found her, she thought, rather than vice versa, in a small antique shop she'd wandered into. Framed in teak, it had delicate mother-of-pearl patterns decorating the dark brown wood; patterns of stars or maybe snowflakes, and of flowers—peonies and roses. No jasmine, however. The marked price was so cheap that it had to be triple checked by the shop assistant, who shook his head in incomprehension as she handed over the money.

Yes, it was indeed strikingly lovely, so much so that she would sometimes find with a shock that she'd been gazing into it for much longer than she realised, her mind completely blank, as if waking from some sort of hypnosis.

This morning, she was alert but finding it difficult to go through her usual litany of good fortune. Even the fragrance from her perfume failed to revive her spirits. The weather forecast on the radio predicted more icy winds and the possibility of snow. She would wear an extra layer for her run this morning, she decided, and she wondered about Gabriel.

When she arrived at the school, she was panting but feeling fit and ready for the day ahead. It wouldn't take her long to wash and change into her school clothes, but as she jogged through the gates and approached the entrance, two angry parents waylaid her, calling out her name.

"Ms. Lai, is it?"

Both wore thick Max Mara coats—she recognised the brand and the fragrance of Le Labo Santal. They introduced themselves curtly as the mothers of Peter and Simone, and no—they wouldn't make an appointment and would not even wait for her to change. Barely able to contain her fury, Simone's mother explained how her daughter had arrived home the previous afternoon "sobbing her little heart out" upon finding that black paint had been daubed all over the lovely silk purse she'd brought into school for show and tell. Phoning Peter's mother, she learned that the same thing had happened to the cricket cap ("An *England* cap, for God's sake.")

Their children had both named the same culprit.

"It's that strange new boy." Simone's mother's face twisted as she spat out his name. "Gabriel."

Serena was shaken by the news. She stammered out an apology, saying how dreadful it was that these precious heirlooms had been damaged. "Can the paint be cleaned off, perhaps?" she inquired. "After all, it is water based."

"Cleaned off!" came the contemptuous reply. "Cleaned off a fragile silk purse! No, it can't be 'cleaned off.' The purse is ruined."

"Besides," added Peter's mother, who seemed calmer, "that isn't the point. It's all very well the school taking in these refugee children, but from everything Peter has told me, this boy Gabriel could well be an illegal. Probably came on one of those small boats. Anyway, we don't think he belongs here, not in Henry Pottinger." She gave Serena a frosty look. "And to be perfectly frank, we don't think you do, either."

"Accepting foreign children is one thing," added Simone's mother. "But employing foreign staff is going too far. And someone from China, too! We've been expecting something like this to happen for some time."

Serena remained calm, saying she was sorry they felt this way and would investigate the incident and present a report to the headteacher.

"By the way, I am from Taiwan, not China," she added.

Ignoring their further protestations, she turned her back on them and entered the school. She had ten minutes to wash, change, and recover her composure.

The morning was difficult. Simone and Peter were evidently still upset, and the rest of the children quietly excited, as even very young children are when there is trouble in the air for someone other than themselves. When the head bustled in to talk with her during morning break, Serena was not surprised to hear about the angry phone call and the resultant appointment the two mothers had made for the following morning.

"But who is this Gabriel?" she asked. "You mentioned him to me yesterday."

Serena began to explain, but the head did not appear to be listening. "Is he here now?" she interrupted, casting her eyes about the outdoor play area.

"He isn't in this morning. I think perhaps he only comes in the afternoons."

"But he shouldn't be coming at all!" The head was clearly very cross about the whole affair. "He isn't on our books, and I know nothing about him! And I certainly haven't been given any funding for him. It's been a nightmare, I can tell you, trying to get hold of the financial support we were promised for the Ukrainian kids, never mind them throwing another one at us from God knows where. Look, I'm chairing a meeting of the heads of the local independent schools this afternoon, so if he shows up, tell his mother to take him away and not to bring him here again. Tell her to contact one of the local authority schools instead." She paused and forced a smile at one of the children who called out a greeting to her and let out a sigh. "This isn't Syria, or Palestine, or wherever she's from. We do things differently in this country." As usual, she was in a hurry to be somewhere else. "In the meantime, get to the bottom of this, will you? Get a report to me later this evening. And I'll see you properly in my office tomorrow at lunchtime."

Serena could have mentioned that Gabriel's mother hadn't appeared yet, that she might not appear today, but she said nothing, just nodded her assent and watched the head leave. If Gabriel came, as she was certain he would, he would not be sent away out into the freezing cold. Instead, she would welcome him and help him and establish his innocence.

THE MUSICAL INSTRUMENTS had been spread around the tables and the children were all happily on task.

Lunch time had passed without incident and the children were more settled now. Rumours that it might snow overnight sent a collective frisson of excitement around the class, and she'd been able to channel this energy into songs about snow and snowmen and winter wonderlands. She then set children the task of making their own music to capture the feeling of snow falling: first gently, then thickly, then in a blizzard.

She sat at the piano, surrounded by the Bluebirds, working out an accompaniment to the tinkles of their sleigh bells and the gentle taps on their chime bars when she became distracted by the music coming from the Robins table. Peter was tapping out a gentle rhythm with a drum and maracas, while Simone and Maria were each playing a recorder. Together, they had worked out how to play a simple version of the opening of the tune from the musical box. As they did so, Serena found that, unwittingly, she had begun accompanying them rather than the three children surrounding her. Then, as everyone apart from herself fell silent, she looked up and her heart thrilled to see that Gabriel had, indeed, come again. He stood in the same spot, wearing the same clothes, his right arm slightly raised in the same curious gesture she had noticed the previous afternoon.

Serena had already decided what she would do when he arrived. Immediately going over to the doorway, she stood beside him and set the children to find their own notation for the music they'd composed or of drawing a picture to illustrate the story it told. Gabriel's hand felt as cold as ever as she took it and led him over to the Robins table. She smiled and told Maria to join the Wrens for a few minutes while she sat Gabriel down near the radiator and asked Peter and Simone to sit opposite him, placing herself in between.

"Now, let's see if we can agree about what happened with the black paint yesterday, shall we? Peter? Simone?"

Peter and Simone both looked very uncomfortable while Gabriel stared from one to the other of them.

"Gabriel? Gabriel, can you look at me, please?" She knew the importance of eye contact when communicating with a child, so she tried her usual technique of positioning her finger in his line of sight, intending to move it to her own eyes once he focused on it. When this didn't happen, she decided not to press it further.

"Now Peter, did you see Gabriel put black paint on your cap?"

"He had the brush in his hand."

"Yes, but did you see him with the cap in his hand, too? No? Simone, what about you? Did you see him touch your purse?"

Both children looked frightened and shook their heads while Gabriel continued to stare at them.

"And did you see him near your bags after I had asked you to put them away?"

"No," blurted Simone, "but my mummy says…"

"But your mommy wasn't here, Simone, was she? Well, was she?"

Serena was talking in her sweetest of voices, smiling, but her eyes were telling a different story.

Neither child spoke.

"Now, I'm wondering if there might have been some kind of accident. I saw how both of you painted a lovely outline of the vase. Ooh, now help me. What colour did you use? Peter, do you remember what colour you used? It was black, wasn't it? I'm sure it was. And you, too, Simone?"

Neither child could deny this, but they both looked increasingly unhappy.

"Let me tell you what I think might have happened. I think you might have dripped some paint, quite by accident, of course, on those lovely, lovely things. It's so easy to do! And maybe you didn't even notice! And then, when you put them away later in your bag, those naughty little drips ran all over the cloth. And how could you notice this? How could you, how could anyone, when they were both tucked away inside your bags? Hmm?"

Both children began to sob.

"I didn't, I didn't…" wailed Simone.

"I know, honey." Serena tapped the back of her hand consolingly. "You didn't mean to. Of course you didn't. That's why it was an accident. It was no one's fault. Not yours, not Peter's…and not Gabriel's. Can we agree on that?"

But Peter shook his head and stared at Gabriel with hatred in his eyes, a look that Gabriel met unflinchingly.

"No," he shouted. "No!" And with that, he shot up from his seat and ran out of the classroom.

Serena remained as calm as ever, calling on one of the boys from another table to go check where Peter had run to, taking Simone by the hand to sit with Maria while she walked around from table to table, studying the children's work, complimenting them on how lovely it all

SEVEN CURSES

was. The boy returned to say that Peter was in the toilet. Serena waited a few more minutes before asking him to try to bring Peter back into class. "Tell him he isn't in trouble. Not one tiny little bit!" she added with a smile.

Subdued but still clearly upset, Peter returned sheepishly behind the boy and went over to sit with Maria and Simone. It was only then that Serena noticed Gabriel was nowhere to be seen.

"Gabriel! Gabriel! Did anyone see Gabriel leave the classroom?" The children were visibly alarmed by the sudden panic in her voice.

"Shall I go and check the toilet again, Miss?" the same little boy asked.

Serena ignored him and instead ran to the boys' toilet herself, flinging open the door and rushing inside.

"Gabriel!" she said, relief in her voice as she saw him standing near the wall by one of the cubicles.

Then she froze. Faeces had been smeared all over the wall behind him.

"Gabriel!" she whispered in horror. "What have you done?"

He spoke to her for the first time. "Not me!" he said in an accent she couldn't place. "Peter. Not me." As he spoke, he raised his right arm, his index and middle finger curiously pressed together, as if to show her that this hand, at least, was clean.

PETER DENIED IT, of course, while the helpful little boy who had gone to fetch him remained stubbornly silent. But Serena refused to believe that Gabriel had been responsible. She knew the children didn't like him and strongly suspected this was an act of revenge concocted by Peter and his friend and that Gabriel was wholly innocent. Her immediate concern was to protect him from further vindictiveness rather than to pursue the incident further.

The best thing to do, she decided, was to bring the children together and read them some of their favourite stories till home time. Gabriel could sit over in his corner by the radiator, out of everyone's line of vision. This tactic worked well enough; so much so that no one saw him leave the classroom. Once again, when the home time bell rang, he'd already disappeared.

Serena watched impatiently as the children were collected by their parents, taking care not to meet the frosty glare of the two angry mothers. As soon as they were all safely gone, she set about cleaning up the mess on the wall of the boys' toilet. She knew the caretaker's routine and where he kept his materials and managed to complete the job before the heavy trudge of his footsteps sounded outside.

Ten minutes later, when she emerged from the staff toilet dressed in her running gear, he was standing some distance away, giving her a curious stare. She blushed but ignored him, quickly stepping through the door and running through the school gates.

But instead of turning for home, on impulse she headed in the opposite direction, across Monks Common and towards the churchyard. Kneeling in the far corner behind the yew tree and out of sight, she took the perfume bottle from her pocket; but no matter how much grass she pulled at or scraped away, there was no sign of the stone plaque with the Chinese character, not in its usual spot nor anywhere nearby. The area was disturbed and looked as if some wild animal had been scrabbling there. She finally gave up the search and leant back on the yew tree, tears spilling from her eyes and chilling her cheeks as they fell. In the rapidly fading light, she headed for the lichgate as the first flakes of snow began to fall.

SHE SPENT MUCH of the evening sitting by her window, watching the thick flakes tumble and swirl around groups of laughing students engaged in frantic snowball fights; *just like kids*, she mused. She thought of her own children and wondered if they were having as much fun playing in the snow with their parents.

But not Gabriel.

She imagined him in a dark, empty room, lonely, cold and hungry, in need of all the comfort she could offer him.

That night, she slept poorly. Ernest had sent her a short message saying they needed to talk over the weekend, without specifying when exactly. Was there a problem of some kind, perhaps an illness in his family or difficulties at work? The anxiety made her restless and, when she did eventually doze, her sleep was troubled by a memory that transformed into a traumatic dream.

There were screams and shouts and insults being hurled. Serena tried to remain calm, but Xie Fei was out of control. Her inconsolable rage had been brought on by the sudden news of her boyfriend's death, a tragic accident, which she nonetheless blamed on Serena.

But in the dream, it took on a demonic quality; Xie Fei grew larger, her rage carrying a destructive energy that smashed everything around it. Serena fled the apartment, fearing for her safety. When she returned an hour later, Xie Fei had vanished, never to reappear, most of her belongings ripped, torn, or broken and scattered about the flat amidst the wreckage of the furniture. The university authorities struggled to understand how a young woman had managed to carry out such a powerful act of destruction in such a short period of time. The dream portrayed it as a superhuman explosion of rage brought on by grief and anger experienced on an epic scale.

The following morning, Serena felt and looked more exhausted than ever. She unscrewed the top of her perfume bottle and inhaled its fragrance, but once again, the smell of jasmine failed to work its magic.

"Mirror, mirror on the wall…" she began, but her morning litany stuck in her throat, sounding hollow and false as she gazed at the black circles around her eyes and the lines furrowing her forehead.

The radio was broadcasting the chaos brought on by the overnight snowfall, heavier than had been anticipated. There were also reports of another boatload of would-be asylum seekers capsizing in the English Channel, with many of the dead feared to be mothers and their young children.

Listening to the tragic news, she failed to hear the snap of the letter box in the door to her living room, nor see a sudden draft lift the envelope and send it drifting under a nearby shelving unit.

She did, however, catch the "ping" from her laptop and was unsurprised to read that the school would be closed for the day. A second email arrived immediately, this one also from the head and addressed directly to herself rather than to all the staff, acknowledging the report Serena had sent the evening before but, more immediately, asking if she could possibly get to the school before it opened. Many of the surrounding roads were impassable, and none of the other staff lived close enough to make it there on foot. An email had been circulated to all the parents and the local radio would also announce the school closure, but the head was concerned the news might not reach the refugee families. They might, after all, be used to this kind of weather and think nothing of trekking through deep snow to get their child to school. Serena replied she would, of course, do anything she could to help, hoping that the head would bear this in mind as she read the report.

She was dressing to leave when her laptop sounded for the third time. With a mixture of fear and anticipation, she looked at it. The subject line was stranger than ever: "*...and he shall be my instrument of justice.*" Serena frowned and shook her head. It sounded menacing, but what could it possibly have to do with a little lost child like Gabriel?

When she opened the message, there were lines of musical staves that indicated nothing but silence. An eerie silence, the silence of the grave, she thought. Her hand trembling, she closed her laptop and remained motionless for several seconds.

The snow of the previous evening had frozen into a layer of ice, upon which a later fall in the night had deposited a fresh, white, treacherous blanket. Running was out of the question, so Serena wore her warmest jacket and trousers and a pair of walking boots as she trudged along the track, unnerved by the silence and stillness that surrounded her. The building site was deserted, although she could see a light glowing from inside a wooden hut some distance away. No footprints led to it, however, and she wondered briefly if a watchman had been stranded there overnight.

The caretaker was expecting her and had already opened the school gates. At the entrance to the upper school, she found two mothers waiting under shelter, smoking, while their two children, boys of about ten years of age, were busy building a snowman in the playground, shouting to one another in their own language. Serena managed to make herself understood and the women, who remained expressionless, called their children over and left without comment.

There was no sign of any parents or children outside the lower school, only the caretaker, waiting for her inside the doorway. He told her the piano tuner, who lived close by, would be taking advantage of the empty classrooms to work in the lower school later that day.

"You won't want to hang around," he said. "'Tis freezing in here. No heating on, see. Not 'til Monday now." He sniffed.

Serena could feel how cold it was as she sidled awkwardly past him. "Of course, but I'll stay for half an hour or so in case any late comers show up. And I'll be back again early this afternoon." She was thinking of Gabriel, of course.

The caretaker shrugged. "Suit yerself." He nodded towards the far end of the building. "Any road up, I'll be down there, in the boiler room. Just pull the door to when you leave." And he strode off, leaving her alone.

The piano tuner arrived before she left. He was standing just inside the doorway when she saw him, changing into a pair of soft-soled shoes, his boots placed neatly by the door.

"Will you be here long?" she asked. "It's very cold!"

He acknowledged her with a nod of his head and picked up his bag. "Depends on the state of the instruments," he answered. "One or two of them may need quite a bit of work, I've been told. Anyway," he added, setting off towards the staircase, "I'll be okay. I'm wearing my thermals." He gave a little laugh and disappeared up the stairs.

Soon she could hear the sound of scales and harmonics and the occasional 'ting' of a piano tuner. By now, the cold had crept into her fingers and toes. "Let me bring warmth where there is cold," she muttered to herself and set out to cross Monks Common towards the small town beyond.

MONKERTON HIGH STREET was largely empty with many of the shops closed. Just one café was open, and Serena sat gratefully in its warmth for over an hour, leafing through a newspaper a previous customer had left on the seat. She seldom read or listened to the news, as she found it so depressing. Today, the paper devoted several pages to the tragic loss of life overnight in the channel. The photographs of the drowned bodies scattered over the beach, many of whom were children, particularly upset her. She put it aside and left, fastening her coat and pulling up her hood as she stepped outside.

At the back of the high street there stretched a large car park, alongside which a series of peeling wooden staircases led up to several rented flats situated above the shops. Run down and in varying states of disrepair, they looked cold and unwelcoming, with wooden boards fixed across some of the windows. Serena examined them as she walked along the entire length, wondering if she might catch a glimpse of Gabriel. It was in accommodation such as this that he had probably been housed, she suspected. There was no sign of him, however. Disappointed, she set off once more across Monks Common, but not in the direction of the school.

There were footprints in the snow leading to the church, so she wasn't surprised to find its doors unlocked. Her regular visits to the graveyard were always in the evenings, in darkness or in twilight, and she'd never actually set foot inside the church before.

When she entered and looked about her, she found the interior a lot less impressive than its outside appearance. Patches of damp were visible on the walls and there was a pervasive and unpleasant dank, musty smell in the air. It was surprisingly empty, too, apart from the lines of wooden pews, a table with a few untidy piles of well-worn hymn books and a dingy-looking painting, somewhat out of character, hung on a wall beside the altar, where the flame of a tall candle cast a dim light over the open page of a large prayer book placed next to it.

The dull echo of her footsteps and the whistling of the wind were the only sounds to be heard as she walked over to take a look. A light above the painting could be operated by pressing a plastic switch to its side. This she did and let out a gasp of shock at the image that lit up before her, an image of bodies entangled with other bodies, of plump, pale-skinned babies lying bleeding on the ground, of distraught, fair-haired mothers pleading to dark-skinned, grim-faced soldiers with Asiatic features, their arms raised, blood-stained scimitars in their hands.

As a Christian she knew the story of the Massacre of the Innocents and shouldn't have been surprised, she supposed, to see some commemoration of the scene inside a church named after the slaughter wreaked by Herod in his vain attempt to kill the future King of the Jews. And she felt deeply moved by its depiction of maternal grief. Nevertheless, in her opinion, it was hardly a subject fit for a religious house where young children could view it. A plaque at the side provided the name of the artist, one of the lesser-known painters of the late Victorian period, whose other works celebrated various victories of British imperial forces in different parts of the Empire.

Turning away, she caught sight of the prayer and was surprised to see that she knew it. "*Oh Lord, unseal unseeing eyes,*" she read. "*Help me find truth where there are lies...*"

Where had she heard that recently?

Before she could recall, a loud bang resounded round the church as its doors blew open, releasing cold gusts of screaming wind into the building. The flame on the candle next to her flickered and went out as she turned and let out a cry.

Gabriel stood in the doorway, a dark figure etched against a white, swirling background of snow, a storm that must have begun since she'd entered the church. He wore the same clothes as always and stared unblinking in her direction.

"Gabriel!" she called out above the deafening noise. "Gabriel, come inside. You must be freezing."

But he paid her no heed. Instead, he turned and disappeared into the blizzard raging outside.

THE SNOW BLEW into her face and fell so thickly that Serena could only distinguish a dark, hazy shape as, leaning into the full force of the wind, she stumbled towards the entrance to the lower school. She was almost upon the caretaker before she could recognise him, his thick black jacket and red woollen hat flecked with white patches of ice and snow. The wind howled so loudly that she had to call out at the top of her voice to make herself heard.

"Gabriel! A little boy. Did he come in here? I can't see his prints anymore."

The caretaker appeared more than a little surprised to see her again.

"Didn't think you'd be coming back in this lot," he called out. "I was just about to lock up."

"No, no, he must have come here. I know he must have."

SEVEN CURSES

Another one of his curious looks darkened his face as he answered her. "Well, I ain't seen no one!"

"He was heading in this direction. I saw him, just about. Disappearing through the snow outside the church. But I lost sight of him, and then of his tracks in the snow. It was falling so fast. I called out, but he couldn't hear me. I could hardly hear myself over the wind. He was coming here. I *know* he must have been coming here."

All of this she spoke as if to herself, brushing past the caretaker, not noticing the look of consternation on his face, her words blowing away in the wind as she pushed the door open.

Once inside the building, Serena leaned her back against the door and forced it shut, panting heavily in the sudden relative quiet, the wind now more of a deep whistle than a raging roar. She looked about her. There were no signs of wet footprints or drips on the tiled floor or on the polished wood of the stairs. Just a few tinkling notes sounding from one of the pianos upstairs. The piano tuner must still be here. He'd said that the job might take a long time, after all. What if the caretaker had locked him in? But then her stomach leapt. *His boots.* They weren't where he had left them and were nowhere to be seen.

"Gabriel!" she whispered and ran up the stairs.

She paused on the top step to listen. The playing was louder here, of course, the sound coming from a classroom at the end of a corridor to her right. She ran along it, calling his name again, pushing the door open, only to stop in sudden surprise. There was no one here, no one at all, and nothing to be heard above the sound of the wind outside other than her own heavy breathing.

But then it started again from a different room, very quiet but faster this time, a tune she recognised. Mozart, was it? Surely it was coming from the ground floor. How could that be?

As she turned and ran back to the staircase, she slid awkwardly on the damp trail her boots had left on the polished floor, twisting her ankle.

With a sharp cry of pain, she was stooping down to massage it when she heard the laughter of a child accompanying the frantic playing that seemed out of control to her ears. It must be Gabriel. And someone was with him. His mother? Could she be a musician?

Breathless, and calling out his name again, she hobbled over to the stairs, clinging tightly to the banister rail and descending them as quickly as she could, ignoring the pain, lured on by the sound of the music. *There*! It must be there!

She staggered along another corridor and flung open the door to a classroom, panting harder than ever; but once again the silence was abrupt and there was no one here, no sound from the piano, only the howl of the wind and the rattling of a casement window that had somehow been left open. She limped across the room to close it, when she began to hear music sounding once again, very faint this time. And she recognised Bach's gentle melody, Gabriel's tune, drifting to her ears in gusts on the wind. She almost smiled. Of course! Her classroom, his haven. His home in the storm.

"Gabriel!" she sighed, her voice soft and gentle, as if daring the brutality of the storm to silence it. She closed the window and made her way there. This time, she knew there was no need to rush.

He stood in the middle of the carpet, facing away from the door as she entered it. The first thing that struck her was the warmth. Had the caretaker forgotten to turn the heating off? That seemed the only explanation. But thank God he had! How could Gabriel have survived otherwise? Then she noticed that although the music continued to play there was no one at the piano. Perhaps it was coming from the music centre at the far corner of the room, although it didn't sound as though it was. And who would have turned it on?

These thoughts were secondary to her concern for Gabriel and her joy at having finally come close to him. Slowly she walked up to him and, feeling the cold radiating from his thin little form, she put her hand on his shoulder.

SEVEN CURSES

At first, he did nothing. Then he turned about sharply to face her, so sharply that Serena had to let go of his shoulder and take a step backward. For the first time, he gazed into her eyes, a long, concentrated stare that held them fixed to his own, hypnotically so. These were not helpless eyes, she realised, neither were they pleading eyes. Rather, they were commanding eyes. But commanding her to do what? Then slowly he raised his right hand in his curious gesture, then his left hand as he spread his arms wide. Her face brightened. So, *this* was his command. To hug him, to love him, just like the little girl in the park.

"Gabriel," she said in her sweetest voice. "You don't have to command me to do that!" She took a step forward and bent down, whispering, "There, there, your mommy loves you," as she embraced his thin, cold body. And as she put her arms around him and closed her eyes, he put his around her.

His grip was surprisingly strong. And warm, she noted, and growing warmer as she basked in the joy of his embrace. But as his grip continued to tighten, and the warmth became more intense, spreading across the whole of her back, she became uncomfortable.

"Gabriel," she said, loosening her own grip and opening her eyes. "Gabriel, you're hurting me. You don't want to hurt me, do you? Let go a little."

He gripped her tighter still, and she felt as if his arms were burning into her. Fearful now, she struggled in vain to free herself, forcing her head away from him to look into his eyes again. The shock took her breath away.

These were not the eyes of a child—they were scarcely even human. The menace she saw in them, the hatred and sheer malevolence—the look was the same as she had seen in her dream, in the eyes of Xie Fei, the eyes of a demon.

In the same instant she realised that the heat she could feel, now unbearable, was not coming from Gabriel but from the room behind her. She began to cough as only now she noticed the smoke enveloping her. Terrified, she turned her head to see tongues of flame licking their way up the walls and across the floor, onto tables, shelves, and into display cabinets. They consumed the map of the world and the children's paintings pinned next to it, including Gabriel's, realising now, to her horror, that the white flecks of paint were never meant as ash but as snow.

She screamed and screamed again, struggling with all her strength, but still Gabriel refused to ease his grip. Soon she could scream no more, only cough uncontrollably. She tried to utter his name one final time, "*Gabriel*," but the coughing wracked her chest, and she collapsed into unconsciousness.

IT WAS THE caretaker who saved her. Concerned by her earlier behaviour, he decided to check the building to make sure she wasn't still inside before securing the entrance. Only when entering the playground that led to her classroom had he caught sight of the red glow of flames from within its windows. His scarf wrapped tightly around his mouth and nose, he'd managed to drag her, eyes streaming, into the playground, then carry her across to the main building before calling 999.

The bad weather hampered things greatly after that. The ambulance crew were barely in time to provide Serena with the oxygen she needed, and flames had spread to the main school buildings by the time the fire service arrived. The resulting damage would take months to put right.

Serena only learned of this later from her hospital bed. Her burns were not severe, but the smoke had damaged her lungs, and she might have scarring and shortness of breath for the rest of her life, a grim-faced doctor explained. She found it hard to speak and, when she did, her voice sounded husky and harsh. This, too, could be permanent. But the doctors all told her that she was fortunate, very fortunate, to be still alive.

Of Gabriel, there was no mention.

No one had been recovered from the classroom other than herself, and no bodies were found in the burnt-out ruins. When she persisted with her questions, the nurses urged her to rest with assurances that it wasn't uncommon for severe smoke inhalation to affect a victim's mental state. Their patronising tones irritated her.

She spent many long hours trying to make sense of what happened to her, trying to understand why Gabriel, whoever or whatever he was, had been so hostile, rewarding her warmth and kindness with cruelty, her love with hatred. She began to have irrational fantasies, imagining him as the vengeful ghost of an abused or neglected child, or as some other kind of malevolent spirit. But why seek vengeance on *her*? This she would never understand.

She called Ernest. He sounded apprehensive as he answered the phone, as though he knew something must be wrong. When she uttered his name, he was shocked, saying her voice was unrecognisable. She explained there had been a fire in her classroom, an accident, but that no children had been hurt. She didn't mention Gabriel and, already breathless, she offered no further details. He expressed his shock and offered words of comfort. When she asked when he would fly over to see her, there were a few seconds of silence before he replied.

"Did you not receive the card I sent you? It should have arrived by now."

"No. What card is this?"

He didn't answer. "Call me again once it's arrived and you've read it." He paused. "And take care of yourself."

The conversation unsettled her, and she texted her current flatmate, asking her to look out for a card from her husband and to bring it to her as soon as it came in.

That afternoon the head came to visit her briefly, as composed and as smartly dressed as ever.

"The insurance will cover the repairs," she told Serena. "Meanwhile, we have enough capacity in the undamaged parts of the school to keep it open. Health and Safety will be a pain, of course. We've sealed off the entrance to the lower school and relocated Miss Meredith's class to one of our music rooms. Not ideal, but the parents are being very supportive." She gave a brief smile. "Don't worry about yourself. We'll pay you sick leave up to the end of term. Of course, you won't be returning for the summer. It wouldn't be a good idea, even if you were fit enough, which you evidently won't be. Some of the parents are holding you responsible for the fire—no, no, don't get upset. I've sent a letter out explaining that investigators are baffled and can find no evidence as to how it started. Others are blaming this Gabriel, whoever he was. It's a useful theory, that, and I'm quietly encouraging it. Neither the police nor the local services know anything about him, though, and he seems to have vanished from the face of the earth."

She left, leaving Serena with a get-well card and a box of Black Magic chocolates.

The following morning, her flatmate arrived with a bunch of flowers. "Jasmine, your favourites! They were delivered anonymously yesterday. Someone knows what you like! Do you have a secret admirer, perhaps?"

Serena forced a smile, knowing that she was trying her best to cheer her.

"Did you find the card?" she asked, putting the flowers aside without comment.

"Yes. Eventually. Under that ugly shelving unit by the front door."

Serena took the envelope eagerly and her flatmate left her alone to read it.

The picture on the card was pretty, a watercolour, a bunch of flowers that she recognised as lily of the valley. The message inside was brief.

Serena, we have been journeying through life together for many years now. You love me, I know, and I have loved you. But it seems, like many travellers before us, we have reached a fork in the road we've been sharing and that our destinations from now on must no longer be the same. I have always been honest with you and will be so now. I must tell you that my journey along a new road has already begun.

SEVEN CURSES

Your friend Angela and I have been close for some time and, more recently, we began an intimate relationship. Last week, she told me she is pregnant with our child. This was neither planned for nor expected, but the sudden and unanticipated joy that flooded through both of our hearts guided me into realising that destiny had already made the choice for us.

As I contemplate this new beginning for me, for us, I know that you, who for so long yearned for a child, will understand my joy and will wish the two of us—soon to be three—all the future happiness, prosperity, and fulfilment that I now, with all my heart, wish for you.

Take care of yourself, forever,

Ernest

Serena could make no sense of what she read. All she was aware of was a growing sense of nausea swelling inside her stomach and her chest. It was the smell of the jasmine, she was sure, irritating the scar tissue in her lungs. In a fit of breathlessness, she leant forward and swept the flowers on to the polished floor where they skidded into a corner, the petals crushed against the wall. Exhausted and breathing with difficulty, she lay back against her pillows and noticed a small card, half-hidden in the folds of her blanket, that must have fallen out of the bouquet. Still in a daze, she picked it up and read the message handwritten in blue ink.

> *"Oh Lord, unseal unseeing eyes,*
> *Help me find truth where there are lies.*
> *Let me seek warmth where there is cold*
> *And make me wise ere I grow old."*

She read it as if for the first time. Then she read it again, aloud, in cold realisation, as bitter tears poured from her eyes and streamed down her cheeks and onto the card, where the ink began to run and stain her fingers blue.

CURSE SIX
ICE

Six is the crone with heart of ice

Who'll fail to heed her own advice…

ONCE THERE WAS a professor of Children's Literature who didn't like children one little bit. She lived at the end of a quiet little road in a large, round house, painted white, with a flat roof that made it look rather like a huge cake covered in frosted icing. At least, that's what the two children who were unfortunate enough to live next door to her thought.

Theirs was an old, rambling Victorian house with four floors, more rooms than I could ever care to count, and more windows than there were rooms. In the winter, when it was cold and dark outside, they would sit together secretly at one of these windows—the one that gave a clear view of the professor's front garden, with its neat lawn that sloped steeply away from the house, down to a large pond right in the centre—and gaze across to the roof where they spotted her quite often, a wineglass in one hand and a cigarette in the other. Actually, they were rather hoping to catch sight of her flying away on a broomstick but hadn't done so yet.

You see, although they didn't know she was a professor—they didn't even know what a professor was—they were fairly certain she was a witch. If ever they played with a ball in the street, she would shout evil words at them for making noise; and if the ball ever landed on her lawn, she would make it disappear forever. Once at Hallowe'en, the boy had been foolish enough to try to trick-or-treat her and was given a chocolate cake with magic cream inside that had been so hot that it burnt his throat and

SEVEN CURSES

made him cry. Just the previous week, the little girl had built a snowman, only to see it flattened by the witch when she reversed her car over it, leaving behind a heap of slush, a battered cap, and a squashed carrot that had once been its nose.

"I *hate* that story!" the witch had called out with a vicious cackle as she drove away.

And she definitely *looked* like a witch. She was small, thin, had long, untidy hair with grey streaks and a fierce face with sharp, cold eyes. Once they saw her leave her house wearing a flowing black cape and a strange black hat, looking just like a teacher from Hogwarts.

It was true that she didn't have a cat, black or otherwise, but her garden was often visited by a flock of big, black, noisy birds—crows, I think, although they might've been ravens. (Can you tell the difference? I'm not at all sure that I can!) One day, the boy spotted a frog hopping away from the pond and he thought it more than likely that it had once been a handsome prince. (Actually, it wasn't a frog, it was a toad—but who on earth has ever heard of a Toad Prince?) Strangely, they'd not seen any sort of man near the house—young or old, prince or peasant, handsome or otherwise. Nor any woman either, for that matter. Grown-ups, they concluded, were far too sensible to visit a witch for dinner.

Although they didn't know she was a professor, or even what a professor was, they wouldn't have been at all surprised to learn that she hated all the stories they loved, and not just *The Snowman*.

No, it wouldn't have surprised them at all.

"Fuck research! Fuck conferences! And fuck the Vice Chancellor!"

The sound of heavy stumbling and clumsy door-rattling announced the arrival of a rotund, unkempt male figure who now stood on the threshold of the pokey staff room. He sniffed the air disapprovingly before letting out a drunken roar.

"Fee-if-fo-fum!
This place smells worse than the VC's bum!"

She didn't have to look up to know who it was.

"Hello, Ted. As sober as ever, I hear."

Ted Davies, Professor of English, staggered into view with a half-bottle of Grouse whisky in one hand and a copy of *The Tale of Squirrel Nutkin* in the other. He waved each about in turn and belched loudly before speaking.

"Ah, nectar from the Heelands! And one of the great classics of world literature! This should be the essence of university life, not fucking research!" He threw the book on the table in front of her; a provocation as he knew she had no fondness for animal stories. Without saying a word, she brushed it onto the floor.

He pretended to notice her for the first time.

"Well, well, if it isn't Calamity Jane, the notorious bad girl from Kiddy Lit Rock."

Jane knew from weary experience that the more he had had to drink, the more verbose he became.

"Alone in the staff room she sits, with only a pair of doctoral faeces for company."

He caught sight of the can of aerosol poking out of her bag.

"In splendid isolation, she sprays her poison into the very air she breathes. The cold winds of winter that blow relentlessly outside these darkened windowpanes outmatched only by the icy blasts of commentary that chill the bones of the poor, weak students she has at her mercy."

He collapsed noisily onto a nearby chair.

"You're looking unusually content today, Jane. Just been chairing the winter exam board, have you? Gunning down the gormless, hanging high the hopeless? Ah, yes, that must be it." He belched again and began to chant one of the silly rhymes he was fond of inventing.

SEVEN CURSES

"Hey, hey, Professor Jane Kaye
How many kids have you failed today?
Was it five or was it ten?
Stabbed to death with your red pen!"

Old Ted was appalling, but she suppressed a smile as she was rather proud of her reputation, which extended far beyond the University of Northwestern England. Renowned and feared for her critical acumen and acerbic wit, she was known to enjoy seeing young scholars visibly grow pale if ever she entered a room where they were about to deliver a conference paper. More than once the intimidating tone of her questioning and the relentless prodding of any weaknesses in their argument had publicly reduced even more established academics to tears, while her most favoured students relished the mockery with which she demolished not only rival academics but the established classics of children's literature.

"Yes, yes," continued old Ted.

"Even the best will be blasted away
By the icy critique of Professor Jane Kaye.

"Whereas the original Calamity Jane loaded her shotgun with bullets of plain old lead," he continued without a pause, "our Jane arms herself with the far deadlier ammunition of theory! The Frenchier the better! Barthes, Bourdieu, Baudrillard, Badiou, the appalling Bruckner and the barbaric Butler (not French, that one, but just as bloody lethal!). Anyone else whose name begins with the ballistic blast of the letter B? My ageing brain fails me. But fortunately, not my poetic soul!

"Fear the name of Calamity Jane.
In her new book, she's at it again!
Potter and Graham, Lewis and Dahl,
Shot down dead cos she hates them all!"

He swallowed a slug of whisky from the bottle.

"Ah Jane, Jane, who will be left to defend the children's classics once Ted treads the corridors of learning no more? Who will remain to sing of your deeds once your worthy opponent is gone?"

A combination of age, outrageous behaviour and *hashtag metoo* had finally caught up with old Ted, who was about to retire at the end of term. But he hadn't quite gone yet.

"You know, Jane, you may be no Doris Day, but you're not too bad for an embittered fifty-odd-year-old spinster. Whip crack-away, hey?" This remark inspired him to song. Arms spread apart, he bawled:

"Professor Jane Kaye
Is no Doris Day
But I wouldn't say no, no way,
To a roll in the hay!"

She'd finally had enough. With a sigh, she placed the essays on the table, put her pen away in its case, picked up her bag, and rose to her feet.

"I always wondered what Ted was short for and now I know—Tedious! Your rhymes are more annoying than Squirrel Nutkin's—and don't forget what happened to *him*." She nodded a glance towards his crotch. "He lost his tail."

"What?" Ted feigned hurt and surprise. "You won't sleep with the enemy just the once, for old time's sake?"

She strode over to the door, then turned to give him one of her withering looks.

"If any woman went to bed with you, Ted, sleep is all she'd get."

She left him silenced at last.

WINTER WAS HER favourite time of year; the colder, the better. Snow had been falling at regular intervals for several days now and the forecast was for the freeze to continue. The thought of this made her happy as she trudged along the empty seafront of the small seaside town to where the University of Northwestern England had recently moved its Arts campus.

She halted, shuffling herself further inside her thick, black coat, tightening the white woollen scarf around her neck and pulling further over her ears the hat she had brought home from a recent holiday in

SEVEN CURSES

Iceland. The children's funfair spread across the sands in front of her in frozen abandonment, its big wheel, helter-skelter, waltzer, and other assorted rides still and peaceful, the melancholy beauty of the sight enhanced by a covering of ice and snow.

She avoided walking here in the summer months when it was at its noisiest, crowded with children and adolescents seeking cheap thrills and the cheaper tastes of salty burgers, sugary buns, and ice creams. The sight of young people stuffing themselves with such rubbish sickened her. Candy floss for the masses, she thought, moments of empty enjoyment, an all too brief escape from the utter pointlessness of their lives. The cold truth of winter was much more to her taste, and she despised such superficial pleasures just as she despised all stories that sought to shelter readers of any age from the bleak fact that, in life, there was no such thing as a happy ending.

Most of the cafés along the front were closed for the season, but there was one, she knew, that stayed open in all weathers—the Nightingale Coffee House tucked away on a small side street. There was so little traffic today that she was able to cross the road to approach it without having to wait for or dodge the leather-clad bikers who swarmed the area during the summer months. She had nothing but contempt for these young men with their greasy clothes, greasier hair, and garish tattoos, despairing at the state of a culture that seemed to make a virtue of such antisocial ugliness.

The windows of the café were opaque with frost and condensation. And she was pleased when she entered to find that, once again, she would be the only customer this morning. She sat at her usual table, drew the hand cleanser she always carried with her out of her bag, and rubbed a generous drop carefully into her palms and fingers while waiting to be served.

The owner allowed her to smoke when it was this empty—provided she bought a pastry and an extra coffee. He would even bring an ashtray over to the table she always sat at, the one in the far corner next to the window. He would place it down ceremoniously between the slim vase, which always contained just one fresh flower, usually a rose, and her packet of cigarettes—always the same brand, Dunhill menthol. There she would sit and read, send emails or mark essays, or even, as today, just gaze out across the narrow street and the vista of the seafront beyond.

The condensation was so thick this morning she had to keep using her gloves to wipe the glass clear. Even then, ice on the pane clouded the view from outside, so she was taken by surprise when a face suddenly appeared only inches from her own, staring directly at her but apparently unable as yet to see her.

A young face. A foreign face, glittering in the pale sunlight reflected by the frost. Most likely a face belonging to one of the Chinese students who lived on the nearby campus, she thought. Instinctively, she leaned away when a gloved hand began to wipe at the window from the outside. As the frost cleared, first one eye, then two seemed to see her for the first time and offered her a brief smile of recognition that puzzled her. The face pulled away from the window. She followed the blurred form of its owner through the plate glass of the windows as it made its way around the corner of the café and opened its door.

The figure of a tall, slim, young Asian stood in the open doorway, wearing a hat of white fur and a coat of distressed white leather, also trimmed with fur. The tight blue jeans tucked inside a pair of leather boots emphasised the length of the legs. A small black shoulder bag hung loosely over the left shoulder. Before she was able to decide if they were male or female, a blast of icy wind blew through the still open door. The napkin under her saucer billowed violently, rattling the spoon against the cheap crockery, and the smoke from her cigarette blew into her face. At the same time a sudden stabbing pain in her right eye made her cry out. Something sharp and cold, like a shard of ice, had flown into it. She felt for the napkin and lifted it to her face. If it was ice, it was surprisingly stubborn, refusing to melt or flow out in the hot tears that had begun to stream from her eye. If anything, the cold was growing more intense the more she wiped at it.

"I am so sorry," said a gentle voice—a male voice—foreign, soft, and musical in its tone. "Please allow me to help."

Without waiting for a response, a delicate hand took hold of the napkin and began to dab at her eye.

"It's a nasty piece of grit, I'm afraid," said the young man. "There, I have it. You have cried it out. Everything should look better now." And he replaced the napkin expertly between her fingers without ever touching them with his own.

This had all happened so quickly that Jane had had no time to decide if she was grateful for the assistance or annoyed by the intrusion. As she dried her tears and her vision began to clear, she looked up at the young man and saw him properly for the first time as he stood within touching distance, smiling down at her. His figure, slim, elegant, yet athletic looking; his skin, smooth and glowing, as if it had absorbed the glitter from the sunlight where he'd stood on the other side of the frosted glass. Above all, it was his eyes. Foxy eyes, attentive and alluring. But also birdlike, each shaped like a tiny feather, the plume tapering upward. Was he Chinese or Japanese? Korean, perhaps?

"May I join you?"

"Yes. Yes, of course." Just five minutes earlier, she couldn't have imagined welcoming anyone to her table.

He sat down with the grace of a dancer and peered into her eyes. She felt a physical movement inside of her, like the unclenching of a fist around her heart, a feeling as powerful as it was unanticipated.

"Your eye, it is looking much better, I think."

"Oh, yes. It sees perfectly, thank you."

"I am Sozo," he said after a brief pause. "From the Tohoku region of Japan. Perhaps you have heard of it?"

She shook her head, aware she was smiling unintentionally.

"There was a very great earthquake and tsunami there some years ago, when I was a teenager."

A frown replaced the smile. "Oh, yes, I think I remember it," she lied.

"I and those I cared most for were lucky," he said. "But it changed my life." Before she could ask in what way, he added. "And you are Professor Jane Kaye."

She expressed her surprise and was more than a little pleased to be recognised by this beautiful youth.

He took off his hat and placed it on the table, white on white. At the same time, he shook loose his hair, black as coal, which seemed to part naturally over his right eye, while a fringe fell thinly over his left eyebrow.

"I recognise you from the photograph on your website. You look less severe in the flesh."

Stupidly, she felt herself blushing at his mention of flesh.

"I made the journey here mainly for artistic reasons," he continued, "to sketch and photograph the frozen wasteland out there, the desolate beachfront. Ever since the earthquake, I have been interested in desolation."

She said nothing, just studied him intently as he drew from his bag a slim, white cigarette holder and a pack of cigarettes.

"And for the fireworks tomorrow night," he continued, "when the Chinese students will celebrate their New Year."

She watched as his long, thin fingers drew a cigarette from the packet—menthol, she noted, his taste like her own.

"In Japan we call them *hanabi*, which means 'fire flowers.' Pretty, I think."

Without force or effort, he slotted the cigarette into the holder.

"I haven't seen anyone use one of those for a long time," she said.

"This holder? Oh, I don't like getting my hands dirty."

Jane glanced at the yellow nicotine stains on her fingers and placed her hands under the table on her lap.

"It looks very elegant, I must say. Is it ivory?"

"No, white jade," he said and smiled enigmatically. "I am Asian, not a colonist. I bought it in an antique shop in Beijing."

Gracefully, he slid his packet across the table towards her.

"Oh, thank you, but I do have my own."

She reached for the Dunhill and, with a shock, realised that they weren't there.

"That's strange," she muttered, searching through her bag. "What could have happened to them?"

"It is of no matter," he said, "These are menthol. You like menthol, yes? Then keep the packet. I have more."

The cigarettes were French, Royale Club Menthol, a very stylish brand. Without waiting for an answer, he picked up the cigarette holder and wiped it carefully with a clean napkin before passing it to her, actions once again executed with all the graceful elegance of a dancer. She was pleased to see him prioritise cleanliness but at the same time felt disappointed at his having removed any trace of his lips from the stem as she placed it between her own. Then, leaning towards him to draw on the flame he offered, she sucked the cool smoke down into her lungs and her head went slightly giddy.

"My goodness," she laughed. "These are very cool." Her eyes sparkled. "And do I look cool with this?" She struck a pose that she imagined a flapper from the 1920s might have adopted.

"Oh yes," he said. "Very cool indeed."

There were a few seconds of silence.

"Tell me," she asked, "why on earth would you have been looking at my website?"

"I have been studying over here. A fine arts degree. Now I have a job waiting for me and an idea that I am sure will be lucrative. I hoped you might help me develop it."

She was flattered, pleased, and intrigued all at the same time.

"Well, Fate has led you to me, it seems. Do you want to discuss it now?"

"Oh, could we do it in a more formal space, in your office? I would prefer that."

She could not deny that the thought of seeing this beautiful young man in a room of her own was a pleasurable one. Before she could respond, a tube of spent ash dropped from her cigarette onto her scarf. She brushed it off and noticed with dismay the grey mark it left on the white wool.

"We must conceal that," he said and, taking the rose from the vase, he snapped the flower from its stem. In no time, he had found in his bag a pin with which to attach it over the offending stain. As he leant across the table, she felt the coolness of his breath on her cheek.

Once she paid her bill, it was agreed he would call on her the following morning. He said he knew where to find her office. As they left, she asked in an offhand manner where he'd been studying and greeted his reply with an expression of surprise.

"What a coincidence!" she remarked. "I was there just a few months ago."

"Oh," he said. "Was it an enjoyable visit?"

She pulled a face. "Not at all. The conference was boring and the accommodations below par. Not at all fresh or clean enough. I had to complain more than once and was disturbed during the night when someone along the corridor was taken ill."

He bade her goodbye with a slight bow, and she watched him disappear around the corner where, unseen, he slipped a pack of Dunhill cigarettes into a wastepaper bin.

Later, as she walked back to her office, she thought it odd that he'd neither ordered a coffee nor smoked one of his cigarettes. And odd, too, that the owner hadn't bothered to ask him for an order, seemingly unaware of his presence. It was later still, when she took off her scarf, that she realised how cold she had been in the café; and it was only then that she noticed the worm in the heart of the rose.

SEVEN CURSES

That evening, Jane sat on her white leather sofa, knees drawn up to her chest, reading through the proofs of a recent article submitted to a journal she edited. She always brought work home, and part of her fierce reputation among colleagues stemmed from her intolerance of any academic who refused to work as many hours as she did. This evening, however, she was finding it difficult to concentrate. The smoke from the cigarettes the young man had given her seemed to have clouded her brain. At one point, she realised she could recall nothing from the last two pages, her mind distracted by an image of the boy from Japan standing in the doorway of the café.

"His legs," she muttered to herself. "His legs, longer than my life."

Hearing herself speak these words brought her to her senses. She sighed and put the proofs aside. The cigarettes were on the table beside her, but she never smoked within her own living space. Inside a café was one thing; she could leave and not have to tolerate later the stale, lingering tobacco smells. Picking up the lighter, the pack of Royales, and pouring herself a full glass of chilled white wine from an open bottle she had in the fridge, she walked into the hallway where her coat hung from a peg.

A minute later, wrapped up tightly, she pushed open the door at the top of the stairs that led directly on to her roof, her favourite smoking haunt. Here she could relax for a few minutes, surveying the regular geometrical pattern of houses and rooftops, of lights shining haphazardly from windows, of side streets lit dimly by too few streetlamps, and the glimpse of shoreline and sea in the distance bathed now in the soft glow of a waning moon. The freezing weather did not in any way dissuade her; quite the opposite. She loved the way the pale moonlight cast its cold, blue light on the whiteness of the snow and how the frost in the air added a further chill to the cool menthol as she breathed it deeply into her lungs.

"Longer than my life," she repeated absently as she leaned on the glass balustrade that ran along the outside of the roof.

In her darker moods, she'd recently begun to reflect on her life for the first time with some regret. Even as a young girl, she'd been the clever one, the sensible one, never one to lose her head. Ruthless ambition and dogged determination had made her successful. But now thoughts of missed opportunities and lost chances preoccupied her. She had for many years been alone but never lonely, having prioritised work and the pleasures of the mind over those of the body. She prided herself on being the polar opposite of old Ted, with his sexist bombast and umpteen ex-wives, lazily putting fun before fame, whoring before hard work. But now, as she gazed over the frozen rooftops where several crows could be seen, irregular patches against the white snow, she wondered ruefully if her choices had been as wise as she'd always thought them to be.

She emptied her wineglass, then took another deep draw on her cigarette, enjoying once again the cool stab of pleasure at the back of her throat as the smoke made its descent into her lungs. There was no doubting the strength of this brand, the mild dizziness induced by each successive inhalation, the visual power of the pictures it conjured in her imagination.

Suddenly her mind was filled with memories from the previous October, images of the disturbance in the corridor outside her room that'd woken her soon after midnight. She'd noted with annoyance at the time that she'd barely been asleep for an hour as the noise of shouting, banging, and weeping had dragged her back into consciousness. Groggy with sleep, she'd staggered from her bed, pulled on a dressing gown, and opened her door to investigate just as a stretcher was being wheeled away at speed by two paramedics. She'd seen the long black hair of a young woman, evidently in great distress, following close behind and the flashing lights of an ambulance throbbing like the rhythm of a heartbeat through a window halfway along the corridor. A woman in the room opposite to Jane informed her that a young Asian man had collapsed from a sudden asthma attack some thirty minutes before the ambulance arrived. She'd heard one of the paramedics suggest it could've been an allergic reaction to the air in the corridor, or rather, the air spray, whose lingering smell he could still detect. Jane said nothing, marvelling at how deep her sleep must have been for her to have woken up so late in the drama.

On returning to her room, she looked for a few seconds at an empty can of air spray in the wastebin before shrugging her shoulders dismissively. When she checked out the following morning, she'd refrained from making further inquiries about the boy, assuming asthma would be relatively easy for paramedics to deal with.

Having hardly thought about the incident since, Jane wondered why it came to her mind now.

Of course. It was the coincidence of Sozo, also an Asian boy, studying at WMU where that awful conference had taken place.

She finished her cigarette, feeling for the first time the chill of the night air penetrating through the warmth of her coat. Stooping over, she stubbed the butt into the rooftop ashtray at her feet, enjoying the sizzle of the ice as it doused the still luminous tip, and shivered her way over to the door which she had to tug at several times before it gave way and slid slowly open. For a brief moment, she almost panicked and resolved to bring a shovel and some de-icer up with her next time.

Back in the shadows of her living room, lit only by the reading light that shone on the abandoned article, she let out a sigh that signalled it would remain abandoned for what little was left of the evening.

CLOSING HER OFFICE door behind her, Jane paused to look about the room. Everything was, of course, as neatly and tidily arranged as always. Even her desktop, polished and dust free, had on it only a bottle of water, a glass, and two piles of theses stacked so evenly that they presented themselves at first glance geometrically, as a pair of matching cuboids. She needed this sense of order to begin her day, but this morning, it felt particularly reassuring.

The can of air freshener was on a shelf to her right. She sprayed her room as usual but was taken aback by what sounded like a ghostly breath outside her office door as she replaced the can on her shelf. The experience was eerie enough for her to peer fearfully out into the corridor. Of course, there was nothing there, but it had added to the discomfort she was already feeling.

She'd had a very unsettled night, unable to sleep as images of Sozo kept invading her mind, each time making her heart race and sending an adrenaline rush through her stomach. When she did manage to doze off, unusually, she'd been disturbed by a dream, or rather a nightmare.

In it, she'd been alone in this very building, working late as she often did, when the room began to shake, and the floor slid away beneath her feet. Rushing out onto the corridor, she found it long and empty, a place she didn't recognise. At its far end stood Sozo, calling and beckoning to her, his voice obscured by the noise of falling masonry. She ran towards his outstretched hand but as she reached for it, the ground beneath her dropped away completely, and she was falling into blackness when she awoke with a start, her heart beating so violently that for a few minutes she had feared for her health.

Sozo had said so little about the purpose of this meeting that she'd been unable to prepare her mind for it. Instead, and to hide the tiredness evident in her drawn features, she prepared her face, taking more time than usual with her make-up. She also combed her hair with care, tying it into a neat bun instead of allowing it to fall freely about her shoulders, as she often did. She was never over-dressed for work, but today she chose a black dress to wear together with a smart leather jacket, a combination intended to flatter her slim, petite figure.

He arrived at 10:00 a.m. precisely, dressed as he had been the previous morning. He entered the room with a slight bow, which she found charming. Scarcely seeming to notice the efforts she'd made to look attractive. However, his immediate attention was drawn to the books on her shelves. He asked politely if he might look at a few and she smiled her consent, delighted to see him use the hand cleanser strategically positioned on a small table inside her door without being asked to do so. A set of volumes with colourfully designed covers had evidently caught his eye.

"So many fairytales!" he said, leafing carefully through a luridly illustrated picture book, whose popup images illustrated some of the best-known French tales. "Why so many?"

She let out a short laugh. "Know thine enemy! The first rule for any academic wanting to make their mark."

"And how are they your enemy?" he asked, his eyes fixed on the enormous jaws of a wolf that emerged threateningly from the book as he turned a page, within which cowered the tiny figure of Red Riding Hood.

"So many versions are sentimental and make impossible promises to children." She pointed at the book he was holding. "That one I like. Red Riding Hood without the hunter. Death and deception without rescue and redemption. The world as it is." She laughed again. "Unlike other animal stories that I despise."

He replaced the book carefully and pulled out another.

"What's wrong with animal stories in particular?"

"Oh, not all of them. Just those that paint them as twee and cutesy, like *The Wind in the Willows* and *The Brambly Hedge Folk*. Animals are wild and savage. They inhabit a world without mercy. As, in all honesty, we all do. Humans are animals, not the other way round. It is better for children to learn the truth as early as possible."

His eyes flashed with interest as he replaced the volume in his hand and chose another with a blue colour, well-thumbed and less ostentatious.

"Surely not all animal stories are like that. Foxes, for example. They get a particularly vicious press in many of your traditional tales I have always found."

She smiled. "Ah yes. Mr. Fox—cunning, sly, and dangerous. Never to be trusted. I must admit to a fondness for him."

She stood up and selected a small picture book, a version of *The Gingerbread Man*.

"Here," she said, opening it to an illustration of a fox swimming in a river with only the head and shoulders of the gingerbread man emerging from its jaws. "The world is full of dangers. Go off running in search of happiness in the delusion of freedom, and you will more than likely end up being eaten alive. If not by a fox, by something or someone equally treacherous."

He seemed genuinely interested in what she had to say, so she continued, selecting two books from different shelves.

"This picture book is both witty and true. *The Sweetest Fig*, by the author of the original *Jumanji*, no less." She opened it and showed him pictures of a fussy-looking Frenchman, evidently obsessed with cleanliness, and his poor, long-suffering dog. "In the end, however, through a delicious mixture of magic and luck, the dog gets his revenge. Not happiness, mind you: *revenge*. And this novel here, for teenage readers, is narrated in the voice of a disabled boy called Midget, who is horribly abused by an older brother, whom everyone regards as his saintly carer." Again, she turned to the end of the book and pointed to an illustration of a drowning figure. "Midget engineers his revenge in the form of a brutal murder, something his brother thought him incapable of. Cruelty, hatred, vengeance. And human arrogance and blindness. These are the stories children need to read, children of all ages. Not the sentimental twaddle they are all too often fed." She paused. "*Cinderella Without the Prince*. That's the title of one of my articles."

Sighing, she replaced the books in their proper order and saw he was leafing through the one he had picked up earlier. Irritated, she said, "I'm sorry, I've been in lecture mode." The book he was looking at, she noted, was a critically acclaimed selection of global fairy tales edited by a famous feminist author. He had it open at a black-and-white picture in which an old woman lay on a sloping roof, wrapped in what looked like a sheet of ice, while a young man sat inside her house drinking wine. It was illustrating a story entitled *Young Man in the Morning*, one she had not yet read herself.

He looked up and smiled at her without comment and replaced the book on her shelf.

"Shall I sit down?" he asked and waited for her consent before doing so.

Once again, she marvelled at the grace and lightness of his movements. The room felt colder than usual, so she bent to the radiator and turned up the heating and noticed him looking at her with evident interest. He'd been listening to her, after all.

"Tell me, have you always felt like this?"

For an instant she thought of her very different youthful self, the avid reader of the great nineteenth-century female novelists, the lover of Jane Austen who had written her thesis on *Persuasion*. But that was before her one long-term relationship had ended cruelly in deception and betrayal.

"For all of my mature years, yes," was all she said.

"I have a gift for you," he said after a slight pause, flipping open his bag and drawing from it a grey ceramic pot with oriental script—Japanese, she assumed—painted in black down its length. A thing of beauty, she marvelled, as he placed it carefully on her desk. At first, she thought it was a vase until she noticed the cork stopper.

"It's a bottle!" she remarked in fascination. "Like something from the *Arabian Nights*. If I uncork it, will I release a genie?"

"Just sake." He smiled. "Have you a glass?"

Without waiting for a response, he leant across the desk and picked up the empty glass next to her water. She shivered at his proximity as she watched him uncork the bottle and pour her a shot.

"Just a taste for now," he said, "while it is still chilled. It is always best to drink sake chilled."

Unlike old Ted, she never drank alcohol in her office. Only ever in the evenings, after work. But the expectant look on the face of Sozo dispelled her resistance.

"Well, just a taste…"

She held his gaze as she brought the glass hesitantly to her lips. *What the hell?* she thought and recklessly downed the whole shot in one. She gasped. "It's cold… So cold!"

"Just wait," he whispered.

It was as if the chill from the liquid, upon hitting the warmth of her stomach, let off a vapour that exploded like a jet of steam up through her chest, her throat, her cheeks, straight to her brain, which for an instant seemed to swim in giddy ecstasy before her eyes cleared, and she found herself gazing at the impassive face of Sozo which appeared, in the coolness of his stare, more beautiful to her than ever.

She was too overwhelmed to say anything. Finally, he began to talk to her of his project. He'd been employed by a leading Japanese company to assist with the production and design of a new series of animated stories for children.

"As I read around the subject, I came across your work. I found your writings most impressive."

Jane flushed with pleasure at these words of praise coming from his mouth.

He knew of her uncompromising attitudes he went on to explain, and he thought they would suit the Japanese market.

"There has been too much of an emphasis on 'cute' in our culture in recent years," he said. "There is an appetite for change, I am certain, and I think your harsh ideas will suit our market and help steer that change."

He went on to ask if she might advise him on the choice of stories. She knew nothing of Japanese stories or Japanese culture, she confessed, but would be pleased to assist him in any way she could. He nodded and thanked her, and she was disappointed to see him immediately rise and prepare to leave.

"The Chinese New Year celebrations and the fireworks will take place tonight," he said. "Then I will leave in the morning."

"Oh, so soon?" she blurted out, then felt her cheeks go red. "Oh, this drink. It's so strong!" she remarked, hiding her cheeks with her hands in embarrassment. "I mean, shouldn't we discuss this more?"

"I must leave tomorrow. I will send you an email."

"This evening then. Come to dinner at my house." A pause. "I need more details from you so I can begin to think, to plan…"

He said nothing.

"My roof," she said suddenly. "It's flat. It'll provide you with a great vantage point for photographing the fireworks. You need not miss anything of the celebrations. I eat late as it is. Besides," she said, finally, "I can't possibly drink this sake on my own…"

She held her breath and felt a rush of excitement when he nodded his acceptance. They fixed a time, and she gave him her address. He told her, somewhat apologetically, of his specific dietary requirements and then left.

Once he had gone, she sat at her desk for several minutes, distracted, scarcely believing her boldness, her silliness. She felt hot, blaming this on the effect of the alcohol, and reduced the temperature on her radiator. Unable to work, she decided to visit The Nightingale, then shop for this evening's meal. As she fastened her coat and scarf, she began to have more sober, professional thoughts about the evening, and tried to dispel any thoughts of romance from her mind. But as she stepped out into the corridor, she was greeted by the call of a familiar, unwelcome voice.

"Jane! Jane! Snow queen of my heart!" Old Ted approached but suddenly halted, sniffing the air. "Good God, Jane! Have you been *drinking?*"

Embarrassed, she said nothing as she hastened to lock her door.

"Ah, Jane, there is no need to drink on your own! Come and have a few with me this evening." He gave her a lewd smile and lowered his voice. "Then I can introduce you to the old dick before I leave. How about it?"

Resentful and furious, she turned on him.

"Old! Old is the only true word you've said for weeks!" she sneered and walked off, her mind suddenly made up.

Why not? she thought to herself. *Just this once, why ever not?*

"Did you see Fantastic Mr. Fox on the witch's lawn last night?"

The children were quietly playing one of their board games on the floor, quite close to the window they called their spy hole. It was the little boy who had asked the question.

"Of course," answered the little girl.

"It was white, pure white," he added. "I didn't know foxes could be white."

"Well, it did have a streak of red in its tail," added the girl. "Anyway, how do you know it was a *Mister* Fox?"

"All right then. Fantastic *Mrs.* Fox."

"Now you're being silly. Foxes don't get married."

"How do you know? They might in a story."

"Well, this is real life, not a story."

A pause.

"You would have to say Fantastic *Ms.* Fox," the girl said eventually.

"Isn't there a special word for a Ms. Fox?"

"I'm sure there is, but I don't know it."

"Anyway, I wonder what he or she wanted?"

"They."

"They?"

"Yes. Instead of 'he' or 'she,' you should say 'they.'" The little girl was quite the bossy school ma'am at times. "It's neater. Ms. Peasey told us in English class last week."

"Oh," said the boy. "So, I wonder what *they* wanted?"

"Well, it prowled around her pond and then just sat there, staring up at the house."

SEVEN CURSES

"You said 'it,' not 'they.'"

The little girl ignored him.

"Do you think *it* will come back again tonight?" he asked, trying to get it right.

A mischievous light sparkled in the little girl's eyes.

"Oh yes, I'm sure she will. Shall we stay up and keep watch?"

The little boy looked very confused now.

"You just called it…"

"Sssshhhh!" said the little girl.

IT WAS THE sake that kept her excitement high and her stress at bay. Jane wasn't used to entertaining anyone for dinner, least of all such a beautiful young man. Given what he'd told her, she decided to keep things simple and to present him with options. Two steaks and two fish fillets lay raw on the table on separate plates, ready for him to choose from—both could be grilled very quickly—along with the vegetable stir-fry of shredded cabbage and carrots she had already prepared. Or he could have the salad of lettuce, rocket, and spinach if he preferred it. Simple. As for the drink, she always had plenty of wine. And there was the sake, of course. She had only poured the one glass for herself and replaced the bottle in the fridge so there was plenty still for them both to share.

She checked her watch and felt the butterflies flutter in her stomach, already churning from the warm strength of the exotic spirit. He was due to arrive in a very few minutes. Music? Should she put on some music? What would he like? She had no idea. What might appeal to a visual artist from Japan with the figure and grace of a dancer? She was scrolling through Spotify when the doorbell chimed. Her heart thumping, she paused in front of the mirror in her hallway and took some time to check her appearance before opening the door.

There was nobody there. She stepped outside and looked around the garden. The path had been cleared so there was no sign of any fresh footprints. There were animal tracks on her lawn, and she thought she saw the shadow of a large cat slink into the bushes to the side of the house, nothing else.

It's those bloody children from next door, I'll bet.

But on glancing up at the window where she sometimes caught sight of them spying on her, she saw the profile of two little heads quickly disappear from view. Beginning to shiver in the cold—she was only wearing a thin dress of white silk—she went back inside and kicked the door shut behind her in frustration.

There was a cold draft coming from somewhere, raising goose bumps on the naked skin of her arms and legs. Following it into the obscurity of her lounge, she saw the curtains billowing in front of the French windows that led directly out to her rear garden. Had she failed to close the doors properly earlier? She couldn't even recall opening them, but in the semi-drunken state she was now in, it was difficult for her to remember. She drew the curtains apart and cast her eyes over the snow covering the dormant rose bushes and empty flower beds and saw that the fresh animal tracks from her front door had continued on to the lawn in the rear.

She was about to pull the doors closed and turn when a slim silhouette stepped silently and gracefully out from the shadows that darkened the far side of the garden. It stepped into the light, its face in profile, and she thought she recognised the fur-lined hat and the fragile beauty of the face.

"Sozo!" she whispered, her heart leaping in her chest, only to sink once more as the figure approached her and spoke. Although the movements were as graceful and the facial features remarkably similar to those of Sozo, the voice was distinctly female.

"Don't be alarmed," it said as Jane stood there frozen in shock. "I rang your bell, but you took so long answering I thought I might catch you at the back of the house."

"Who are you, and what are you doing here?" Jane's voice was harsh and nervous as she readied herself to slam the door in the face of the young woman if she came too close.

"The Japanese boy you are expecting. I have a message for you."

Jane's heart sank further, and her shoulders drooped. He wasn't coming. This was a disappointment, she realised now, that she had secretly been fearing all evening.

"Well, what is it?" Her voice was quiet, its tone resigned.

The young woman took a step forward. Like Sozo, she too was beautiful, of the same height and build and wearing similar clothing, though there was what looked like a red belt tied loosely around her waist. Jane wondered if she was his sister, and her body began to shiver violently.

"You are cold," said the woman. "I think I should come inside."

Jane had questions to ask, so she moved aside, telling the woman to remove her boots and carry them through to the front door before joining her in the kitchen. Taking the bottle of sake from the fridge, she sat at the table in front of the now pointless plates of food and poured herself a glass. The alcohol had the physical effect she desired, a delicious melange of ice and fire. It intensified the sense of pleasurable giddiness but failed to dull her apprehension as the woman entered the kitchen.

"You're his sister, aren't you?" Her voice was slightly slurred. "You look very like him."

The woman shook her head. "I am Chinese, not Japanese."

Jane's expression of surprise lingered for just a few seconds.

"Well, what are you then? His girlfriend come to warn me off?"

The young woman sat down elegantly, positioning herself directly opposite Jane at the table.

"Professor Kaye, I have come to warn you. Things are not what they seem."

Jane scoffed. "What do you mean?"

"You know nothing of this boy. And yet you invite him to your house."

Jane's cold stare bore into the eyes of the girl, who nevertheless held eye contact and remained cool and impassive under her glare. This imperviousness annoyed Jane greatly. How dare this young Chinese nobody, whom she was sure she'd never met before, presume to come to her house and speak to *her*, an eminent scholar, in such patronising tones!

"Listen, young woman. I'm old enough and wise enough to look after myself. I certainly don't need advice from a mere slip of a girl like you."

The woman continued as if Jane had not spoken. "Sozo is handsome and charming, I know, but believe me, he is no prince come to rescue you." She paused briefly. "And besides, I thought you mistrusted fairytales."

Jane's eyes flared with anger.

"Listen, Miss Hu-Hu or whoever you are—if you have a message from him, then say what you have to say and leave."

The girl didn't flinch.

"Cast your mind back to last October, on the young Asian boy taken ill outside your room after you, in your usual nightly drunken state, emptied an entire can of air freshener along the corridor."

Jane reddened but didn't offer a denial.

"He died on the way to hospital." She paused. "You didn't know that, did you? And you certainly didn't care enough to find out."

The colour drained from Jane's face. "Of course, I didn't waste my time making pointless inquiries about a person I never knew and an incident I refuse to take any responsibility for. Who exactly are you, anyway?"

"Just answer me this. What if I told you the young man who died was also called Sozo? That he was also an artist and photographer?"

Jane frowned in confusion.

"Well, even if I were to believe you, what of it?"

The young woman leant towards her.

"How do you know this isn't him come back to take his revenge on you?"

Jane's frown changed to one of incredulity. She studied the woman's face for a moment, noting that it remained completely serious. Then she laughed, loud and long.

"Young woman, if I don't believe in fairytales, I certainly don't believe in ghost stories."

The Chinese girl sighed and leant back once more in her chair.

"Yet you believe that such a handsome young man could be interested romantically in a woman such as yourself? Have you learned nothing from these stories that you write about?"

Jane was speechless in her fury. With hatred in her eyes, she watched the young woman draw a book out of her pocket and place it on the table. It was a famous volume of fairytales, published by Virago, the same that Sozo had briefly held in his hands while in her office earlier that day.

"Here," said the woman. "You should read these again. Especially the section on *Sillies*."

There was no sarcasm in her voice, her tone as cool and as impassive as ever. She rose from her chair and looked down at the twisted features of the older woman.

"I didn't intend to make this visit, but I began to pity you. After all, hope and desire are all too human, I suppose, despite everything." She headed for the front door and slid her feet into her boots, calling out as she did so, "But thank you for the final proof of your callousness. Goodbye, Professor."

Jane picked up the book and threw it at the woman. It missed her, flying out into the night air. In a rage, she pushed back her chair and heard it clatter to the floor as she raced over to the open door, screaming out a stream of abuse. But in those very few seconds, the young Chinese woman had disappeared into the darkness.

THERE'D BEEN NO fresh fall of snow, but gusts of wind blew into the air flurries of white, powdery flakes that'd previously settled on the branches of the tall trees that formed a boundary between her lawn and the street beyond. On one of them, a flock of crows had alighted just a few minutes earlier. From where she stood, all their eyes appeared to be focused on her.

"A murder of crows," she said out loud, at which, as one, they rose into the air and swooped towards her, circling overhead, cawing loudly, defiantly, black shapes against an even blacker sky. The sight in no way disturbed her. For some reason, it brought to her mind the scene from the animated version of *The Snowman* where the boy was gliding through the air to the strains of that awful song. At one point in his flight, a drunken man in a party hat sees him up in the sky and looks questioningly at his glass of champagne for an explanation. She held up her own glass of sake to the pirouetting birds, mockingly offering them a toast.

"Here's to you, you murder of crows," she repeated before swallowing its contents and hurling the empty glass through the air, disappointed to hear it land with a thud in a patch of snow rather than with a smash on a harder icy surface. Then, with a rather drunken smile, she recalled a meeting of the English department earlier in the year when the closing five minutes had been hijacked by old Ted who insisted they exercise their collective literary talents to invent portmanteau terms for prostitutes. A flourish of strumpets had been one offering; a volume of trollops another. A professor of Middle English volunteered a gaggle of ginders, which no one other than himself had understood or been amused by. Old Ted had chosen 'a selection of pros' as the winner. A rather dull choice, Jane thought at the time.

"A selection of pros, a murder of crows," she muttered then flung the cigarette holder over the balcony, too, watching the tip of the final Royale Club menthol leave a glowing trail through the air before being snuffed out in a snowdrift on the far side of the pond. This sent the crows careering off towards a neighbouring house where they settled untidily on the rooftop, their attention turning once again towards her.

"Shit!" she called out, regretting her action immediately. Then, "Fuck off, you murderous birds!" as if blaming them for her rashness.

Ever since that little Chinese bitch had left thirty minutes earlier, she'd been feeling murderously angry. Who the fuck was she? Why had she been nosing into her affairs? How'd she have the audacity to come to Jane's house and accuse her of killing someone she'd never even met? And what the fuck had she meant by suggesting that Sozo was some malevolent spectre returning to haunt her? What kind of moron did she think she was dealing with?

She shivered, which was strange as she could hardly feel the cold, wrapped up as she was in her coat, hat, and scarf and with the alcoholic fuel of the sake still burning inside her. But she wasn't so drunk as to ignore such a physical warning. Turning towards the door, she gave a start as a sudden explosion echoed through the streets behind her, and she sensed the sky grow lighter. Looking up, she saw the first of the fireworks erupting into the winter sky, circles of white, purple, and orange light blossoming intensely and fading as quickly before other patterns followed in their wake, surging into the air where they flowered in petals of beautiful, fiery colour before disappearing forever.

"Fleurs du feu, fleurs du mal," she said out loud, unaware of why the phrase had suddenly sprung to her lips. Flowers of fire, flowers of evil. Evidently, it'd been inspired by the bitterness she felt on realising that Sozo was not here and would not be coming. After all, this had been the lure, the chance to capture images of the fire flowers from this wonderful vantage point.

And it was, indeed, quite marvellous. The display held her transfixed, and she lingered there, waiting for it to continue. But after two minutes of darkness and silence, she concluded that the display was over. "The light gleams an instant, then it's night once more!" she said, puzzled by how short-lived it had been. The famous quote from *Waiting for Godot* seemed wryly apt as here she was vainly waiting for Sozo.

Once back in her kitchen, Jane remained dressed in her coat and hat while emptying the bottle of sake into a fresh glass. The renewed bodily warmth emboldened her to venture out once more, this time to recover the jade cigarette holder she admired so much, for itself rather than for its nature as a gift, she told herself. Leaving her door slightly ajar, she steadied herself against the slipperiness under foot and walked out onto the lawn.

It was much easier to find than she feared. In fact, it protruded from a snowdrift and, perhaps in some freakish effect of moonlight reflecting from the ice on the pond, was glowing luminously in the shadows.

"Like a will-o'-the-wisp," she muttered as she bent over uncertainly and picked it up. It was clearly clogged with snow and ice, so she raised it to her lips and blew on it, hard.

"Good evening, Professor."

The voice came from behind her. Startled, she turned quickly, her hand raised to her heart in shock.

"Forgive me for startling you. And for being late."

It was him this time. Definitely Sozo. Standing behind her, close enough for her to reach out and touch him if she dared. He was still dressed in his clean white leather and had a large camera case draped across a shoulder.

"The light gleams an instant..." she repeated softly to herself.

"I'm sorry?"

"The fire flowers," she said. "You've missed them."

He smiled.

"No, not at all! That was simply a test run. The display proper will begin in," he consulted his watch, "less than ten minutes." He paused, then said. "I wasn't going to come, you know."

"Then why did you?"

"I came because of you."

She led him into the kitchen, her anger and confusion dispelled, having given way to a giddy sense of drunken pleasure.

"No time for the meal, then!" she said, picking up the glass of sake she'd left on the table and waving her free arm in the direction of the plates of raw food.

"Later, perhaps," he said. "After the hanabi."

Then he looked at her as if a sudden thought had occurred to him.

"I have an idea," he said. "Can we go up to the roof now?"

He studied her with a professional eye, nodding slightly and smiling. She found herself enjoying the experience of being gazed at appreciatively in this way. She wanted him to see her in the white silk dress she'd chosen especially for the occasion, so she replaced her glass on the table and held his gaze as she began to unbutton the coat. But he quickly held up his hand to stop her.

"No, not here, Professor Kaye. Not yet."

"Oh please," she interrupted him in mild irritation. "Jane. Call me Jane. At least for this evening."

"Jane, then." He maintained a professional air as he spoke. "I have glimpsed the white dress beneath the coat. I think some photographs of you dressed in white, in the snow, with the fire flowers lighting up the black sky behind you could be...well, quite spectacular."

Jane said nothing at first. Then, in a voice intended to sound deliberately cold: "I'm no model."

"Ooh, I don't know." He smiled. "You struck a convincing pose yesterday when I gave you the cigarette holder." He pointed to it where it lay on the table next to the glass of sake.

"Besides," he continued, "they will be my gift to you. Not for public display. Something private between us."

The idea of being aestheticised in this way was entirely novel for her. With anyone else, she would have refused. She shook her head, however.

"It's cold, too cold up there."

"Oh, don't worry. We will be done in a very few minutes. Trust me."

Really, she'd already made up her mind. "Just this once," she said. "Why ever not?"

She turned and walked towards the stairs, aware that he was following her a few paces behind. When they reached the roof and stepped into the freezing cold, he began work immediately.

"First, I will try a few practice shots with your coat on. These will be without the flash."

He encouraged her to be natural, to lean back, arms outstretched against the balustrade and face him, smiling; to gaze up at the sky in wonder; to stare over the rooftops as if lost in thought. Despite the blowing wind and the freezing temperature, she found herself warming to the task, dancing from one pose to another as he snapped pictures, uttering words of encouragement as he did so. Occasionally she glanced over to catch his look, but it was always hidden behind the cold, glass eye of the camera.

"Now, quickly, take off your coat for me," he said. "The hanabi is due to commence any second now."

Despite herself, the lust rose from the pit of her stomach as she undid the coat, staring directly into the eye of the camera behind which, she knew, the warm, feathery, foxy eye of Sozo was looking at her and at no one else. She let the coat slide down her body to reveal the tight-fitting dress of white silk.

"Nice!" he said. "Very nice!" And she felt a warm thrill surge through her as the camera flashed and the first of the fireworks erupted in the sky behind her.

For the next few minutes, Jane was aware of nothing but her performance, her dance from pose to pose which became increasingly ecstatic the more the flash of his camera blinded her, and the explosive echoes of the fireworks deafened her, resounding as they did from frozen rooftop to frozen rooftop. All this against the backdrop of the fire flowers themselves, their beauty bathing her gloriously in vividly changing colours that shimmered on the thin white silk of her dress.

Then he stumbled over the discarded coat, still in a heap on the ground, and seemed almost to drop his camera. It was only natural, therefore, that he should stoop to pick it up and throw it over the rail of the glass balustrade. But before it could settle, it was caught by a sudden gust of wind that blew it into the air, and she watched in amusement as it sailed over the garden, sleeves flapping in a ghostly fashion, before it landed, arms outstretched, hanging from the branches of the same tree where the crows had earlier been gathering.

"I will run and retrieve it," he said, lowering his camera into its case.

"Oh, leave it," she said. Her voice was panting in the sudden silence as she placed her hands on the balustrade rail to gaze at the expanse of winter sky above, inky black once more.

"Look," she said, regaining her breath. "It's all over now, anyway."

She heard no reply. Turning her head, she saw that he had vanished. For a second, the door to her staircase hung still and slightly ajar; but then some great force, probably a sudden gust of wind, seemed to grasp hold of it and slam it shut. As the loud bang faded slowly away, like a farewell echo from the firework display, she became aware of the cold intensifying by the second. The dampness between her thighs now felt like a coating of ice, the ache of it spreading upwards, penetrating her insides.

Gasping out loud, bent double, she tried to remove her hands from the balustrade, but they'd become stuck fast. With a loud scream, she finally yanked them clear and staggered backwards, leaving a thin layer of skin, raw and flaky, behind on the rail. Looking down at her hands, now hurting dreadfully, she saw droplets of blood oozing red around her still white palms. Stumbling over to the door, shivering uncontrollably, she grabbed hold of its handle. The pain was excruciating as she pulled at it again and again, unable to grip it properly. In growing panic, she called his name. Her teeth chattered and her voice shook so much that she could scarcely get the words out.

"Sozooo! Sozooo, help me!"

Then, at last, she heard his voice reply to her, not from the other side of the door but from the garden below.

Barely able to control her movements, she slid over to the balustrade and saw him gesturing and calling to her.

"The door," he shouted. "It's stuck fast. You will have to jump!"

"Jump? Impossible!"

"It is your only option," he called. Then, "Otherwise you will freeze."

He looked and sounded calm, his face benign and reassuring.

"Trust me. I will be able to catch you."

She saw him try to reassure her with a smile.

"You are small and light, like a bird. Climb over the balustrade and jump into my arms!"

As she gripped the rail, the pain in her hands became more unbearable than ever. Hauling herself over the balustrade, the cold from the glass penetrated through the thin silk of her dress into every inch of her body. Her screams were constant now but almost inaudible as the wind had sprung up once more. At last, she slid down the outside of the glass, crying out as she nearly slipped off the thin ledge, beyond which there was a steep drop onto the lawn below. She looked up and saw that the crows had returned to their tree and were watching, silent and expectant. Her coat, flapping beneath them, had evidently not frightened them away.

"Jump!" called Sozo, his voice drifting away into the wind. "You must jump now."

Hauling herself to her feet, Jane stood for a second, her hair blowing wildly about her face, her dress billowing in the wind. She saw him spread out his arms, whereupon she let herself fall away into the icy air.

And in that split second, he revealed himself to her as the woman he really was.

SEVEN CURSES

A YOUNG FEMALE police officer was the first to find the body.

It hadn't taken long for Jane's disappearance to become a cause for concern at the university. Everyone knew she never missed lectures, tutorials, or departmental meetings, and no one could recall the last time she'd been ill. After three days' absence, during which time she failed to respond to either emails or phone calls, two colleagues drove over to her address to investigate. No amount of bell-ringing or door pounding had produced any kind of response. On peering through windows, however, they noticed the glow of electric lamps and ceiling lights, despite the fact that it was a sunny, if very cold, day. Fearing an accident of some kind, they immediately informed the police.

When the two officers arrived, they entered the house through the unlocked patio doors at the rear of the property. Drawn by an unpleasant, sickly smell, they made their way carefully into the kitchen, where they found on a table putrid plates of uncooked food—discoloured meat, stinking fish, shrivelled piles of sliced vegetables—along with an arcane-looking cigarette holder and an empty stone bottle patterned with oriental script of some kind.

Discovering nothing else untoward on the ground floor, nor in the bedrooms upstairs, they proceeded up the staircase to the door that led onto the flat roof. Once they unfastened the bolt and gave the door a firm push, a carpet of fresh, virgin snow lay before them, offering no clues. If the missing professor had been up here, they concluded, it hadn't been recently, as it had snowed lightly on the two previous evenings. Spotting the snow-covered outline of an ashtray on the ground near the balustrade, the female officer approached it to inspect when her eyes were drawn towards a black coat hanging in a twisted, frozen form, half-hidden among the branches of one of the trees that bordered the garden below.

A few minutes later, in the garden, while her colleague had been tentatively examining and photographing the coat, she discovered the sodden remains of a book of fairytales lying half-buried under a layer of frozen snow. Thinking nothing of this discovery, her gaze shifted to what looked like an icy trail leading from a spot beneath the roof down the sloping lawn towards the pond.

Her boots sank deep into the crisp whiteness as she trudged slowly over there. It was rather a large pond, she mused as she crouched down to take a closer look at it. Thick ice covered its surface, which was rendered completely opaque by an additional layer of snow. She leant forward and brushed it away with her right hand, protected as it was by a black leather glove. After a few seconds, she let out a horrified gasp.

A pair of eyes, lifeless as glass, stared up at her from the frozen face of a dead woman, as if trapped within the wrong side of some ghastly mirror. Long strands of hair floated eerily in the water beneath the ice, like tangles of thin water snakes writhing in slow motion around the pale blue skin of her cheeks.

The sudden sight of this coffin of ice held the female officer silent and transfixed for several seconds, hypnotised in horror, a spell broken only by the sudden sound of crows cawing from the tree nearby. Looking up, she saw them circling above her partner as he cowered beneath them, waving his cap frantically about his head as if fending off an anticipated attack. The sight struck her as so absurdly comical that, despite the shocking nature of what she had just uncovered, or perhaps because of it, she erupted into an uncontrollable fit of laughter, the loud peals ringing out in an eerie chorus as they blended with the shrieks of the crows—a fitting anthem, she later thought, to mark such a grotesque and terrible death.

Later house-to-house inquiries revealed little. No one had seen or heard anything unusual. At work, too, colleagues of the dead woman expressed nothing but shock and incredulity. One old professor said he'd noticed that Professor Kaye had been drinking at work recently,

SEVEN CURSES

but he himself reeked of alcohol while being interviewed, and the claim had been scorned by all other colleagues and hence dismissed. There being no evidence of foul play, the coroner's verdict was suicide, but the reasons for her taking her own life remained a mystery and a matter of pure speculation.

Only two people, in fact, knew what had really happened but, for one reason or another, nobody thought to ask them, perhaps because they were children.

EVERYONE LOVES FIREWORKS, don't they? Especially children. I'm sure we can all agree on that! So, I know you won't be at all surprised when I tell you the little boy and the little girl had been straining at their window, *oooh*-ing and *aaah*-ing together as they watched them soar through the sky, screaming with glee at the sound of the bangs and whizzes and booms that echoed loudly and delightfully around their very own street.

But if anyone had asked them—which nobody did, by the way—whether they preferred the sight and sound of the fireworks to the sight of the witch dancing crazily around her rooftop, I am not sure what their answer would have been. You see, it was such a funny dance! She made them both laugh as she slipped and stumbled clumsily over the ice while someone whom the little girl said was dressed "just like an arctic fox" took pictures of her with a very expensive-looking camera.

But why was the witch being so silly, asked the girl out loud, to be dancing around in a thin white dress when the weather was so cold that neither of the children had taken off their coats all day, even though they hadn't ventured outside for one single second!

"Oh, look!" the little boy called out. "The witch's cape has flown off without her!"

"And look!" the little girl replied, "the foxy lady has gone down to fetch it for her!"

"Not a woman, a gentleman!" said the boy.

"No, I think it's a lady," said the girl firmly.

They weren't going to agree, that was plain, but then they both let out a groan when the fireworks stopped altogether. Their groan sounded a bit like "*Ooooooohhhhh!*" and was the kind of sound you make when your grumpy uncle has eaten the last chocolate biscuit, or when you wake up and find the snow has melted overnight before you've had the chance to play in it, or when you think it's Saturday, but it isn't and you have to go to school after all. Anyway, the witch was still there to amuse them with her funny dancing. And now it was very funny indeed because her whole body was shaking!

"Like a maraca!" said the girl

"Like a shaker!" said the boy, at which the little girl tutted loudly.

"Shaking like a shaker? That isn't very good! Ms. Peasey would put a red line through that and keep you in at playtime until you thought of something better!"

The boy's face reddened, and he turned his head away but then pointed down to the garden excitedly.

"Look, look, the foxy man is waving at us!"

And indeed, he was! Instead of fetching the witch's cape, he'd gone across the lawn, past the pond, when he seemed to spot them in the window overlooking him.

"She isn't at all cross with us, is she?" said the girl, still insisting that the arctic fox was a female. And they both waved back, as she (or he) pointed up at the roof, as if telling them to look at the silly witch. Which they did and became very excited because she was beginning to climb over the glass wall. And very funny she looked, too, as she nearly slid off the roof altogether.

"Do you think she's going to fly this time?" asked the boy, giggling.

The girl looked serious for a moment as she watched the foxy lady in the garden below call up to the witch and spread out her arms.

"Well," she said, "she will be very foolish if she does. I mean, her cape has already flown off without her and she hasn't anything like a broomstick to sit on."

"Even if she had, she's shaking so much I think she would fall right off it!"

This thought made them both laugh so much that they almost missed it when she *did* take off. At which point they both stopped giggling and let out a gasp as, instead of flying, the witch dropped from the air like a stone; and instead of catching her, the foxy person stepped back and let her hit the ground with a crunch. The children looked on in wonder as the witch slid down the slope of ice, as if on an invisible sleigh, straight into the middle of the frozen pond.

"Oooh!" said the little girl, shaking her head. "Ms. Peasey told us we must never ever try to walk across a frozen pond because in the middle…"

A cracking sound could be heard, growing louder and louder.

"…the ice is very thin…"

And the children watched in silent fascination as the surface of the ice split in two and the witch sank out of sight beneath it. *Plop*! Just like that!

For a moment or two, nothing moved. Then the foxy person spun about and looked up at them both, at the same time describing a perfect circle in the air with their right arm. Then, they placed their right hand on their left shoulder and bowed, ever so gracefully.

"She's taking a bow!" said the girl. "Like an actor at the end of a play!"

"We must clap, then, mustn't we?" suggested the boy.

The girl gave a serious, brief nod. "Yes, we must! It's only polite."

"Yes," the boy agreed. "And I think you were right. He looks like a woman now. And we should thank her for getting rid of the witch for us."

And so, they both clapped loudly as the foxy person looked up and gave them a wicked little smile and a final, graceful wave before disappearing from sight.

CURSE SEVEN
CHINA ROSE

Last is the poet who will find in hell

A fitting place for poets to dwell...

"WILL YOU SIGN this too, please, Professor James?"

A new volume of Rimbaud's poems was placed neatly on the table alongside the copy of Dominic's own book, a study of the nineteenth century French poets known collectively as the *poetes maudits*, or "accursed poets."

"I particularly appreciated your commentary on *A Season in Hell* in chapter seven. This poem has recently become a favourite of mine." The young woman held out an elegant-looking fountain pen, waiting for him to take it.

Dominic was flattered to be asked to sign a copy of poetry written by one of his literary heroes. It helped dispel some of the irritation he felt at being detained a moment longer than necessary in this dingy room above a local library, where the assistants were noisily clearing away the ranks of uncomfortable chairs that'd only been partially filled for his lecture. Just a few of those attending had actually brought a book for him to sign.

"I haven't used one of these in quite a while!" he said with a smile. A few drops of ink dripped on to his palm as she handed it to him. "And now we see why," he added ruefully.

"Oh, I'm sorry!" she said, but he didn't acknowledge her apology.

"And what name should I dedicate it to?" he asked, pulling the copy of the poetry book towards him.

"Rose," she answered.

SEVEN CURSES

"Just Rose?" He was used to Chinese students adopting an English name, but they would often couch it within their given names in the written form.

She smiled her assent and so he wrote on the title page: "Dominic and Rose both love these poems and the spirit of poetry they embody." He signed underneath with his usual flourish and handed the book back to her. She read what he'd written and nodded her appreciation as he turned his attention to his own book.

"The pen," he heard her say, without looking up. "Please accept it as a gift."

Why on earth...? he thought impatiently as he wrote: *"To Rose. May poetry always be a blessing in your life and never a curse."* He'd used this quip before, of course, but when he looked up, the girl called Rose had already gone. Nonplussed, he closed the book and glanced down at its darkly gothic cover, *The Song and the Curse* emblazoned in yellow and orange flames over a labyrinth of tunnels and thin, shadowy figures, evidently intended to represent the doomed poets themselves. Far too sensational for his taste, and as if to confirm the misgivings he had expressed to the publisher, here was a copy, abandoned by its owner in front of the author's own eyes.

He dropped the pen onto the desk in some annoyance and watched as it rolled a few inches before settling. It was slim, light, and elegant in appearance, blue with a chrome pocket clip. But it didn't look expensive and had the initials U E carved into the cap. He had no use for it. The room was empty, and he could see the one remaining assistant hovering impatiently over by the door. Hurriedly, he gathered his things together and gave her a brief smile of acknowledgement as he passed her, the pen remaining on the table, already forgotten.

The Holiday Inn at the edge of town was hardly the most salubrious of places to stay, but at least it was only for the one night. Public lectures and book signings on weekdays were scheduled for the evenings, so it was always going to be too late for Dominic to drive back home to Cambridge.

He'd long since lost his enjoyment for such events, finding them increasingly tedious, albeit necessary, to sustain his reputation as a public intellectual. After all, appearances on radio discussions chaired by Melvyn Bragg and Arts programmes on BBC2 had been as instrumental to his being offered the chair at Cambridge in the previous year as had his wide range of academic publications. Besides, that his reputation should extend well beyond the narrow confines of academia had always been personally important to Dominic James. Fame, he wasn't afraid to admit, mattered to him.

After a light salad supper and one glass of cabernet, he retired to his room to call his wife for a brief chat and to check if everything was fine at home. Abandoning his job at WMU hadn't troubled him, despite the angry, at times tearful, protestations of some of his doctoral students; uprooting his family had, however, been stressful, particularly for his two boys, who were both of secondary school age. But he was certain in time they would come to appreciate how much better it was to live among the glittering spires of Cambridge rather than the shabby dreariness of a bleak city in the West Midlands.

His wife told him that all was well, but it was the tone of her voice rather than her words that reassured him; for halfway through their conversation, he'd ceased to listen to her, becoming preoccupied by the ink stain on the palm of his hand, which he'd been unable to wash off. When he'd looked at it earlier, its shape had reminded him of a small, wild animal, but now it looked more like a flower. Snapped out of his silent reverie by a sudden, irritable query, he pleaded tiredness and promised to send a text when he set off for home the following morning.

SEVEN CURSES

Instead of preparing for bed, however, he sat in front of his iPad at the tiny desk in the corner of the room and searched the internet for images he could use in a forthcoming keynote lecture he'd been asked to deliver to the French Academy. It was the first time this prestigious body had invited him to speak, and it rather thrilled him. He'd only once before attended a conference they'd organised, when he'd delivered a paper on Marguerite Yourcenar's *Oriental Tales*. Not because he liked them particularly; he'd chosen them to address the conference theme on influences of the East on contemporary Western literature. Evidently, it'd been better received than he had thought at the time, for they'd invited him to talk about his new book, in particular the chapter on *Hell and the Demonic*. He smiled and, not for the first time, mused about how he, an ordinary, hard-working, law-abiding family man, was so attracted to literary figures like Byron and Rimbaud, wildly unconventional and very different from himself.

His train of thought was interrupted as an unexpected image filled the screen. It was Umberto Eco, signing a copy of his novel *The Name of the Rose*, smiling enigmatically into the camera. Dominic was wondering what link he had mistakenly pressed when, with a shock, he noticed the distinctive-looking pen that the author was holding between his fingers. It was slim, elegant, and blue, exactly like the pen the young Chinese woman had offered him as a gift.

He sat back in his chair and stared at the screen, his heart beating fast. Umberto Eco. U. E. The successful academic who had made the transition into renowned artist had done so as the owner of a pen identical to the one he'd just carelessly abandoned. Could it be the same one? He shook his head. "Don't be ridiculous!" he said out loud. How could a young Asian woman possibly come into possession of something so precious? And even if she had, why on earth would she have wanted to give it to him?

The thought lingered, however, like an ear worm or an unwelcome melody as it struck such a deep chord within him. For like many other academics, he had found inspiration in Umberto Eco's success; but unfortunately, like practically all such academics and to his intense regret, success as an artist had eluded him. His own book of original poems, published almost a year before, had disappeared without trace, hardly noticed by critics and public alike.

That night, however, he dreamt that he was, indeed, a poet—a *renowned* poet, writing verse that would live on long after all his academic works had been forgotten. A poem of mystery and beauty that flowed from somewhere deep within his soul and onto the page in sublime, musical cadences. A poem written with the very pen that he might well have inherited from Umberto Eco.

He woke up in the early hours in a state of fevered excitement. He could remember it, every word! Half asleep still, he scribbled down the verses he'd dreamt. Everything flowed so easily onto the page until the last stanza. There *was* another stanza, he knew, but he could no longer recall any of it, not one word. In weary desperation, he went back to bed, hoping that in sleep he would remember what he couldn't recall while awake.

The dream, alas, did not return, and when he read what he had written the following morning, his heart sank. This was parody, not poetry.

"It's Tennyson, you idiot!" he swore to himself. "Pure bloody Tennyson!"

Tennyson, whose poetry he'd been forced to learn off by heart at grammar school, was definitely not one of his heroes. Shaking his head in sorrowful disbelief, he nonetheless slipped the poem into his briefcase.

Later, as he breakfasted on muesli, black coffee, and wholemeal toast, he couldn't rid himself of the irrational thought it would've been a different, much better poem if he'd written it down with the right pen. Umberto's pen. He chided himself at his silliness but nonetheless went out of his way to visit the bookshop opposite the library before driving back to Cambridge, telling himself he might as well check if the pen had been found while he was in the neighbourhood. But it hadn't, and throughout the long drive home, he could not shake off a feeling of loss and regret.

"What's that mark on your hand?"

Dominic had driven home without stopping and now sat at the kitchen table, drinking a cup of red bush tea with his wife, when she spotted the ink stain.

"Oh, this. It leaked out of a pen someone lent me to autograph the new book." He paused, then held up the palm of his hand. "Tell me," he asked, "what do you see in it?"

"What do you mean? It's just a messy blue stain that you ought to scrub off."

"No, I mean, do you see a picture of any kind?"

"Oh, don't be silly, Dominic. You sound like Freddie, practising amateur psychoanalysis on any poor victim he can find." Freddie was seventeen years old and the elder of their two sons.

Her husband smiled and took a book from his bag.

"Well, this should keep him occupied for a while. I just bought it this morning for him." He dropped a copy of Freud's *Interpretation of Dreams* onto the table. To his surprise, a troubled look darkened Callie's face. "What's the matter? It may be fantasy, but it's hardly pornography."

"Dom, do you have to go to this conference next week? Where is it again? It's in a castle, you said."

"Le Lude, near Anjou." He sighed. "Look, I'll only be gone for a few days, a week at the most. And you know I can't turn down offers like this." She was still frowning, so he stretched his hand across the table and gave hers a squeeze. "And it won't be that long before the boys are off to university, and you'll be free to come with me on these trips whenever you like."

But her frown deepened, and she shook her head, glancing towards the book.

"You'll think I'm silly but hear me out." She gave a deep sigh. "I had a dream last night, an awful dream, very, very vivid." She looked at him. "I don't normally dream, as you know, but this one frightened me." She gave a short, nervous laugh. "I had to get up and make a drink to calm myself down."

"So… What was so bad about it?"

"It was you. You were in some kind of gloomy, underground chamber, lit by hundreds of candles of different sizes—some tall, some very short. I'd been walking along corridor after corridor, calling your name. When I entered, you were there at the far end, your shadow flickering large on the wall behind you. It all looked grotesque. Threatening." She paused. The memory was obviously upsetting her.

"Go on," he said, frowning.

She let out a deep sigh and continued.

"The candle beside you on the desk was very short, its flame sputtering as though it might die out any second. You were sitting, crouched over a wad of paper, looking tired, thin, much older, scribbling away with a pen. There was an old-fashioned ink bottle next to your hand. Whatever it was you were writing, you were obviously not satisfied with it as you kept scratching it out. But the worst was when I called your name. You heard me and looked up." Tears were now welling in her eyes. "You stared straight at me but didn't recognise me. You saw me, but I could tell you didn't know me as your wife and the mother of our children."

SHE QUICKLY PULLED herself together, of course, trying to make light of it, saying they didn't need Freud or even Freddie to interpret that dream. There was the chapter she'd read and hated in his new book, the one about hell, and the highly unusual fact that this conference was taking place in a castle far away. Not to mention her unhappiness with Dominic spending so much time travelling recently.

She waved away his apology, acknowledging that, of course, she didn't expect him to start organising his life on the strength of something as irrational as a dream. Neither of them was religious or superstitious. Besides, withdrawing from a commitment at such a late stage would greatly damage his reputation for reliability, no matter what excuse he offered to the conference organisers. And an invitation by the French Academy was indeed special. She knew all this; she was herself an academic, after all, and a deeply rational woman.

Dominic had said nothing, only nodded his assent and promised to be back as soon as he could.

Now, as he drove the BMW along the quiet roads near the River Loire, he regretted this promise, wishing he could stay here longer and enjoy the mild March weather, the early signs of spring and the beautiful French countryside. And the space. Not just the geographical space that surrounded him, but the psychic space within him, plagued in recent months by restlessness, a growing dissatisfaction with his current life that he couldn't shake.

It made no sense, but ever since he'd reached the pinnacle of achievement as an academic, he'd come to realise that this was not, at base, what he desired. The ambition that'd driven him in his thirties and forties had been fulfilling, but now, in his fifties, that sense of fulfilment had evaporated. For having reached the summit and gazed into the future ahead of him, he saw only repetition, boredom, and pointlessness. And when he retired, what then? Academic fashions changed so rapidly these days; it was hard to believe that many people would still be reading him, and fewer still once he had "passed," as they said—a euphemism he despised. So, what would he have achieved of lasting significance in his impeccably bourgeois life?

Unlike the poets and artists he wrote about, whose lives were shorter than his but whose work persisted well beyond their deaths, he would quickly be forgotten.

This was the crux of the matter. Dominic James no longer wanted to be Dominic James. Instead, he had a growing longing to be among the select group that Dominic James wrote about. A writer of immortal lines of poetry, verses that would, long after his death, move and inspire, shock and astonish, help shape the emotional lives of women and men. The excitement of having a first volume of poetry published had quickly dissipated into a feeling close to despair as he came to realise his abject failure as an artist.

It wasn't fair. He knew all the poetic devices. He could analyse metaphor and metonymy, scrutinise simile and synecdoche, dissect tropes and tautologies, but couldn't apply this knowledge in any memorable way to his own poems. Reading through them again, what he originally saw as clever he now saw as crass, images intended to be dazzling as predictable and dull, insights meant to be original as mere platitudes. Subsequently, he tried to reconcile himself to his shortcomings as a poet by celebrating all the more his success as a critic, but the restless, hungry feeling persisted. And the dream of the pen, the one he'd so carelessly let go, was haunting him as a symbol of his desire for an alternative life, the life he'd once yearned for as an undergraduate, when he'd written and performed poetry at live events and had verses published in student magazines. Those dreams had vanished over time as the realities of wage earning, marriage, and children had replaced them with other, more worldly ambitions, only to resurface in recent months with surprising forcefulness.

And at the heart of this nostalgia was Petra, his first great love, the music scholar who could play Debussy like no one else—light and airy, misty, finding delicate contrasts of colour and shade as her fingers skipped effortlessly over the piano keys, and her long black hair seemed to hover and swirl in accompaniment to the music. She, too, had been wild and unconventional, a typically gifted artist. One evening she'd abruptly ended their relationship, devastating Dominic for months afterwards.

He was wistfully recalling her—her dark, foreign looks, her beauty and his youthful dreams as he drove into a small town on the banks of the river and stopped for coffee and a sandwich at a quiet café where he could sit outside in the pale sunshine.

While eating, he picked up a copy of a regional paper a previous customer had left on a nearby table. He read how a local farmer, missing for several days, had been found dead in a field; how a poem about a wild animal, written by a teenage girl, had won a local talent competition; and about a local man in his fifties who had lost all his savings after investing them in a ghost crypto account. Apparently, a young Asian woman had befriended him online with the promise of a romantic relationship. Cleverly, she spent weeks grooming him before encouraging him to invest just a small amount that had appeared to realise genuinely high daily profits. If he invested the rest of his savings, she promised he would have enough money to treat her lavishly when she visited France in a few months' time. On transferring the funds, however, his crypto account went dead, and the woman went silent. Dominic shook his head in disbelief as he read, muttering contemptuous remarks about such men and their midlife crises, before calling the server over to pay his bill.

Next to the café was a small librairie[12], where he scanned the shelves for a few minutes before finding a book he thought perfect for Alfie, his younger son, now fourteen years of age and a budding linguist like his father. Dominic still had a fondness for this charming story, and his heart felt lighter as he paid for it. Once back in the car, he wrote a short message on a card he'd also bought and placed it inside the book's front cover before dropping it onto the passenger seat beside him.

A few kilometres beyond the town, he noticed a sign that caused him

---

12 French word meaning "book shop."

to slam on the brakes, sending the book hurtling against the dashboard before rebounding violently back on to the seat. Glancing fearfully into his rear-view mirror, Dominic was relieved to see no cars on the road behind him, only an old man in blue overalls some distance away, cycling slowly in his direction. Quickly, he reversed a few metres and halted in front of the sign that'd caught his attention. Yes, there was no mistaking what he'd read. Pointing down the minor road to his left, the words *Chateau Rose par ici*— 'this way to Chateau Rose."

Just as he'd dreamed it in the poem, the poem that now lay on a crumpled sheet of paper somewhere in his study at home.

But it was also very much alive still in his mind as, gazing at the sign, he began to recite it aloud to himself.

"A river runs through central France
Where I was driving, quite by chance,
And was it fate or happenstance?
A sign appeared that caught my glance
'This way to Chateau Rose.'
Was it the promise in the name?
Was it some fairy's evil game?
I chose it not but still I came
To visit Chateau Rose

I glimpsed its towers as I drove through
An ancient, tree-lined avenue
Of oak and aspen, elm, and yew
So still, despite the wind that blew
Along the lonely track.
I parked beside an outer wall,
Beneath the towers, grey and tall,
And sure I was a voice did call
'There is no turning back.'

SEVEN CURSES

And who was she that waved her hand
From casement high where she did stand,
The mistress, surely, of this land?
Was it a warning or command
A promise or a threat?
Her scarlet dress, her coal black hair,
Her almond eyes, her sultry stare,
This Chinese Rose, she held me there,
As if I owed some debt."

The final verse still eluded him, annoyingly so, yet he knew it was there in his memory, somewhere. It might be worthless as art, but he sensed it held a message for him if only he could remember it. He also had a strong feeling he would find out what this message was if he took that road.

The more sensible thing to do was to carry on to his destination, of course. He checked on his maps app and could find no mention of the chateau, so he had no idea how long the detour would take. But he was tired of always following the safe road, the one well-travelled.

"Do what one of your poets would do, Dominic," he said to himself aloud. "Leap into the arms of mystery and embrace her!"

He pressed the indicator decisively and took the left turn, only vaguely aware of the cyclist approaching him from behind.

THE OLD MAN in the blue overalls wobbled to a stop, steadying himself as his left foot hit the ground, a look of puzzlement on his craggy face as he listened to the sound of the car's engine disappearing into the distance. For a minute, further down the road, he thought he'd glimpsed a signpost on the corner here, where he knew there never had been a signpost before. Now he was reassured to see only the small, ancient menhir that had always been there. He shrugged and screwed up his eyes as he resumed cycling into the direct line of the sun. It must have been a trick of the light, he muttered to himself, and he wondered if the Englishman knew where he was going.

As it turned out, map or no map, the route to the chateau was so complex that Dominic never would've found it if not for the series of signposts that guided him through a network of roads, each smaller and more isolated than the last. Finally, after driving along a dirt track through a dense wood for what must have been over a kilometre, he pulled out into a clearing and paused, the engine still ticking over as he looked about him.

The building was hardly large enough to be called a chateau, but it was nevertheless lovely and beautifully maintained. From where he sat, gazing across the cropped lawn and neatly shaped hedgerows, he admired its smooth walls of polished pink granite, its tall windows, elegant mansard roof of blue slate, bordered on each side by tall, conical turrets topped with intricately carved fleurs-de-lis that pointed upwards to the clouds now gathering in the sky above them. So very, very French.

And nothing, really, like the chateau imagined in his poem.

There was no long avenue lined with trees, no blowing wind, no outer wall, and no woman waving to him from one of the high windows. In fact, there was no sign of anyone here apart from himself.

He parked the BMW to the side of the track, thinking he would at least take a quick tour before resuming his journey, hoping to find an answer to what had drawn him here in the first place. A gust of wind rustled the bare branches of the surrounding trees, where the first buds of spring were only just in evidence. He stood still for a while, once more looking about him. With no sign of a car other than his own, he wondered if there was a garage to the rear of the property. More than likely, the owner was out somewhere, most probably buying provisions. But it was wise to make sure before exploring the property.

He strode across the clean, white gravel path that bordered the lawn towards the steps, also of pink granite, whose carved balustrades—eighteenth century, surely—curved their way up to the large oak door which was painted the same shade of blue as the roof tiles.

It opened as he approached, and he let out a short gasp as the woman from his dream stood before him.

Her hair was thick and jet black but cut stylishly, parted on the left and swept across her forehead, a short fringe curling neatly over her right eye. Her silk dress was tailored in the traditional Chinese style with the high mandarin collar and fitted in a way to emphasise her figure. Pale blue in colour, it was covered almost entirely by an intricate pattern of red roses, a design he might have considered vulgar if worn by anyone else. And, as in the dream, she stared at him, her almond eyes showing no expression as he stood there, stunned by the sudden surprise of her beauty.

He stammered out an explanation for his presence in his near perfect French, nonetheless apologising for how ridiculous it must sound. As she listened, she tilted her head and pouted a little, scanning him with a look that struck him as vaguely predatory and which added to his embarrassment. When she spoke, her French was perfect, with just the hint of an accent.

"Well, the least I can do is let you have a look around since you're here," she said, opening the door wide as an invitation for him to step inside. He did so, gazing up at the broad marble staircase that spiralled between the landings of the two floors above, and heard her turning a key in the lock behind him.

"This place is remote. I always think it best to be extra careful," she said.

He turned to see her looking at him, her head cocked slightly to the side again, staring like some cute but semi-wild animal. This seemed to be a feature of hers. The hint of a smile played along her lips— scarlet, like the roses on her dress.

"But I can tell you're a cultured person, no one for me to fear."

She walked past him through a door, beside which a large vase full of roses stood on a small mahogany table. There was an animal-like quality, too, in the way her body swayed as she moved and in the twitch of her nostrils as she paused to breathe in the scent of the flowers, pink and in full blossom.

"Roses are a favourite of mine. It was the name of the chateau that first drew me to it, in fact, although it actually refers to the colour of the stone—*le granit rose*—and has nothing to do with the flower. But you see, Ch'iang Wei, or Rose, was the name of my grandmother back in China."

"Ah, your 'Granny Rose,'" he said in English, but she gave no indication of having understood the pun or even of having heard him. Instead, she held a flower out towards him and placed it in the palm of his hand.

"Tell me," she said, gazing at the ink stain that still persisted after all these days, "why do you carry the tattoo of a fox in your hand?" He was about to explain when she appeared to lose interest. "No matter. You carry a rose in it now, too."

He stood there, lost in thought for a few seconds. The book he'd bought Alfie also had a fox and a rose at the centre of its story. Another strange coincidence.

He followed her from room to room, each one decorated in exquisite if identical taste throughout. There were lacquered wooden cabinets and desks with thin, delicate legs and intricate carvings of birds and flowers on their panels and drawers. Some were painted in tasteful shades of pink, green, or blue, decorated with paintings rather than carvings. The landscapes and figures they depicted were pastoral, with trees and rivers and birds flying overhead, with men in fine clothes on horseback and women with flowing skirts on swings or in open carriages. But none of these were suggestive of France.

"Chinoiserie[13]," he said, and she smiled.

"Inherited from the previous owner," she explained. The sonority of her voice, the melody of its tone, gave it an otherworldly quality. "Apparently he'd never been to China, but like so many cultured men of his generation, he found the aesthetic fantasy of the orient irresistible."

Dominic said nothing but could empathise with this previous owner, whoever he was. He marvelled out loud at the wallpapers, the rugs, the polished tiles, the vases of varying sizes, mainly filled with different coloured roses, although there were some with orchids, jasmine, and peonies, the hint of their fragrances permeating the air and adding a subtly different quality to the atmosphere in each of the rooms.

The few questions he asked were polite but focused on her rather than on the chateau and its furnishings. Apparently, she hadn't lived here long and never met the previous owner, who died while still in possession. She lived alone but was often away travelling. This much he learned, but little else. The source of her great wealth—for indeed it must be vast for her to be able to buy and maintain a property such as this—she didn't disclose, nor did he feel it discrete to ask. It nonetheless added to his fascination.

One of the rooms was different. Smaller than the others, it was practically empty of furniture apart from a table near a window at its far end. This contained just two small pieces of pottery, a dish and a bowl, both fashioned from porcelain in shades of a delicately nuanced pale green. The design looked distinctly modern to his eye. He mentioned this, and she frowned.

"On the contrary, these are by far the oldest items in the house. Song dynasty, over a thousand years old. Among the few items I brought here myself." She picked up the bowl with her long, slim fingers and handled it without undue care as he watched her, intent on hiding his embarrassment.

---

13 **Chinoiserie**: a style in art (as in decoration) reflecting Chinese qualities or motifs.

"What about these photographs?" He crossed the room to a wall on which several, all monochrome, hung neatly in frames. There was a notable echo from both his footsteps and his voice, so empty was the room. "These are yours, too, I think." He pointed to one of an old woman taken in profile. Her face was lined with age, but nonetheless striking. "And this lady here. Is she your grandmother? She must have been very beautiful when young." He permitted himself a confident smile, which was not returned.

"No. She is, in fact, my great-grandmother, dead for many years now. But yes, she was very beautiful. An actress and a dancer who performed in the Beijing opera. Local women were jealous and called her the 'jade-faced fox fairy.' Which implied she was also a seductress of wealthy and influential men."

She did not say whether there was any truth in this, and he didn't ask.

"She didn't have an easy life, so my grandmother told me."

There was a hint of sadness in her eyes before she turned to a painting on another wall he thought he vaguely recognised. It was a scene set at night, coloured almost entirely in shades of grey and dominated by two hawthorn trees in the middle of a field. The season was evidently winter as the trees were bare of leaves. The looming shape of a dense pine forest could be seen in the distance. Most striking of all was the group of foxes surrounding the trees, all pure white apart from a reddish streak in their tails.

"This is a most impressive piece of work," he said. "The style is not at all Western. Is it Japanese?"

"That's right," she said. He felt pleased with himself. "The original is, anyway. By an artist from the nineteenth century called Utagawa Hiroshige, famous for his woodblock prints. This is my version of it, painted in oils."

He was genuinely impressed and told her so.

"It's a talent I have discovered very recently," she replied and moved to stand alongside him. He caught her scent for the first time and swallowed hard.

"The white fox is special in Japanese countries," she continued. "It has the power to ward off evil and protect maidens who need help."

She paused, so he turned to look at her. She was staring at the painting, lost in thought, with what he took to be a mark of sorrow on her face.

The next room was obviously a library, with shelves of books bound in red leather stretching from floor to ceiling. On a table at an angle, a thick French copy of Dumas' *The Count of Monte Cristo* had a shiny metal bookmark protruding from the final pages, as if she was currently reading it and was almost at its end. He looked up to see a slim ladder hanging from a runner that would allow easy access to the higher shelves.

Forever drawn to books, he glanced at the titles. They were in French, which was unsurprising, but every one appeared to cover a different aspect of Chinese culture or history. There were volumes of traditional tales, of classic works of literature that Dominic had heard of, but few of which he'd managed to read in English. One of them he recognised in translation as *Dream of the Red Chamber*, the first volume of which he'd read in the Penguin edition some years before. There were volumes of Chinese art and art criticism, of the country's history and geography, and of poetry written by Chinese poets from ancient times. Some of their names he recognised, others he knew nothing about. From the way the young woman was looking at him, he felt she was relishing the discomfort of his ignorance.

"I think I should go now," he said, looking at his watch.

"Oh, take a look at this before you do," she said, suddenly speaking in English and pointing to a signed, framed photograph on one of the shelves.

Dominic approached and glanced at it, then stood still, wide-eyed. "How is this possible?" His voice was scarcely more than a whisper.

"Apparently, he was an acquaintance of the previous owner." Her

English was perfect, slightly accented like her French, but this time he thought he recognised her voice. "He got the idea for the novel that would make him famous while on a visit here, discovering the chamber that lies beneath the cellar. And he decided to commemorate this inspiration in the title."

Dominic stared in disbelief at the same photograph of Umberto Eco that had appeared unsolicited on his laptop several days earlier; although he said nothing, she could evidently read in his eyes the question he wanted to ask—"Who exactly are you?"—a question that she answered only partially.

"You were right, Dominic. It *was* his pen, the very same. And you now have a second chance to accept my gift. And this time you will have the chance to test it, too. Come. I'll take you to it."

DOMINIC WONDERED IF it was wise to follow her, but trailed after her, nonetheless. Unlike some of his colleagues, he'd never been a philanderer; beauty for him had always centred upon aesthetic appreciation rather than sexual desire. But there was some quality in this woman that operated like a magnet on his willpower. Watching the natural, graceful way she moved, he imagined her feet dancing over piano keys to a melody by Debussy.

So, he followed her. Into a yard to the rear, where it would have been simple for him to skirt around the side of the chateau, find his car and drive away. Instead, he walked behind her to a small outbuilding, inside which was an ancient-looking door that she opened with an impossibly large key. He hesitated before stepping through it, but step through it he did, watching impassively as she unhooked an antique lamp from the wall to her left and lit the candle within its glass casing. The new light illuminated a flight of spiralling stone steps that descended, steep and well worn, into the darkness below.

SEVEN CURSES

"The cellar leads directly to the underground chamber that so fascinated your hero. He wrote the first drafts of the opening pages there, in fact." She spoke without looking at him as she made her way down the steps, evidently confident he would follow her. Which he did, stepping gingerly and holding on to the wall for support.

Once in the cellar, she held the lamp aloft. From the patch of light where they stood together, he could see that it was long and rectangular, with a vaulted brick ceiling and large barrels lined along one of the walls. She saw him looking at them. "All empty now," she said, reading his thoughts. "Wine is not my drink. Stay close to me."

There was a rough oak door barely distinguishable at the far end of the cellar. As she walked over to it, the flickering candle cast wavering shadows across the floor and on to the wall. The door led into a narrow tunnel hewn directly, if roughly, out of the rock. Dominic was quite a tall man and had to crouch as he made his way along it for what seemed an inordinate length of time. The smell was earthy, and the walls became increasingly moist and slimy as they approached what sounded like flowing water. Suddenly, the tunnel opened up before them, and in the light of the lamp, he could see they'd reached the bank of an underground stream at least five metres wide and flowing very fast. There was no telling how deep it might be.

She must have seen the worry on his face. "Take my hand," she said. "And close your eyes. I will lead you across."

Again, he hesitated as she stretched out her hand towards him. Then, obediently, he closed his eyes and took it in his own, whereupon the effect was immediate and extraordinary. It was as if they floated above rather than walked across the water. When he felt the earth beneath his feet again, he opened his eyes and, gazing down at his shoes, which he could only just make out in the light of the lamp, he saw no sign of dampness. The woman was already walking into the darkness ahead and he stumbled after her, by now more apprehensive than curious. After several metres, she stopped and turned.

"We're here," she said simply. "Just follow me up these steps."

They were to her right, seven of them, and led to a door identical to the one that had led them out of the cellar. A key was already in the lock, which she turned.

"Come, take a look."

She stepped through the door. He followed her out of the darkness.

The room was cavernous, but not large. Like the tunnel, the ceiling was hewn out of bare rock, as were the walls, to which lamps identical to the one she held were attached at even distances, glowing dimly to provide just enough light to see comfortably by. The fact that they were already lit, he found rather sinister. He told her so, but she ignored him once again as though she hadn't heard.

Instead, she made her way across the floor of paved flagstones to the large, old-fashioned desk, thick and sturdy, that dominated the room. There she placed the lamp. Behind the desk stood a chunky wooden chair with a red cushion on its seat. She bade him sit down while she took a few short steps over to the divan positioned along the far wall, against which he could see a line of embroidered cushions. She sat with silent gracefulness, drawing her feet onto the bed and curling her knees up towards her chest. Her eyes sparkled in the candlelight, and he was briefly unnerved by the effect it had on her gaze, that struck him now as seductive, though paradoxically overlaid with a quality of innocence.

Once seated at the desk, his attention was drawn to the small bookcase to its side, filled as it was with volumes bound in red leather, similar to those he had seen in the chateau's library. He began to lift up the lamp, the better to see them.

"There are candles and a holder in the desk drawer, the one on the right," she informed him.

He put down the lamp and opened the drawer to find a thick, squat candlestick holder made of brown pewter alongside what must have been over two dozen candles and several boxes of matches. He fixed a candle into the holder, lit it, and held it in front of his face, gazing about the room, whose whole appearance now struck him as eerily familiar, like something he'd seen on a stage or imagined in a dream. Or perhaps seen in a painting. The quality of the light shining in the darkness, the age and style of the furnishings, brought to mind Caravaggio. Even the woman herself, in the way her hair fell loose across her shoulder as she leaned back on the bed and fixed him with a nonchalant, almost amused look, made him think of Titian's *Venus*, radiating light in the darkness.

She pointed a casual finger to a small table in front of her that he hadn't noticed before, where oranges were laid out on a pale green plate reminiscent of the pottery from the Song dynasty he'd seen earlier. She helped herself to one and cut out a segment with the sharp blade of a silver fruit knife, fashioned in the shape of a dagger. There was a small jar of salt on the table, and she sprinkled a few grains that melted like snow on the flesh of the fruit that she then sucked, puckering her lips, before biting into it, slowly wiping away with her thumb the juice that trickled below her bottom lip and glistened red as she licked it clean with the tip of her tongue. He mopped his brow with a table napkin, loosened his collar, and watched the sensual dance of her fingers as she dipped them into a small bowl of rose water to clean them. She then cut another segment and leant forward, holding it for him to take. He noticed again the long, thin quality of her fingers as he did so, the fingers of an artist, he thought, rather like Petra's. But when he bit into the fruit, its juice tasted bitter, and he screwed up his face as he swallowed, whereupon she smiled with what appeared to be a look of pleasure, or perhaps of satisfaction.

"So. You have visited the underworld and tasted the fruit of the fairies, Dominic. That's good. You will find the pen in the other desk drawer, the one on the left, with all the paper and ink you will need to try out its power."

Sure enough, when he slid the drawer open, he found the pen lodged neatly between a pad of paper and the wooden frame. He took it out and stared at the initials U.E., shaking his head.

"I don't understand any of this. Why me? Why here?" He looked up. She stared at him, her head cocked to one side in that manner of hers. "And who exactly are you?"

Once again, she helped herself to a slice of orange, followed by the ritual cleansing of her fingers before she replied.

"It's a long story, a fairy story, really. It ended when my life changed profoundly, so profoundly that I can only describe it as a death followed by a rebirth as someone far stronger and more powerful than my former self." She leant forward ever so slightly. "And I know you have a strong desire to be reborn, too, as your true self, as the poet you always longed to be. That pen you are holding," she nodded towards it, "it's really only a symbol of the real gift I'm offering you—the chance to let go of your old life, as I did, and reinvent yourself here in this chamber, away from the distractions of the world, the demands of your career." She paused very briefly. "And those of your family."

He found it hard to hold the intensity of her stare.

"But I can't," he answered eventually. "I must go. I'm expected. The Academie Francaise…"

"… Is just an old boys' network with a few old girls thrown in for appearance's sake! Dominic…" She sighed and softened her tone, almost purring now. "No one will miss you for a week. Surely?" She stretched out her hand across the table and gently caressed the back of his.

She was right. No one would. He'd told Callie the phone signal might be very weak here, and that she shouldn't worry if she heard nothing from him. He looked about the chamber—strangely atmospheric, a good place to dream. To write. He looked at the woman who called herself Rose and fancied once again he could see something of Petra in her, this time in the way she was looking at him.

"But how could you know all this about me?"

She seemed to consider for a moment how much she needed to explain to him.

"It's one of the powers I now have since my rebirth. The ability to see people's hidden desires." She paused. "Some I choose not to help. Those who desire power for their own petty ambitions. Or sex—so pathetic. Or love and admiration—so weak. But some people I choose to help. You, for instance. I always admired the breadth of your knowledge, the clarity of your insights. I wanted to study under you once, you know. Before."

He nodded, rather flattered. If she really could read people so well, he could see why she admired him over those with the other desires she'd mentioned.

"And today, if I am not mistaken, you seemed to be expecting me?"

She turned his hand over gently, and with her forefinger followed the outline of the fox—most definitely a fox—on his palm.

"Oh, lures, charms, enchantments..." Her lips twitched in and out of a brief smile. "I have access to those now, too."

The electric touch of her finger made him ignore—or was it accept?—the improbable implications of everything she was telling him. His will power ebbed away in her direction, and she must have realised this, gently removing her hand from his as she eased herself out of the divan with natural, animal grace. She looked about the chamber.

"These walls. They are rather bare. I'll do something about that." Walking towards the door, she said, "You must be very tired. I'll come again tomorrow, but I think you ought to sleep now."

Overcome by a sudden intense weariness, Dominic took the few steps over to the divan and lay his head down on one of the cushions that still held the impress of her body. Her lingering scent, too—it surrounded him, and his head began to swim as he drifted off immediately into a deep and dreamless sleep.

When Dominic awoke, he had no idea whether it was morning or not, as no natural light could ever reach this chamber. He looked at his watch. Annoyingly, it had stopped, evidently soon after he'd entered the room on the previous afternoon.

He sat up and helped himself to one of the oranges still on the table beside him. The dagger Rose had used was no longer there, so he peeled it with his fingers. When a jet of juice spurted from it over his fingers, he recalled the way she'd slid her thumb under her lip to wipe it clean as she ate. The taste seemed less bitter today—sweet, even—and he swallowed it greedily, then helped himself to another.

He cleaned his fingers in the rose water as she had done and felt in his pocket for his phone—it would at least give him the time. But his pocket was empty, and he realised he must have left it in the car. Letting out a sigh of frustration, he thought he'd need to retrieve it later. Or perhaps Rose might fetch it for him.

Standing up to stretch, he saw, much to his surprise, in the flickering half-light, a painting hanging on the wall above the bookcase. It was exactly the same as the one he'd seen the day before in the room that contained the priceless pottery. The candles in both the lantern on the desk and in the candlestick holder had burned down overnight into nothing more than stumps. Those on the walls had completely burnt out. Quickly, he replaced the candle in the pewter holder with one from the drawer and held it up to study the painting once more.

"Yes, it's the same one."

Her voice startled him, and he let out a gasp as he turned to see her standing by the door, motionless in the shadows. He hadn't noticed her earlier and certainly hadn't heard her enter the chamber. She emerged into the candlelight and crossed the room silently to stand next to him. Today she wore a loose-fitting red dress that exposed the pale amber skin of her neck and shoulders. Her scent was different, too; subtle, but with something wild about it, he thought, before dismissing this as utter foolishness.

"Sometimes I look at this painting for so long that I feel I lose myself in it." She stared at it almost wistfully. "Tell me, how many foxes do you see?"

Dominic counted them. "Twenty-three."

She nodded. "Sometimes I imagine I see a twenty-fourth."

He counted them again. "I'm fairly certain there are only twenty-three…"

She whirled away from the painting and pointed to the desk.

"Today I suggest you read," she said. "I've selected two volumes. One you know already, but he is worth revisiting. The collected poems of a significant nineteenth century French poet who was a teacher like yourself." She smiled. "And no one remembers him today for his teaching, of course. This second will be new to you. He died young and is known as the ghost poet of ancient China. Translated into French in this rare volume."

He picked up one tome then the other, opening each in turn, flicking through their pages, lifting them to his nose and relishing the touch and the smell of leather and paper of such fine quality.

She watched him, amused.

"They're beautiful," he said. "I will love reading these."

"And when you're hungry, there."

She pointed to the table, which now displayed a spread of bread, cheese, apples and a jug of water. He was becoming used to her conjuring tricks and expressed no astonishment. She turned as if to leave him.

"Will you be joining me later? For lunch?"

"Oh no. You need the time on your own."

"Oh, my phone," he remembered. "I must have left it in the car. The keys are…" Once again, he searched in his pockets but found nothing.

"I have them, don't worry. They're safe. And you won't be needing your phone."

"But my watch appears to have broken. To know the time, I…"

"Oh, time, time," she interrupted. "Time is another distraction to be discarded, a trap from which I have released you, Dominic. Time has no place here. There is just yourself and your poetry."

"And you, of course."

She paused. "Of course."

He laughed nervously. "It seems our roles have reversed."

"Meaning?"

"Meaning that you wanted me to be your mentor and now you are acting as mine."

"Your mentor…and perhaps your muse?"

HE FOUND IT such a pleasure to read with a creative rather than a critical eye, losing himself for hours in the mysterious visual worlds evoked by each of the poets, luxuriating in the beauty of their imagery. Noting those images on paper that he found particularly striking, he attempted various translations into English, playfully mixing the metaphors and symbols of different poems into short, new poems of his own.

After what must have been several hours of such play, he devoured the food hungrily and, lantern in hand, left the chamber for the first time only to stop at the stream, where he stripped off his clothes and washed as best he could, not daring to step into the water that rushed like a torrent into a narrow underground passage to his left and which he could hear plunging downwards to greater depths. The distance across to the opposite bank seemed much greater than it had the day before—an optical illusion, he thought, as the lantern seemed unable to cast any light beyond the fast-flowing water.

He realised for the first time that he would never be able to return safely across these waters alone.

Later, he lay on the bed and dozed. When he awoke, the light from the lamp's candle had burnt out, and he stared into a darkness that revealed no shapes, no shadows, nothing of the room around him. Unnerved, he lowered himself carefully off the bed and crawled across the floor, groping ahead of him until he found one of the desk legs, then feeling gradually upward until he located the drawer, its handle, and slid it open. He cursed when he felt inside and found only paper—it was the wrong drawer. Once he had the correct drawer open, he quickly found a box of matches and, fumbling at it, spilled many of them onto the floor. Finally, he managed to strike one alight, but he still breathed uneasily until he could use the meagre flame to locate and light a fresh candle, which he quickly secured in the pewter candlestick holder.

Dominic hated the darkness—the absolute nature of its blackness—and vowed never to let the candle go out again. He looked again inside the drawer and saw his supply had already notably diminished; he must ask Rose to bring more for him.

His eyes were drawn to the painting, and he wondered ruefully if, instead of counting sheep, the Japanese counted foxes to help them sleep. He numbered them as twenty-four. Surely this was wrong. He tried again. Twenty-four, there was no doubt. He scrutinised the picture closely. One fox seemed to be slightly further from the pack, as though prowling in the direction of the forest in the background. He couldn't recall noticing it before. Perhaps this was the one he'd missed?

When he slept again, he dreamed vividly of Rose. She was wearing the same red dress he'd last seen her in, the one that fell loosely off her shoulders, as she crawled on all fours across the floor towards him. Her face, as beautiful as ever, also had more of a feral quality, in the way her nose twitched and her head moved slightly but sharply in different directions, as though seeking the scent of a particular prey, while her eyes displayed an expression both timid and wild, what the French call *farouche*.

As she drew closer to him, a pale shudder of nakedness let slip that fragrance he had smelled the day before—a promise of wild delights, of a life less empty of ordinary dreams. He felt giddy as the touch of her lips rippled across his cheek, but she drew away before he could respond.

Now the image changed, and he grew cold as she ran ahead of him into a mist, her dress slipping lower and lower from her shoulders but never quite revealing her full nakedness before a rising swirl of vapour covered her completely.

He awoke, the images still fevering his imagination as he recalled their beauty, not without a pervasive sense of loss. Once he'd bathed and eaten, he returned to his desk and picked up Umberto's pen. By the time Rose reappeared—and he had no idea at all what time this actually was—he'd scribbled and discarded a number of verses, but there were two he'd put aside, though neither yet had a title.

She picked up the first of these without waiting for an invitation.

Elusive spirit
Woman
I wish to perpetuate your amber flesh
Your hair hovering drowsily
Dark with perfume
Did I love a dream?
Cruel illusion
Triumphant error of an ideal Rose
Whose fragrance faded
Weeping like a spring
This dawn is a rebirth
Also a death.

He held his breath as she read it, admiring the stylish traditional dress with the mandarin collar she wore, which today was white with a faint silver floral design and red edging.

"Well, better than your usual offerings, don't you think?"

He inclined his head with a weak smile of agreement, disappointed by the lukewarm nature of this response.

She replaced it on the desk and picked up the second one.

SEVEN CURSES

The smile
That hid the red edge of her lips
Blossomed into laughter
A drunken bloom
That made the space between them shiver
And her kiss
A subtle lie that grazed his cheek
Her breath
Becoming hoar frost on his skin
A cold but pure delight
It lingered still
A fragile tang of beauty
Like twilight.

She pouted when she finished and gave him an inscrutable look.

"Dreams," she said, glancing once again at the paper in her hand. "Some people's secret desires are so evident they are hardly a secret at all. And some, along with fears and anxieties, declare themselves in dreams. But you know your Freud, of course."

She placed the poem on the table, this time in front of the poet. "You probably think these honour me in some way. Or perhaps it's a youthful, lost love you describe, her ghost finding shape in my body. But just read the last line for me."

He didn't have to read it.

"Like twilight," he said, almost in a whisper; then, clearing his throat, he repeated it more loudly. "Like twilight."

"Now say it again, just the vowel sounds this time."

Puzzled, he looked at the words.

"I—I—I…" he said.

"And again."

"I—I—I!"

"In other words?"

Understanding clouded his expression.

"It's about me," he said, surprise in his voice. "It's all about me."

"The woman in these poems, whoever she is, is just a peg upon whom you hang your desires, your sense of impotence, your self-pity. I quite like them, I do! *Triumphant error of an ideal Rose.*' Is that line really yours? *'A fragile tang of beauty.*' But the emotions are juvenile, Dominic. It's quite pathetic, really."

Her words utterly deflated him.

"I wasn't always beautiful or desirable, you know." Her tone had changed, as though she was confiding in him. "When I came to the west to study, first in Paris then in your country, I was rather plain, very easy to ignore. Just one more quiet Asian student, good for college finances but little else. Easy to abandon, quick to forget."

She paused and gave him a harsh look whose significance he failed to comprehend.

"I find that very hard to believe. What happened when…what you call your rebirth?"

She moved to the painting and gazed at it for a few seconds before she answered.

"My parents both died when I was a little girl, so I was brought up by my grandmother. I was a difficult child, and she often shouted at me, saying that I must have been swapped for a fox fairy when I was a baby. Sometimes, when my behaviour made her very angry, she would threaten to throw me out of the house and invite the fox fairies to take me back. Fox fairies," she stretched out her hand slightly as though she might caress the foxes in the painting, "those semi-immortal female spirits I used to read about in folktales and ghost stories, forever young and beautiful but also cunning and cruel."

She seemed to be fondly recalling this grandmother, now most probably dead.

"I see now that she was worried about me growing up in a way that would make it difficult for me to fit into ordinary society. Of course,

I *liked* hearing this, that I had fox fairy blood in my veins. It made me feel rather proud, even though I never believed it. I wasn't pretty, just a bookworm with very few friends. But my grandmother did warn me that one day, if I didn't learn to control my temper, the fairy spirit that lay dormant within my soul might rise up, summoned by some powerful, uncontrollable emotion."

She paused and turned to face him.

"I was never happy at your old university. I was patronised, humiliated, ignored, insulted… I know many other Asian students felt the same. But I was assaulted, too, and even poisoned—can you believe that? Each offence I could manage on its own, but with one piling up on top of the other, I felt I was being crushed under the pressure. Outside I looked calm—we Asians often do. Inside I was a volcano ready to explode."

It was clear from her face whatever events had finally caused this explosion had been traumatic, perhaps too traumatic for her to talk about.

"Then, imagine the single person you care about most in the world, the person who keeps you sane, who alone seems to make life bearable at times, is suddenly snatched away by acts of such selfishness, such carelessness…and so unnecessarily. You're helpless as you see him, unable to breathe. You're with him when he dies. What do you feel? Sorrow? Grief? Of course you do—but later, you feel *rage*, such immense rage swelling within you, surging through your blood into every muscle, taking over your body, transforming you…"

She looked again at the painting.

"…then taking you home, back to the forgotten lands of your ancestors, to where fairies and demons show themselves rather than remain hidden, speak rather than remain silent, where they sing and dance their magic into existence. Their magic, their charms…" Her face hardened once more. "Their curses."

Her anger was cold but palpable. He waited for her to speak again. When she did so, she'd regained her usual composure.

"Do you know what has made me beautiful? Power has made me vengeful, and vengeance has made me beautiful. Can you write that into a poem, Dominic?"

He said nothing, unsure if she was being serious or mocking him.

"If you must dream me into a poem, dream me as the fox, not the rose—the sorrowful fox, the vengeful fox, the fox who must be feared."

She left him as abruptly as she'd appeared, once again doing so without him seeing her leave and before he had made his request for candles. At least there was food and water on the table.

Later, he looked again at the painting, specifically at the white foxes. He still counted twenty-four and was surprised to see that the fox that stood alone in the field was closer to the wood than he remembered.

He lay on the bed and tried to sleep. Her story left him troubled and fearful. No matter how fanciful it sounded, her anger had been real enough, as had her thirst for vengeance. Although relieved at not being implicated in her misfortunes, he needed to leave. The place was losing its charm. How many days had it been? He was still trying to decide as he drifted off to sleep.

DOMINIC DID DREAM of Rose—or rather of Rose-as-a-fox—and spent the hours after waking writing his dream into verse, composing two poems from the powerful visions that had come to him in the night. He called them songs as there had been music, too—strange, sinister music in his dreams. And a repetitive chant, a curse. As an afterthought, he tried playfully to dispel the underlying fear he now felt in the form of a short children's rhyme. Then he waited.

For a while he thought she would not come today—if it was today and not tonight. When she did reappear, she was wearing white, her hair tied back in a ponytail, held in place by a red ribbon that dangled below the knot and half-hidden amid the black tresses. She had a distracted, somewhat impatient air about her, as if she had a pressing need, or just a strong desire, to be somewhere else. He handed her his poems and waited as she read them. So far, they'd not spoken to each other, which he found discomforting.

She read the children's rhyme first and scoffed.

"Oh, don't use me to frighten children," she said. "Children have nothing to fear from me."

He grew increasingly anxious as she read the others, waiting for her judgement. When she finally spoke, she continued to glance through them while holding them in her hand.

"Dominic, these are really not bad. Not bad at all. You've captured your dream quite well. Your dream and my reality."

He heaved a sigh of relief, only now realising he had been holding his breath all this time.

"I did as you suggested," he said, seeking further approval.

She nodded.

"I was close to death, you know. And those emerald hills. You can't see them in the painting. They stretch for many miles beyond the forest."

He frowned, never having thought that there was anything representative or real in the painting, seeing it just as some ideally imagined dreamscape.

"I also like the line about the cowering scholars, powerless now."

She gave him one of her inscrutable looks but then smiled broadly.

"You see? Our plan is working. We will have a whole volume ready by the time you leave here."

Despite the praise, his heart sank.

"Oh… I was thinking I might leave very soon. Surely the week is almost up. It's so hard for me to tell down here." He paused. "Is it?"

She didn't answer but picked up a pen.

"The curse," she murmured to herself and began scribbling underneath the second of his poems.

"You've definitely restored my confidence," he continued. "And my desire to become the poet I always wanted to be. In that sense, I... I am reborn, a...as you proposed."

She shook her head and continued to write.

"Not yet, Dominic. You're not ready yet. You're giving up too soon." Then, in a whisper, "In curses seven, my legacy." Louder now. "There, that completes it!" Putting down the pen, she scanned what she'd written, then took his hand gently in hers.

"Don't disappoint me. Think of everything I'm doing for you, helping you write those immortal lines so the name of Dominic James will stretch into eternity. That's what you want, isn't it? To become... eternal?"

As ever, her willpower was too strong for him. Any sign of resistance faded quickly, and the tension in his muscles weakened. She must have felt this, for she let go of his hand and stood.

"Why not write about your own experience, this time honestly?" she said, turning towards the door. "Revisit that poem you remembered from your dream, the one you told me about when you first came to my door. Why not begin with that?"

This time he did see her leave, and just as she closed the door, he remembered.

"Candles!" he called out. "I need more candles!"

He rushed over, pulled the door open, and called again. Hearing no response, he stumbled down the steps towards the pitch darkness of the stream. Surely, she couldn't have crossed it already. He cried out her name, "Rose! Rose!" but only the hollowness of an echo sounded in response.

He let out a shriek of disgust. Something had brushed past his legs. A rat? Surely it had been too large for that. Perhaps it was nothing but a draft of air? Whatever, he dared not stay out here any longer, and he used the narrow shaft of light flickering from within the open door to guide him back into the chamber. It was only then that he wondered how Rose, since leading him here, had been able to come and go, apparently without the aid of a lamp or a candle of any kind.

The table beside his bed was empty, and he felt a hollowness in his stomach as he realised there was neither food nor water on the table.

HE SLEPT, BUT his hunger and thirst awakened him. He dreamed, however, once again as Rose had suggested he might, of his journey and arrival at Chateau Rose; this time, miraculously, he could recall the final missing stanza of the poem once he awoke. Quickly he wrote it down, as if it might vanish from his mind at any moment. Sitting back at his desk, he read it aloud to himself.

> *"The days have passed, she holds me still,*
> *She is the mistress of my will*
> *And here I stay, she says, until*
> *It please her that I go.*
> *And she has set a task for me*
> *To create lines of poetry*
> *Worthy of immortality*
> *Or rest here for eternity*
> *La Dame de Chateau Rose."*

He wasn't sure if he was recalling the last line correctly, but he preferred this version to the alternative, *"Damned in Chateau Rose,"* which, in any case, didn't scan properly.

In vain, he waited for her to come, too distracted by hunger to read or write or even to think. At one point, he took the lamp down to the stream and stood there, bellowing his tawdry parody of Tennyson into the empty darkness, laughing insanely at the cacophony of distorted rhythm and rhyme that rebounded back to his ears.

Later, after what must have been many restless hours, he managed to sleep but awoke hungrier and thirstier than ever. Taking the empty jug from the table, he carried it down to the stream and dipped it just below the surface, pouring the water he captured greedily down his throat. It tasted sour. It might contain pollutants that could make him ill, but what choice did he have?

Four hours later, he was vomiting violently and lay on the bed for a long time with stomach cramps. He found himself staring up at the painting. Something had changed. He could swear it.

Staggering over to the wall, he leant one hand on the desk and righted himself so he could see it better. Dumbfounded, he saw the fox in the field had almost disappeared, just a small ribbon of red tail marking the spot in the forest into which it had vanished.

He watched the candle in the pewter holder burn down completely before lighting the wax stump that remained in the lamp. He knew he had to get out somehow. When the cramps subsided, but feeling very weak still, he took hold of the lamp and made his way slowly once more down to the stream. Placing it carefully on the ground, he studied the rushing waters. He wasn't a good swimmer, but surely, he could make it across to the other side. Perhaps the stream wasn't that deep.

Slipping off his shoes, he sat on the bank and dangled his legs over the side. The current felt strong. He counted to three, then to ten, before finally plucking up the courage to lower himself into it. Immediately he felt himself being swept under the surface, drawn uncontrollably towards the black hole into which the stream flowed at the far end of the cavern. Gasping for air, he tried in vain to swim towards the opposite bank, splashing violently but helplessly, using all his strength just to stay above the surface.

As he was dragged into the black hole, beyond it the water was, as he had thought, rushing even faster into some cascade, and he would be dragged deeper into the earth if he let it take him.

SEVEN CURSES

Terrified, he stretched up one of his hands to the roof of the tunnel to search for a handhold of some kind. It slid along solid, jagged rock that cut into his skin before it detected a long, thick root which he grabbed hold of in desperation. In his fear, he found the strength needed to drag himself across to the side of the tunnel, where he stretched out his free hand, searching for more roots that might be strong enough to support him against the relentless force of the current. To his great relief, he was slowly able to work his way back out of the tunnel and on to the side of the bank, several metres down from where he'd left the lamp. Using all his remaining strength, he hauled himself out of the water and collapsed onto the wet ground, breathing heavily, his heart thumping, elating in his narrow escape.

His elation, however, was short-lived. Once recovered from his exertions, it became clear his situation had worsened. There was evidently no way he could escape if Rose didn't return. And for reasons he was only now beginning to understand, he felt a dreadful sense of certainty she never would. For he suddenly knew who she was—or, rather, who she had been.

He staggered back to the chamber, the flame in the lantern flickering as the wick burnt out. It died just as he reached the desk, plunging him into profound darkness. Soaked through and aware that blood was seeping steadily from the cut in his hand, he groped for the drawer and pulled it open. He felt inside for the remaining candles and matches but found none. Stupefied, he tried again. It was completely empty. This was impossible. Frantically, he opened the second drawer and swept his hand around inside it. There was nothing but the pen. Not even any paper.

In despair, he took out the pen and sat there, water steadily dripping onto the desk, before hurling it into the darkness while cursing himself, his vanity, his stupidity, and the appalling fate that now awaited him.

THE GENDARME[14] PARKED at the end of the track and made his way slowly towards the car, whose shape could be distinguished through the bushes and undergrowth. Once he had checked the make and the number plate, he returned to his own vehicle and radioed through a report confirming that the car spotted during the helicopter search did indeed belong to the missing British academic.

Picking his way carefully through the long, knotty grass, he made his way back to the car, a BMW, and slipping on his gloves, tried the passenger door. It was unlocked and slid open easily. Leaning inside to scan the interior, he saw no sign of any keys, just a copy of Saint Exupery's ever popular *Le Petit Prince* lying loose on the passenger seat. He smiled; this had been a particular favourite of his when he was young.

Opening one of the rear doors, he spotted a thin leather case behind the driver's seat. He pulled it out and unzipped it carefully. Inside, he found a laptop and a printed set of notes for the speech the professor had evidently intended to deliver at the conference in Le Lude. The conference that did not exist, that the Academie Francaise had never heard of. The gendarme frowned as this discounted one theory—that Professor James had been lying to his wife and colleagues. For some reason that yet remained a mystery, he'd genuinely believed in this fictitious invitation.

Replacing the case where he found it, the gendarme closed the car doors and looked about him. Apart from the wind blowing through the branches of the trees in early bud, there was no sound at all. That was hardly surprising. The place was so remote that it might never have been found if not for the report of an eyewitness, an old man who'd seen a BMW with GB plates turn on to a side road that led in this direction. Even then, the professor must've driven for several kilometres along roads and tracks, ever smaller and more remote, in order to arrive here. The gendarme had struggled to find his way and taken several wrong

---

14 **Gendarme:** a member of a body of soldiers especially in France serving as an armed police force for the maintenance of public order.

turnings, despite the precise geographical location the helicopter had provided him with. More than once, he'd remarked that the route seemed to have been deliberately designed to avoid coming close to any of the cottages or farmhouses that lay scattered among the dormant vineyards along the route.

And why here, after all? What could there be of interest in the ruins of a house that might have been grand in its heyday a hundred years ago but had evidently been abandoned for several decades?

He used his baton to hack a path through the many thorn bushes that thrived in what must have once been the garden and that all but hid the steps that led to a door, half-hidden behind branches of ivy growing thickly up the wall and into the roof. Groping through the foliage, he found the handle of the door, but twist and push as he might, it would not open.

He stepped back and looked upward. This building must have been beautiful once. Now its pink granite walls were stained brown and mottled green with damp. The climbing ivy had shattered all the windowpanes, the guttering had collapsed along with much of the roof, and he wondered about the building's history, its previous owners, about the stories and the people lost within its past.

At the rear of the mansion, he found equal signs of damage and neglect. Before turning to leave, however, he heard a door swinging and banging on its hinges, coming from the direction of what he could see now was a low, crumbling outbuilding, almost hidden by thick, untidy greenery beyond what must have once been a paved yard. He felt the evidence of shattered stone slabs under his feet as he made his way across it.

To his surprise, the door, now wide open, seemed to be secure and in good repair as it swung on hinges which moved freely, as though they had recently been oiled. Switching on his torch, he carefully made his way down a set of well-worn steps into a cellar, at the far end of which, beyond the wreckage of a number of large, ancient wine casks now rotten with age, was another door, this too wide open. Stepping through it, he found himself walking along a tunnel, where he shone his torch on the smooth rock beneath his feet to check for possible obstacles in his path.

He followed its downward slope for some distance and was further astonished when the tunnel eventually opened up into a large underground cavern that contained a fast-flowing stream. Fascinated by this discovery, he stood on the bank and cast the beam of his torch over the rushing water, now flowing high and full with the recent winter rains. He then shone it around the walls of the cavern and across to the opposite bank, where he spotted something unusual.

He made his way along the bank until he stood directly opposite the shape, keeping the beam of his torch focused on it throughout. The closer he approached, the surer he became that he was looking at a human figure lying inert on the ground.

Was it breathing? He thought so but couldn't be sure from this distance.

He called out, "Professor James!" loudly, several times. He thought he saw some slight movement, heard some slight moaning, though it was difficult to be sure given the noise of the flowing torrent.

He quickly realised it would be impossible for him to cross this stream and bring the professor—if it *was* the professor—safely back across with him. Swiftly, decisively, he rushed back to his own vehicle and reported exactly what he'd discovered, emphasising the urgent necessity of an immediate medical and rescue response.

Then he stood and waited, looking once again at the ruins that surrounded him, perplexed at the mystery he found himself involved in.

After a few minutes, he returned to the BMW and opened the passenger door. He thought he'd spotted something earlier on the floor beneath the seat. Yes, there it was, a card of some kind. He bent down, picked it up in his gloved hands, and read the note that had been written inside. The card had evidently fallen out of the book, bought as a gift, and he smiled at the sentiment, his English being proficient enough for him to appreciate it.

"*To Alfie, from Dad,*" he read. "*I hope you will read and enjoy this book. And learn from it, too, as I once did—learn about love from the rose, and wisdom from the fox.*" The gendarme's smile became a frown, and he hoped that this beautiful message would not prove to be the last one uttered from father to son.

Above the ground, the March winds blow
Around the empty, bleak chateau,
Where only thorns and ivy grow
In heavy, putrid air as though
The very stones are rotten.
No more illusions fill the air;
Vanished, too, are roses fair.
The fox has settled in its lair,
Its vengeance spent, forgotten.

EPILOGUE

I was never kind, Akio. You were always much kinder than I. And my vengeance has indeed been cruel. You would not have approved. But you are no longer here. And I do not regret my cruelty.

They deserved their punishment, every one of them, not only for what they did to me and what they did to you—but also for what they would doubtless have gone on to do. Such were the flaws in their very natures.

And they all had their warnings—in words they failed to heed, in dreams they chose to ignore, in signs they refused to read. They were too proud, or too arrogant, or too vicious, or too stupid, or too delusional, or too smug, or too vain. Too blind. Too human, I can hear you say. But when you were stolen from me, so was my humanity. Quite literally. I feel no pity, no compassion, no mercy for any of them. But I, who have known human desire, still understand it, and this has been my greatest weapon.

I find myself thinking of those gods and goddesses whose stories we both loved, for whom humans are playthings. Those who insult them, either wittingly or unwittingly, are brutally punished. How dare they! That is how Rose the Fox Fairy felt after her metamorphosis.

How dare they silence me, insult me, assault me, steal from me?

How dare they separate me from Akio forever?

Arachne was transformed into a spider, Actaeon was torn to pieces by his own

SEVEN CURSES

hounds. If I have been cruel, I am in good company.

So why spare Dominic James? Why leave things as I did, making his discovery possible?

It wasn't carelessness, I assure you.

His good fortune was to be number seven. Lucky number seven.

I'm tired, you see. Tired and bored, and I really don't care anymore.

Where I had once thrilled at my cunning, at the cruel fates I had successfully engineered, I now feel nothing but emptiness.

This man whose intellect I'd once admired so much proved to be just another vain, ambitious, self-centred fool, easy to deceive and easier to seduce.

So yes, I suppose my vengeance is spent, leaving only a hollowness where I had hoped for fulfilment and closure.

What now? What awaits me in the thousand years of life that lie ahead?

The stories suggest I will resurface from time to time to seduce and make love to unwitting young scholars and so sap the life and energies from them. Erotic fantasies written by men, of course, who fear—and desire—women who do not conform to the role of sweet passivity that society still prefers. So no, whatever awaits me, it will not be that. Besides, I have had enough of cowering scholars and have never desired any other man. Or woman.

We used to speculate together what it might be like to live among the gods. How we could devote ourselves to our shared project knowing there was no time limit on what we might achieve. The irony is not lost on me. Now that I've become semi-immortal, I would trade all the years ahead for the few I could have spent with Akio.

Perhaps happiness is time bound and incompatible with eternity.

If that is so, I would willingly and without hesitation trade eternity for Akio, always.

Farewell Song

The night is white with frost and cruel with snow.
Alone beneath a canopy of pine,
The Fairy finds her way through frozen paths.
Her memories, like shards of shattered ice,

Like dying stars whose light no longer shines,
Persist in blue and sterile solitude.
And stripping petals from a fallen rose,
She watches as they drift away and knows

Her last bruised tears, now scattered in the wind,
Will slumber soon upon the frozen earth.
Do gods await her on a distant hill?
She lingers, dreams of exiles, bids farewell.

Immortals feel no pain and no regret.
Does suffering mean that she is human still?
As demons, whispering, urge "Forget! Forget!"
Ignoring them, she knows she never will.

About the Author

J C Lee is the pen name of an Anglo / Chinese, male / female authorial partnership. They share a passion for myth, fairytales, and ghost stories from Chinese and Western cultures, and a taste for good whisky from anywhere. Both are published authors in their own right, but this is their first collaboration in horror fiction.

We thank you for reading and supporting!

Reviews go a very long way in helping both the authors and press continue to deliver high-quality content. If you have a moment, please consider leaving a review on any of our retailers' websites.

Seven Curses by J C Lee
graveside-press.com/seven-curses

CONTENT WARNINGS

In addition to the standard warnings expected of any horror novel, *Seven Curses* contains the following:

Death of a child (off-page)
Derogatory terms and slurs
Sexual assault (off-page)
Sexual themes
Verbal abuse